MW01224090

# Pieces of the Past

## Bree Matthews

authorHOUSE®

AuthorHouse™
1663 Liberty Drive
Bloomington, IN 47403
www.authorhouse.com
Phone: 1-800-839-8640

This is a work of fiction. All of the characters, names, incidents, organizations, and dialogue in this novel are either the products of the author's imagination or are used fictitiously.

Published by AuthorHouse   03/06/2015

ISBN: 978-1-4817-1776-2 (sc)
ISBN: 978-1-4817-1775-5 (hc)
ISBN: 978-1-4817-1777-9 (e)

Library of Congress Control Number: 2013902929

Print information available on the last page.

Any people depicted in stock imagery provided by Thinkstock are models, and such images are being used for illustrative purposes only. Certain stock imagery © Thinkstock.

This book is printed on acid-free paper.

Because of the dynamic nature of the Internet, any web addresses or links contained in this book may have changed since publication and may no longer be valid.

The views expressed in this work are solely those of the author and do not necessarily reflect the views of the publisher, and the publisher hereby disclaims any responsibility for them.

screenplay: adultery, intrigue, private investigators, clandestine meeting -- oh, and let's not forget the incredible fact that, in the end, they simply 'traded' spouses. Anne had to chuckle to herself with that one; Elena got the better end of that deal because her second husband, Rolfe was truly a nice guy. Bryan -- well, not quite so lucky. He and 'his soul mate', Hannah finally married many years later; and would choose to 'divorce' Anne and her family, along with his own first family. Amazing, she thought, how horrible 'Happy Ever After' can go...I had to try for that twice myself. And, then, again, if you think about it, are there really...truly any 'Happily Ever Afters' or is that just a fantasy we are brought to believe as children. Marriage is supposed to be, how does that go... *for better or worse, richer or poorer, sickness and health, 'til death do you part'* ; not until something *better* comes along. But, for Bryan and Elena, there were court battles, custody hearings to which everyone in both families had to pick sides. Anne shook her head - and, I picked the wrong side. Picking family loyalty over the truth. It seems I have always had a bit of a problem seeing people for who they really are...but, never in a million years, would I have thought my own blood - my brother - could be so completely different from the boy I remember growing up with. At one time, I even considered him my 'hero'. I truly can not believe I could have been that bad a judge of character, because when I think of my brother now, 'character ' is a word I would not use. Oh, bother now... back to reality, thought Anne. Back to this little e-mail. Little did she know opening that e-mail on a sunny summer afternoon would change all life as she presently knew it. But, it was hitting the **'Read'** button that could not prepare her for how much her life would change in a **very** short time..

# Chapter One

The Inbox on her computer screen was flashing its knowledge of new mail. Anne often ignored that little icon nuisance as it interrupted her work but, this time something pushed her to open it and see what was the latest 'just can't wait' information one of her friends had sent her. She considered herself to be a current up-to-date person, but in all honesty, she truly did not like the computer age with all of its trappings – Face Book, Twitter – they were unimportant to her. She felt them silly rants of a generation that truly had lost touch with the whole idea of face to face communication. Seriously, a thank-you note sent via e-mail - what happened to good old fashioned *HAND WRITTEN* notes that you actually had to mail; of course, that is if you knew the going rate for a stamp or, better yet - hand deliver, and current mortgage (oops, I mean) gas prices came into play there. Her late Southern Grandmother, Miss Eula Mae, would have had a spell of the vapors over that one. **Aargh.** But back to the present and, that annoying little icon. Noticing that the communique` was from Elena, her former sister-in-law peaked her interest; especially since they had only recently re-connected after a death in the family. Elena, along with her only niece, Jenna and nephew, Christopher, were all collateral damage when Elena and Anne's brother, Bryan divorced years ago. Momentarily, thinking back, Anne remembered that time was awful for everyone; their divorce made the War of the Roses look like a Sunday School picnic. If there could have been a book written on **'How Not To Handle A Divorce'**, the example would have had to be Elena's and Bryan's. Their divorce could have read like some Hollywood movie

# *Prologue*

Joshua lowered his head, coming on level with Anne. Barely grazing each other's lips, the kiss began as an innocent buss for memories long past. What began innocently enough as a soft remembrance of all those many years ago, ignited quickly to escalate to a passion that surprised both of them. The kiss they shared spanned one of nearly forty years of yearning, to which neither would have readily admitted just months ago. With the skilled ease of knowing each other, the kiss deepened into their very souls interrupting all rational thoughts of current obligations. Soft, yet urgent - tasting of each other as if refilling an empty tank. Tender bites of the lower lip; suddenly, feelings were raw and exposed. Exploration of ground so well mapped in their minds, was now rewinding to long ago. Breathing became difficult, standing nearly impossible. Yet, there was no indication either would let go of the moment for fear it was just an illusion - a wanted to dream, but can't have dream. A fluttering of eyelashes, then a moment when their eyes opened, if ever so slowly, throwing them both back into reality. And yet, no embarrassment from either of the moment they had just shared. It would have been useless anyway, because they both understood without a single word, the past was in charge now; their destinies, maybe even life as they both knew it, would - nor could ever be the same again. And, they had truly been in their own private world for, surprisingly, no one in the front café of *The Bistro* was even vaguely aware of what had just occurred in the Foyer, as they mindlessly continued to sip their lattes and check the Internet.

# Cast of Characters

## Main Characters

Anne-Elizabeth Adams Ebersol
John Reed Ebersol
Joshua Crayford Breckenridge
Petra Nemonoweski Cantor Breckenridge

## Supporting Cast

| | |
|---|---|
| John Bryan Brookfield Adams, III | Anne's brother |
| Elena Walters Adams Fossey | Former sister-in-law |
| Elizabeth Emerson Ebersol-Mallen | Anne & Reed's daughter |
| Timothy Wright Mallen | Anne & Reed's son-in-law |
| Brennan Blake Mallen | new Grand-son |
| Emma-Elizabeth Adams Mallen | new Grand-daughter |
| Carey Crayford Breckenridge | Joshua & Gayle's 1st son |
| Liam Sanderel Breckenridge | Joshua & Gayle's 2nd son |
| William Carson Breckenridge | Joshua's brother aka 'Will' |
| Grace-Katherine Butler Breckenridge | Will's wife |
| Gayle Sanderel Breckenridge | Joshua's first wife |

### *The Four Footers*

| | |
|---|---|
| Mags | Anne's Lhaso-Apso |
| Vanna White | Anne's Lab 'Grand-dog' |
| Bear, Raisin & Penelope | Anne's cats |
| Lady, Tramp & Mischa | Joshua & Petra's Cocker Spaniels |
| Chablis, Whiskey & Jack Daniels | Will & Grace's Bichons |
| Henry | Kitchen cat @ Butler Plantation |

The memory of your first love always stays with you, but when it spans forty years - marriages, children, grandchildren, deaths - and then, suddenly reappears in your life, the pieces of the past become new again. This is the story of two people - who fell in love as teenagers, lost love and, through the miracle of life, found love, even if forbidden, once again. With *Pieces of the Past*, you meet Anne and Joshua.

.........................................................................

To Fannie for all you gave in making this book a reality.

# Chapter Two

Hitting the **'Read'** button, Anne waited patiently for the file to load. Since **AOL** was acting as though the communication lines today were made of caramel string candy instead of high speed cable, she rose to refill her empty mug. Pouring the hot spicy cider into her cup allowed the wonderful aroma of cinnamon and mulled spices to invade her senses and momentarily, she was lost in that dreamy world. The loud ding of her computer telling her the file had loaded brought her back to her world. Her comfortable world. Having retired a number of years ago from her job due to health issues. she was given the opportunity to be a full-time mother once again - a role she relished. Now she and her husband, Reed were empty nesters, allowing her even more time to herself; that was, until the twin grand babies were born. Their beautiful grand babies. Born prematurely at only 7 months, it was an honest to goodness miracle they were even here, she thought smiling broadly. And, what precious bundles of joy they are . They couldn't come home too soon from the **NICU**, aka, Neo-natal Intensive Care Unit which had been their home since their births. She wanted to hold them...love them...spoil them. Yeah, she and Reed were going to be doting grandparents, for sure. Casually walking back to the computer, she smiled as she noticed her big black Persian cat, Bear raise up from his puddle of sunshine on the floor and stretch, acknowledge her with one of his ' fingernails going down the blackboard ' meows, then reposition himself for his next four hour nap. Ah, the life of a cat. Well, she couldn't complain either. Her life had been relatively easy since retiring early. Sitting back down at the computer, she began to read Elena's e-mail; a paragraph of catch-up news about her four grand babies; of she and Rolfe's latest travels; but, it was the next sentence that literally jumped off the screen at her. So much so that while she had meant to set her mug down securely on the desk, she missed it all together sending the just filled mug crashing to the floor. Elena hedged at first , but then, said she had been contacted by Joshua...'*her Joshua*' of a lifetime ago. **Whoa** - why was the room spinning? Anne grabbed the side of the desk to steady her thoughts, closing her eyes to bring the room back down from outer space. Being the protector that Elena had always been toward her, she said she had not offered much information to him because she wanted Anne to be aware of his looking for her first. Could she give him her phone number or, what about the e-mail address. Anne's head was spinning...how...where...when did this happen? What was she to do...*why*, **why**, **now**? As she took a deep breath, opened her eyes, then silently willed herself to finish reading the words that were now literally jumping off the page at her. She tried to read and not let her mind wander back. Back to all those years ago..what was it now, at least forty...to that hot summer when everything went wrong...**everything**. What's that she read... Joshua is an ordained Minister? For a moment, she almost laughed; and then, she felt the tears welling up in her eyes. She realized time had changed a lot of things, but she just could not imagine what had transpired in his life to make him want to be a Man of the Cloth. That summer - had that been the determining factor...or something later in life. What could have possibly happened to change her Joshua; Yes - her curly hair, fun- loving Joshua - to offer his life to the Lord. Without thinking, Anne crossed herself hoping that the prayer she had just offered up had been heard. And, then there was the last sentence. Elena had gotten Joshua's e-mail address and told him that she would forward it on to her. There it is ..black and white...contact information - ***jbelieves53@ aol.com*** ...all Anne had to do was use it. Anne was frozen to her seat... goose bumps...tears just about ready to flow. 'Oh what a mess I am,' she said out loud, apparently so loud that Bear grunted at having been disturbed from his siesta. Where to now? Damn... damn the internet. Once upon a time a person could stay off the radar... if they so wanted ...but not anymore.

# Chapter Three

For a few moments, Anne simply sat in front of her computer. She didn't want her mind to start the 'what if' replay for the thousandth time; however, the urge to remember was more powerful than she expected. And, so it was on a warm early summer afternoon, she found herself drifting back..*back*..**back** to the day when it all began...to when Joshua first entered her life and, became her world without her even knowing it. Her mind filtered the images until there ... there ...in the distance...there it all began...***Again.***

Anne's could trace her family's heritage back for generations. Her ancestors had been early landowners having their lands granted to them by the King of England way back when America was still 'The Colonies'. They had always been well to do; but, well to do didn't necessarily mean there were no problems or, that you were 'normal'. Anne's parents were on the social register, and were active members of their community, held professional positions. Members of the Country Club, on committees for this and that. Her father was an Architectural Engineer, her mother a registered nurse; and, they were 'Social Alcoholics' or, what we would today call, weekend drunks. Only on Friday did they have 'fun' with their circle of equally dysfunctional friends. Long before the days of **Al-Anon** for family members was even available, the kids had to figure out how to exist in this world not of their making. So, like kids do, they bond over the same issues. Having to help one of your parents to bed or drive them home (long before Designated Driver was even thought of); or, throw a blanket over the lifeless limp form on the sofa. This was the world of a kid with 'social' parents. Doesn't mean they were 'bad' parents. Monday - Friday - the work week - they were or, truly tried to be the Norman Rockwell painting. It was the weekend that was the albatross. Make the liquor store before closing at 6 p.m. on Friday; make sure the liquor cabinet was fully stocked for the upcoming weekend with their friends. For these kids, a normal life of having a friend come for a sleep over - having your date, especially if your date was not in this 'clique` of parents, pick you up - these were well orchestrated so as not to have to answer too many questions. And you were careful, oh so careful - somehow even as a kid you knew this was not the norm. To walk in to your home, say on a Saturday night around 11:30, your curfew time, and find your parents entertaining, yet again, and everyone feeling no pain... not particularly a sight you want to share with your date or an unknowing friend. There are only so many times you can laugh it off . So you tend to bond with those that are under the same umbrella of shame..and that, is where for Anne, Joshua entered her world.

# Chapter Four

'Joshua' - in the dictionary it means 'Yahweh **saves'** which roughly translated means God of the Hebrews saves. Now looking back, he *was* Anne's salvation in many ways. Tall, my word, he was what over six feet even then at, what 13. Thin with curly hair that just could not be convinced to behave itself, piercing eyes that even at 13 held too much hurt and grief behind them, but a smile, such a smile; one that could light up a football field. Trying so hard to be a man, this young boy was never allowed to be a child almost from the start. Joshua simply fell into Anne's life like a leaf falling from an autumn windstorm. His parents were also members of the 'Group'. After his Father passed when he was only 12, his mother was, perhaps, in hindsight, a little further down the self destruction road than the others. So much so that, she sometimes carried her weekends over to a Monday, as well - even a Tuesday, too. And often, there was no break in the pattern. It could be a continuous event—at least, until the liquor ran out completely. And through all of this, Joshua simply grew up way too fast - smoking at 6, drinking himself at 9, having a full time job at 12. Working all the way thru Junior high and Senior high to the point that he often said school was an interruption to his paycheck...a paycheck that would buy him beer and cigarettes to go for the next week. And, he used to joke, there was no "home life" as his mother didn't like the sole responsibility of her two boys...they learned to fend for themselves quite well. She didn't like to do the 'things' normal Moms did. No Martha Stewart for sure...she didn't like to keep house... to cook..nurture. According to Joshua, 'she could burn cereal'. So he and his older brother, Will grew up mostly taking care of themselves. And, just like all of the other kids in this prestigious circle, he had very few friends. You just didn't let people into your world for fear the embarrassment would be too much to handle. And so, when Joshua showed up at one of the group's soirees, he hardly expected to see anyone even near his own age among the party. At that moment, or so he would later confess, to Anne in great detail... when he saw her standing at the far end of the Game room, his heart fell to the floor. ' Dark hair, dark eyes, tiny -- you were everything I was not. .. You were laughing at something someone had said - and, your laugh was so unique - kind of sweet, yet sexy —sexy?'...and, just how could that be, I wondered to myself...you were only - what 15 at the most? ' Oh great, ' he said he told himself. ' I groaned inwardly ..bet she won't give me the time of day.. oh, but I gotta try..' he related to her...and with that thought and a very deep breath for courage, he said he had found himself just inches away from her. 'You turned around and smiled at me - saying a casual 'hi'. **That was it for me;** *that was it. I fell hard - so hard...'* he later told Anne he had fallen in love with her from the moment he first saw her. A fact he silently held onto ... as it was many years later before she would know. One thing she did know - that was the night for them an unlikely friendship began to blossom.

# Chapter Five

Anne was pulled back to the present by the insistent ringing of her cell phone - just let it go to voice mail...this is more important, she thought. Where was I.. oh, back to when she and Joshua first met...so long ago. She let her mind drift back to that night..to that moment when a friendship was born out of the need to escape. It was a mutual understanding forged without any questions asked - each needing the other; and, it didn't seem to matter what it might have been. The mere fact that they had so much in common seemed ridiculous. Mainly, she remembered with a slight smile, he was younger than she was...so, how could they possibly be on the same level. They would, however, become fast and furious friends, seeing each other nearly every weekend ..not date like, for she would date others, her never even contemplating the possibility that Joshua was interested in her. I mean, after all, Joshua was a couple years younger than her - not date material. He would go with her and her dates, sometimes, tagging along almost like a little brother. In fact, he *was* her little brother in so many ways. With her own brother being much older and already out of the home, it was easy to 'adopt' Joshua. They were confidantes ... co-conspirators.... buddies. At least, until a few years later when he said he actually gathered up the nerve to ask her out on a real honest to goodness date; according to him, he was amazed, nearly floored when she said she would. They dated - and, what good times they had. Not at all uncomfortable like teenage dates can be sometimes. Nothing was ever forced where they were concerned as it all just seemed to fall into place. Their feelings grew - Joshua had told her the depth of his feelings for her grew each time they were together; and, he confided that once he finally got up enough nerve to actually kiss her...a soft tender kiss - his mind was racing, as he wasn't quite sure what the outcome to this would be and, then he related to Anne ...'You smiled at me, that warm sweet smile and asked me.. "What took you so long?" ' He said his heart had soared...and, he knew, he later told her, that his mind finally agreed with what his heart already knew. She was the love of his life and always would be; and, in remembering that moment, Anne found she had a smile on her face, even if it was mixing with the tear rolling down her cheek.

# Chapter Six

Reaching for a tissue, Anne let her mind go back to those special days with Joshua. They went on picnics, long drives, football games - had cookouts with her family, and, on weekends, of course, they were together as most of the parents were gathered to celebrate another work week's conclusion. It was good they were together. They helped each other through a lot, especially in the early days, before they starting dating. She laughed as she tugged at her ear, a habit she had always had. Fingering the tiny diamond stud in her ear, she was suddenly reminded that Joshua had been her co-conspirator in getting her ears pierced... all the rage at that time...but not in her mother's eyes. She had flatly refused when Anne asked her if she could go to the mall and get hers pierced. Not to be denied, she convinced Joshua to help her 'do it herself'. So, on a warm afternoon in the downstairs rec room, while everyone else was away, she and Joshua pierced her ears...with a potato for the stabilization of the ear, a bowl of ice cubes to deaden the lobe (yeah, *that* worked, she laughed to herself), a darning needle, a book of matches and some alcohol, they pierced her ears. And did it hurt...she laughed to herself. Joshua put the earrings in as she couldn't do it; and, with a sense of accomplishment and conspiracy, she pulled her long brown hair over her ears, hoping to remember to keep it that way until they healed. By then, she thought, it would be too late. And, it was Joshua who had constantly reminded her to ' Turn the earrings... as often as you can... ' Thinking back, I lost one of those earrings... when...years ago. Probably during **THAT** summer ...when I lost everything including Joshua...again. Caressing her earlobe, she laughed out loud. And, I *still* have only two holes in my ears, thinking of the young girl who had done her nails the other day – what was it, I think I counted six in each ear. **Oh, My Word.**

# *Chapter Seven*

Reaching for another tissue, Anne stood up....she just couldn't do this anymore ..not again. It had been years since she had gone down this road. It had been such a well traveled road so many years ago..and, she totally blamed herself. She was the one who had sent Joshua away; maybe 'sent' was not the right word. No, she ' let' him walk out of her life...she was the one who, literally, turned her back on him when he left for Tennessee. Hard headed and spoiled, she just could not see what he was trying to do. He didn't want college at this time - he wanted to be out on his own, make a name for himself and a life for them...college would take too long. This was an immediate career path. So, Auburn was out. But for her, it was...college, first...then career. It had to be that way...it was logical...practical ...sensible. So, thinking she had the upper hand with logic on her side, she would not budge. College, then career...simple. No college, no me. Boy, that was intelligent, she thought. I could have been patient...but no..I wanted my way. I was at the point where graduation was nearing - only a year away. All my friends were making career plans, moving on from their college lives...and, my life was being thrown upside down by Joshua wanting to forgo College, and move hundreds of miles away..away from Home...away from me to pursue a career in Marketing with a major retail firm. No, that would not...that could not happen. He needs to go on to college...sure, I'll be ahead of him and graduate first, but, so what? Once I graduate, I can find a job and he can finish school - and, if he goes to Auburn, like he first wanted to, he could retain his place in the Management Program and work part time. A win..win. But, if he takes this job instead...well, okay...he'll be in Northern Tennessee...me at U-Alabama, then eventually back to South Carolina. Hundreds of miles apart. He can't want to 'willingly' leave me to go to 'work' - college, yes, but a job without the benefit of college, not in this day and time. He wants to leave me behind for ...a JOB? Fine. His choice. There won't be an 'us'... I'll move on... start dating... and, then, he'll see what he's lost, choose college, and then, we'll both come back home. And, we'll have our own happy ever after. Ah, but the best laid plans ...do not work. She let Joshua walk away... assuring herself he would come back...even though she told him not to. So, a wounded pride and a bit of revenge plotting, for Anne, that is when stupidity took over. She would move on and feeling justified in that irrational thinking, she fell into a whirlwind of what she mistook for love. Everyone else could see it...blinders, maybe? Perhaps, *if* she had not been so eager for the fairy tale - to believe in Happy Ever Afters... if she had just listened to all the 'doubting Thomases', Joshua included. She hated herself for hurting Joshua the way she knew she had; she hated the way things were left so bad between them...what now over 40 years ago? Maybe he just wanted to cross off something on his Bucket List of things left undone; maybe it was payback time. No, he is a Minister now. He wouldn't do that kind of thing. Oh good grief; what a muddle my mind is in, she thought. Doing her very best Scarlett O'Hara imitation, she said out loud...' Oh, dear, I'll think about this tomorrow.'.. and turned her computer off.

# Chapter Eight

Sleep...not tonight. Anne's mind would not turn off; a migraine had reared its ugly head, and being the true Southern girl she was, she took to her bed. Sleep will force all of this into a ' it didn't happen in the first place bag'; so when I wake up it will have been a very bad and unwelcome dream. Opening her eyes, she felt the comforting warmth of her little Lhaso Apso, Mags nestled beside her. From the other side of the king size bed, she could feel Reed's rhythmic breathing moving the bedcovers. Pushing aside the comforter, she gingerly slipped out of bed. The hall nightlight lead her to the kitchen; since she didn't eat much dinner, she looked over the late night possibilities and pulled out some cheese...um, with crackers, that won't be too bad. Looking at the microwave...Oh my word, it's 3 a.m. Now what she asked herself? I'm not sleepy; the entire world, except me, is asleep. No way, I'm watching tv and, then she looked over at her desk. The computer... can I do this, she wondered? Turning around, she heard Mags coming down the hall. Blinking sleepy eyes that questioned what she was doing up at this ungodly hour, the little dog came to rest at Anne's feet as if to say...'I'm here, you will not be alone in this, Mom.' And with that, Anne turned on her computer.

# Chapter Nine

Whirling to life, the computer flashed its ready button...Anne hit the e-mail icon. She must have reread Elena's e-mail at least three times...now what? I don't think I can do this; maybe I shouldn't do this. I mean it's been too long. There is a part of me that has always been rather fond of the Ostrich Syndrome... bury your head, don't look back, whatever..it will go away. But he started it. Oh, that's mature thinking, she chastised herself. Trying to disengage her brain from such irrational childish thinking, she mindlessly dialed up Face book to see if her daughter had put any new pictures of the twins on her wall. While she did not like the social networking site and, had made her displeasure known to her daughter, Emerson, she relinquished her complaints as she could keep up with the twins' daily improvements by visiting the site ...pics and all. Again, not to her liking; pics of her darlings that **ANYONE** could see. But what are you to do with this younger 'social networking' generation??? And then it hit her, what if Joshua was on Face book . I mean he is a Minister....he probably has a page. Taking a deep breath, she typed in his name,' **Joshua Crayford Breckenridge'**. Now, hit **'Search'** and wait to see if any info would load; when his page appeared before her eyes, she was stunned. There's a current snapshot just as he looks today. Older, well, of course he's older, she laughed to herself. Big smile and holding on to *his* wife. **Her** Joshua was holding on to *his wife*; she laughed at herself for even thinking that! Of course, he wasn't **HER** Joshua anymore. She found herself reading his entire page. He really was a Minister. He was chatting about his love of the Lord...his love for his congregation...his love of all that is

Holy. She looked over pics of his family, his sons, grand children. It was like filling a pitcher at a fountain; the more she read, the more she wanted to know. And then, without thinking it through - something anyone rarely does at 3 a.m. - she hit the **'Message'** icon and waited for it to load. Inhaling deeply, she began to type...wait, what do I say. I can't just blurt out**..' Elena told me you were looking for me.'**..that sounds crazy. No, it must be something vague..a nonchalant - no it has to be a 'meaningful' kind of something. So, tying and retyping, and THEN, retyping yet again, she finally settled on... **'You would not, by any chance, be the same Joshua Breckenridge that I went to the St. Francis of Assisi Senior High School Prom with?'** That was specific and not very vague, was it..she thought..what will I do if it isn't him ? It **has** to be him, I typed his whole name; the picture, it is Joshua..older, but it is Joshua. I mean he will have my Face book address, sure... but I don't have to answer -- right? Quit Face book... I can cancel my **AOL** membership, if necessary... right? And so, satisfied with that irrational 3 a.m. thinking, she hit the **'Enter'** button. Oh, my word, what have I done...I just opened up the lid on my Pandora's Box, she thought. Then, as if suddenly frightened by the Ghosts of the Past, she quickly shut down her computer.

# *Chapter Ten*

Not many people, unless they have to be, are up at 3 a.m. For most people, it is a P.M. factor thing. However, for Joshua Breckenridge, 3 a.m. was not abnormal.. He had always been an early riser and since the phone had awaken him a few minutes ago with the need for a transport, he was now trying to erase the cobwebs from his head. Calling his office, he informed the dispatcher that a transport was needed at a local nursing home for an elderly lady who had just passed. Since beginning his transport service, **A Touch of Comfort**, several years ago, Joshua was enjoying the fact he was providing a much needed service. One that he and his staff handled with dignity and respect for those recently deceased. And it was true; nobody ever passes on at a reasonable hour. So, the middle of the night was not at all unusual for him. Hanging up the phone with his dispatcher, he walked to the kitchen counter and poured a big steaming mug of the coffee intended for breakfast; this will help wipe away the cobwebs, he thought. Normally if he did not have to go out on the call himself, he would work when he was aroused in the middle of the night - or read - maybe outline his sermon for Sunday. It was his turn to preach as Petra, his second wife of nearly 20 years, did so last week. They were a rare pair - both Ministers, him ordained - her not. The deep 'Bible Belt' South had really strong mandates where women Ministers were concerned. They could do almost anything an ordained Minister could do: preach..tend to the souls of the parish, but did not have the label *'ordained'* in their resumes... antiquated thinking, at best. Oh well, only time can change that, he thought. All that did not alter the fact they had shared so much over their marriage; but, it had been their equal love of the ministry that was the strongest. No.. don't want to think about my sermon yet. So, not knowing what he wanted to do at the moment, he walked over to his laptop and turned it on; maybe I can get ahead a bit today, he thought. I could post my daily bible readings early. Punching in his password, he headed to Face book; he saw the **'Message'** icon, but since he always had messages from his parishioners, he didn't immediately go to it . Sitting there looking at the blank screen, he felt as if his mind had suddenly gone blank as well. Since I haven't determined my sermon title yet, best wait on the bible verses as I like to lead up to my sermon..so not just yet...later, he muttered to himself. Let's see what messages are awaiting me, Lord. And there it was....blink again..no it is there. Can it be...oh my word, there it is. Reading voraciously he re-read that simple question at least 20 times...and, then he realized that he needed to take a breath...breathe... breathe... Joshua breathe, he told himself.

# Chapter Eleven

Anyone who has ever seen the world at 3 a.m. knows it can be a bit unnerving just knowing that most of the world is rebooting itself for the coming day. That can be enough to want to try the sleep thing again. But it was different with Joshua; maybe it was the home life that had set his internal clock to want to leave the house as soon as he could to go to work before school ...or, maybe it was the fact that it normally was calm and quiet in the deep of night. Night tends to hide a lot of the dirty things that are visible in the daylight. And, Joshua had plenty of things in his past he would like to forget. Prompting himself back to the present, he raised his head from the cradle his hands had formed .' **Thank you, my heavenly Father...I have found her. After years and years of searching,.. I have found her.'** And then, his mind raced back to when thinking the heavenly Father or anyone for that matter, would have been the furthest thing from his mind. He had been such a lost soul after that summer so long ago. His job had taken him to another state, hundreds of miles away, away from family, friends...away from everything that was familiar. Home. Maybe I should have chosen to go on to college..I mean I did later, but if I had then, well, Anne and I would have been closer to one another..at least geographically. She would have been at U-Alabama, me at Auburn. Well, same state, our schools bitter rivals, wouldn't that have been a hoot..but, we would have been able to make some sense of our lives. And she wouldn't have been caught up in all of that web of insanity ...all because I was not there...I should have stayed...or, at least gone on to College. Hindsight...20-20. By taking that job, we broke up...and, I found

23

myself with no one to confide in, no one to ease my doubts. Anne had always done that for me. Away from her and... from all of the hurt. Sometimes, even now years later, he wondered if he had done the right thing. And, after leaving to take that job, he found himself in a downward spiral of drinking, smoking and looking for anything that would deaden the pain. But, every night, she was there - in his dreams making forgetting useless. I can't go down that path again, he thought..the pain is too much. No, I am past that now, he thought. Looking at the computer screen, he found his fingers incapable of typing. I have waited so long for this moment, he thought. What do I say? Careful, do not be flip or cavalier as she'll see right thru that; don't seem needy, either... she'll run like a frightened kitten. Be open and honest...yes.... honesty, that will be the way to go. Bide your time, Joshua...you cannot rush this. But how can I possibly tell her that now...now ...that .. I have been searching for her for years - wanting to see her. That even now, dare I say it...I still love her. That goes against every principal I stand for as a Minister, but, You know, Father, it is the truth. Save me from Your displeasure, Father, but to You I can not lie. Thinking quietly to himself for a minute, Joshua simply replied to her - **'That would be me - how the world are you, girl?'** Now, the hard part - wait for a reply...and pray, pray hard that I did the right thing.

# Chapter Twelve

Opening one eye to greet the sunshine streaming thru the bedroom window made Anne remember how sleep had alluded her the night before. There is no way it can be morning yet; but, the body slam of Mags against her side proved otherwise. You could sleep late only if you remained motionless; because, if you gave the slightest hint of being awake, you were fair game for the from the bottom of the bed to the pillows **NASCAR** race and, then the sumo wrestler body slam from the 15# concrete ball of fur that was Mags. And, how could you possibly be angry with such joy and happiness even at 7:00 a.m.? So, without further ado, the morning began. The outside walk with Mags and her co-partner in crime, Vanna White, the 130# black Lab grand-dog their daughter, Emerson had graced them with over ten years ago when she moved out to her city apartment; then back in to let the cats outside, convincing Bear and his sister, Raisin that the day had, indeed, begun; starting breakfast before Reed came back from the morning feed. Normalcy. That is what was so special about her life ...simple - comfortable - routine. She and Reed were good together. They had formed a friendship as neighborhood kids growing up and were next door neighbors. She always laughed when she said she had married the *'boy next door'* because City folk didn't understand that in the country, *'next door'* could be what --- five miles down the road. A smile crossed her face as she opened the fridge - let's see, eggs, bacon, biscuits. How many times in their nearly 40 year marriage had the day begun this way? She and Reed were opposites in every possible way - she was petite at only five feet, he graced this world at six feet four inches. Her family was small, consisting of her parents and seven years older brother, Bryan; and even though she had a brother, Anne still felt almost like an only child. Bryan had been in the College and then in the U.S. Army before she was even out of high school. She was college educated, from a genteel Southern family who could trace her lineage back hundreds of years; Reed was a 'good ole boy', as they say in the South, from a huge family of nine..six girls and him, the much wanted boy, the baby..and was he ever spoiled, she laughed. He had seven mothers, for goodness sakes. He was the sports jock, the good looking, hard drinking, partying kind; but, there was also a familiarity in that he was so like her father. He had a deeply ingrained honor about him that truly had come through even in his rough and tumble coming up years. Like volunteering for service at the height of the hated Viet Nam war, while some were traipsing off to Canada to avoid the draft. Anne always felt that because he manned up and volunteered, was the main reason, his tour of duty was spent in Greece and finally England. He never had to experience Viet Nam first hand...they both just attended way too many funerals of those that did. The simple fact they had been friends for most of their lives was an oddity. Anne laughed when she thought about it now...I guess having six sisters didn't hurt, either.. the friend part that is. But, somehow for the most part, they clicked. Oil and water, sugar and salt..some would say, but it worked. Though their courtship and eventual marriage did not sit particularly well with either side of their families; hers, kind of snooty that she was marrying 'outside of her class' and his, that he was 'getting above his raising'. Yes, even in the 70's, the old South - the 'class' thing - remained intact. And yet, theirs had been a good marriage. One of mutual respect . They had talked about that summer after he came back from his military service in England; and then, they never - ever- spoke of it again. They both agreed that whatever had happened to each of them before there was a **'them'** were pieces of their past and, that is were it would to stay. Reed had his skeletons, Anne had hers. Those doors were closed…at least, she thought - until last night at 3 a.m. when I cracked the lid on my Pandora's Box. She shook her head.. what was I thinking…*Face book*?? Really? Maybe, just maybe, nothing would come of it. And with that thought chasing around in her head, she heard the back door close. Suddenly her world went back to 'normal.'

Reed came upstairs to find Anne starting breakfast – his coffee cup sitting on the counter waiting to be filled. Another good morning off to a good start, he thought. Walking over to where Anne stood at the kitchen sink, he wrapped his big arms around her waist, gave her a quick peck on the cheek, then picked up the newspaper and sat down at the kitchen counter. They chatted easily of how the morning had gone so far – two brood cows appear to be getting close to calving, mark it on the calendar for twenty-one days.. 'maternity watch'…; after breakfast, will be going to check the fences in the back pasture as a windstorm a couple of days ago, had broken some limbs down and, you know what happens when the 'ladies figure out there is an opening'. They both laughed as they were used to playing rodeo every once in a while. Of course, it was different in the world of today, as you did your **'roundup'** with trucks or 4- wheelers instead of horses; there was such a 'comfortability', if you will, with the two of them. They had weathered a few storms, some serious, some not so, in their lives together and, finally, they had reached that wonderful world of retirement. All was good…but, they both knew not to take anything for granted. Reed asked Anne about her restlessness the night before; to which Anne replied that she must have just been 'overtired and not able to get comfortable'. Reed countered with …' I knew something was up when I heard Mags jump off the bed to go find you ..' and he laughed. 'You should have seen her - she was so funny…walking through the hall as if she couldn't believe it was time to get up yet..' laughed Anne. ' When did you finally come back to bed, honey?' asked Reed. 'I think it was somewhere after 3, maybe…I didn't really look at the clock..I'll probably pay for the no-sleep thing by late afternoon...maybe I'll catch a nap, later..' Anne said. And with that, they finished breakfast, and the rest of the day started for both of them. Anne had to smile at how 'normal' her life really was.. at least, it was until last night, she chastised herself.

# Chapter Thirteen

Joshua sat motionless at his computer, willing it to flash anything. Message..chat..anything..something. Really?? Come on dodo brain. It is 5 a.m. At this hour? Noticing the time stamp on the message board, he knew he had checked his messages before Anne's entry..crap. Patience, you have waited years for this, you can certainly wait a little while longer. Restless now, he wasn't ready to work on anything - his cell phone was ringing and he hadn't even been aware of it. Answering it, he was thankful as he had a purpose now. A nursing home upstate in Ruther Mills had a resident who had just slipped her earthly bonds and needed to be transferred to a funeral home. I'll take this one. Ask, and you shall receive, he thought - Thank You, Lord, for allowing me to help. It will delay my tortured mind for a few hours. Quickly getting dressed, he left a note for Petra on the kitchen counter. He was off to Ruther Mills for a transport -- he would be back later that evening. Quietly, he dressed and then headed to his car. In the distance, he could just see the beginnings of night's darkness giving way to the tender mercies of the day. Even at 5:30 a.m., he could tell it was going to be another hot one here in Dubrussiae Parish, Louisiana. The air was thick with the fragrance of summer jasmine, faintly reminding him of the honeysuckle from home. **Home**. He hadn't said that word in years. **Home....**back to those days with Anne. Of holding hands... honeysuckle bouquets... twilights dipped in honeyed haze...of laughing eyes, simple ways and quiet nights under the stars...back to her. So, this was the way it was going to be, now, he thought. All the memories ... all the *'what ifs.'* I want to go back and understand how something so good between two people, who truly loved and cared for one another...how it could have gone so wrong. So many mistakes were made, mine, hers, ours. We had something so few people ever have. And yet, both of us threw it away. What is it people say..**'With age comes wisdom'** ; what is so sad about that is by the time you become **'wise'**, you are usually too old to do anything about it. Baby steps, he told himself..baby steps. Inhaling the moist early morning air, he turned the ignition key and said a quiet prayer - 'My Heavenly Father, I once more ask for your guidance as I bring another one of your flock home to pasture... Help me to follow Thy will and handle my designated duty with grace, dignity and faith in Your plan. I ask for Your forgiving love and guidance in all that I do. In Your name...Amen. ' Before he started his van, he paused once more... and said another prayer. And this one, didn't have anything, at all, to do with his job. It was merely..'Thank You, Lord. Thank You'.

# Chapter Fourteen

Pulling on to Highway 17, Joshua saw the milepost ahead informing him to exit 19A for Ruther Mills. Up ahead was a Pilot station, so he mindlessly turned in to fill up and grab something to eat. The morning haze was slowly burning off and the sky took on that watercolor palette immortalized in novels and art...the Lord is so powerful he thought. **Praise be to the Glory.** He looked down at his hand with that wide gold wedding band on it...I wonder why now...why now when I have finally found myself...found my salvation, my purpose in life...found Petra. Why could I have not found her when my soul so needed her...or was she lost to me even then? I must be thankful that I have found her - this was- has been - a mission for me; but, I have already been through so much. Oh, not the Pity Train again. He thought back of all the trials he had endured; he had seen and done way too much to be only 59...sometimes, he felt ancient. I have lived too hard, done too much to have even been considered worthy of being forgiven by the Lord. Tally it up, ole boy. First marriage - a disaster from the start. Attempting to cure the loneliness and in doing so, maybe wipe Anne's memory away, I went on a binge of sorts. Yes, the drinking was always there as a crutch, but I found myself trying to drown her out any way I could. I met Gayle - she was everything Anne wasn't. Yeah, she was small and pretty, like Anne, but that is where the similarities ended. She was looking for an out - and it could have been any unfortunate soul - salvation from her trailer trash life, and she picked me...and such a willing partner I was. So I was the only one surprised when Gayle told me she was pregnant. It never occurred to me...no never..that I was not the father. Maybe what Anne had just gone through prevented me from doing that..I don't know. So, of course, we married; and that was a mistake from the *"I do"*. Thinking back, and chuckling to himself...I mean, seriously, we got married on April 15, Income Tax Deadline Day...really..now I ask, what maybe – only April Fool's Day would have been worse ; but, two great things came out of that insane 17 year union, our, *no* my boys, Carey and Liam. Ultimately, we divorced and, being the mother of the year she was, Gayle moved on to the second of - what was it now – six husbands. She didn't want the boys..but she wouldn't give them up, either. In an out of the courts, until it became clear to everyone, there should be no question who would raise the boys. So when they became troubled young men in their own right, who was to blame, I wonder. I could have done so much better, I know that now. We all went through Hell...I wasn't a good role model; however, things did improve, by the time Carey left, there was only Liam ; once he was given more of a stable home environment, thanks to my marriage to Petra, we were able to salvage a bit of normalcy to our lives. But, before that could happen, I had to find some inner peace of my own. ..because somewhere in the nightmare of all of everyone else's problems, I lost my way. I believed that there was nothing left I could do, nowhere to go - besides who cares anymore. Oh, there was a major pity party going on there...and I am the Guest of Honor. What a freaking mess I have made of my life, and I have, unwittingly, added my boys to the mix. By then, young men.. with their own choices... so what of me, he wondered. So, it was on that cool autumn day, I felt lost and was at an impasse; I remember I got in my car, and started to drive - no destination..and nobody knows where I am, I thought I drove for hours - then seeing a roadside pull off, I finally stopped. Reaching for the glove compartment, I pulled out the 38 pistol I always carried for protection when on the road. Checking to see if it was loaded, I slipped it into my jacket pocket and opened the car door. A nature trail was just ahead - wonder where it leads, I asked to no one. Doesn't matter, I won't be coming back. Plodding along, I was totally oblivious to any other hikers on the trail, head tucked down following this trail I had no idea where to...then, suddenly it opened up to a clearing up ahead. Good, I am tired, so very tired, I thought. Coming out of the umbrella of trees, I saw the mighty Mississippi River in front of me. I had seen the river many times before in my life, but, somehow, today, it was as if I was seeing it for the very first time. It was awesome..so huge - and it went on for miles.. look at the sheer power of the water...how could anyone live next door to such majesty and not see it, really see it? I remember I walked over to a formation of rocks and collapsed in a heap. Why am I here I wondered to myself...I am a failure..I have nothing to show for my life except my sons - and my guidance has lead them down the same worn path to self destruction I have walked so many times. Looking at the awesome beauty of the river, I finally took a deep breath.. can I do this? Can I really do this, I asked myself. I have tried everything to stop the drinking, the self abuse, the hatred that grows like a cancer inside of me...so maybe, just maybe, I can, at least, end my pain. Pulling the gun from my pocket, I was momentarily mesmerized by the way the sun glinted off of the highly polished metal. It is almost pretty, I thought.... this instrument of protection will be my salvation and end my pain. It seemed I was in a trance of sorts; and, then a quick rush of doves scrambling from the underbrush brought me back to the moment; and, then - it was at that moment, I heard a voice. Quiet , at first seeming to be only a whisper. but it was there and it was calling my name..." ***Joshua.. Joshua... you said you have tried everything to change your life... why not try ME?*** " I looked around to see where the voice had come from - there was no one - no one there...And then, I heard it again...this time louder and with more insistence in it***..."Joshua... try ME."*** I was trembling - so hard – I knew, I knew that the Lord, my Lord had saved me from myself. Without even being aware, my death grip on the gun released and I watched as it tumbled over the rocks on its way to the river. And with that, I gave my troubled life over to God. And I thank Him over and over again...for saving a wretch like me. He felt me worthy of saving when I did not think myself worthy of anything.

**Ding - Ding - Ding** --- the gas pump's insistence for attention brought Joshua back to reality.

# Chapter Fifteen

Breakfast done - dishes calling out to be washed and stacked. Morning routine..like every day before. Reaching for the tv remote, Anne turned on Siruis Radio– quickly punching in the number for her favorite station - 60's on 6' as she loved the 60's music she had grown up to. So when the **Gerry and the Pacemakers'** song - ' **Don't let the sun catch you crying…'** came on, she fell back to those wonderful days in high school - the innocence, the camaraderie of friends. It was amazing how you always tend to remember all of the good times, she thought..that is until now. Why am I going over this, yet again, she wondered. I have re-wound it, again, and again, and nothing will change it…oh, if you could only go back and have a second go of it. She smirked as she remembered hearing the 'old folks' way back then … *'You must aspire to live life fully the first go around - have no regrets…you don't get second chances in life'.* Maybe, she could have had that forbidden second chance, but I screwed that one up royally with Joshua. So. no, it would be the third chance…and, absolutely no where is it written you get that -- nobody gets third chances, she thought. And yet, if by some quirk of Fate, you were lucky enough to actually have another chance, how do you displace what you have for what you might have - and, who picks up the pieces if you *do* test fate? Questions..so many questions with no answers. She glanced over the room to her desk willing herself to test fate, she walked over and opened up the laptop, hoping against hope that there would be nothing there and yet, wanting so desperately for something to be there. I am a fool, she thought, a silly irrational fool. Pulling up the e-mails, she re-read Elena's yet again, validating that it was, in fact, real and not some dream she had been privy to. I could e-mail him - after all, there is his e-mail address...I mean that IS his address - no more wondering if he will answer me on Face book...what could it hurt? It's just an e-mail. She carefully typed in the e-mail address, and entered the simple original text of – 'Elena told me you were looking for me.. ...Anne.' ... not the most original opening line for a forty year absence, but at least, it was the truth, she thought. Then closing her eyes, Anne hit **'send'**. There, I've done it...should've just written an e-mail to begin with. This just disproves the theory that with' age comes wisdom,' because here I am doing things at the convergence of my heart's wishes and not my head...oh well, I am probably going to regret this, but it's done now. Moving on to read another e-mail, she noticed that the just sent e-mail had not been deliverable. Odd. She went back and checked the screen name - yes, that was what Elena had given her. So, now what? Write Elena and ask her to give me the address again?? I can not appear too eager ...no, that would not do. Elena would see right through me. Sending Elena an e-mail back, she tried to casually mention-- in the text many paragraphs down – that she had e-mailed Joshua, but that the communique had come back as **'undeliverable'**, and she wrote down what she had used. Don't sound anxious, she cautioned herself; this is going to be a waiting game anyway, because Elena does not check her e-mails very often...it could be days before I hear anything. Oh well, what's a few more days, when you are talking forty years..she wondered. So, over to Face book for some mind-numbing jibber - jabber ...that should take my mind off things. Ah, there were some new photos of the twins their paternal aunt had put up...still don't like the idea of my babies' pics out there for the entire world to see, she mused. But then looking at the tiny adorable little bundles in their Pods, she was grateful to see them. Their Aunt Susan had missed her calling as she was a great amateur photographer, and yet, had chosen to do it only on the side. Anne smiled at the sight of her little darlings in their Pods in the **NICU**, their home now for several months. These were their miracles - so tiny yet perfect.

There was Brennan, the bruiser as he was twice the size, even from birth, of his miniature sister, Emma. Born almost two and one half months early, these little wonders together didn't weigh 5 pounds at birth. And yet, there they were - perfect. Emerson and her husband of five years, Wright had endured so much to get these little angels here; miscarriage after miscarriage.. fertility treatments.. doctors... specialists..additional treatments... and, finally when it seemed all hope was lost, Emerson became pregnant again. And this time..this time, God was looking out for these little ones...Praise Be, thought Anne closing her eyes and crossing herself. And then she saw it, the icon..**'You have unread messages'** Not wanting to tear herself away from the babies, she continued on until there were no more new stories to stall her progress. Here goes, inhaling deeply and closing her eyes, she hit the message retrieval icon.

# Chapter Sixteen

Oh wonderful, I have been tagged to play computer games... yeah. Oh, and the Ebersol family picnic is scheduled for the second Sunday of June at the Pavilion.. .bring a covered dish. Choir Practice set for Wednesday, the 7th has been changed to Thursday instead due to a/c problems in the Sanctuary. Final sale of the summer for Registered Bulls at Lodgensville Farm will be the 17th at 2 p.m. Prior registration is required. Only one more message left - so what are the odds? And then, there it was... staring at her...in black and white.. *'That would be me... How in the world are you, girl?'* And with that, Anne caught her breath, and quickly shut down her computer.

The rest of the day was, as is often said when your soul is troubled, was a blur. Everything was normal...normal. How could everything be normal when in the span of a few days her entire world had been invaded by unwanted hurtful memories. Hurt she thought was so deeply hidden away as to never rear its ugly head, was once again taunting her. Anne tended to her flower garden...the koi pond...walked the dogs....did all of the chores needed for the day. She did everything imaginable to keep from being inside where that damn laptop sat on her desk..mocking her. She and Reed went to the hospital to visit the babies, amazed at their on-going progress...they ate dinner at O'Reilly's Garage, one of their favorite restaurants because of the onion rings. And in the dusk of the summer day, they were once again home for the night. Anne was restless, even Reed noticed it. She passed it off as concern for the babies as now there was talk they might come home next week. She even made herself believe that was it; but she knew, deep down inside that wounded part of her heart, the part she thought she had locked away so many years ago.. she knew what it was. And, now that Joshua was back, it simply wasn't going away.

# *Chapter Seventeen*

Shaking the fog from his head, Joshua realized the loud beeping noise he kept hearing was the insistence of the gas pump to finish the transaction; and, he also realized that his hands were shaking like a leaf in the wind. Quickly returning the nozzle to its pump, he slid his credit card across the scan, took the receipt and headed inside. A Coke and a honey bun - that would satisfy any Cardiologist for a balanced morning meal; well, it would do for the time being. Paying quickly, he was once again back in his van. Ruther Mills was only 57 miles away. Good. I'll have plenty of time - time to do what? Beat myself up again for all the things I could do over if given the chance - or re-think my life - or better yet destroy it? With that, he took a big bite of his not-so-fresh honey bun and shifted back into high gear settling in for the last section of his trip.

The miles clicked off easily as Joshua settled into his routine. He had been right about it being a typical **HOT** Louisiana day; only 7 a.m. and already it was nearing 90. A scorcher for sure.. and the weather forecast called for afternoon thunderstorms. If luck would play out right, he will have already loaded and be headed back to the funeral home before that happened. Thunderstorms... oh.. how he used to love thunderstorms. The loud bangs of thunder –the scary kind that seem to move the ground with its power. Remembering back to what his mother used to say **'that thunder was the Devil beating his wife.'**...odd how that could have ever been accepted into rational conversation...wife abuse, the Devil...really? Ah, and the air after a storm had passed - that was the best part ..the fresh earthy scent that sensed renewal. Washed clean of sins. Funny, he thought, because even before I was saved, I used to think of rainstorms as being a bath to wash away the dirt from your life..sins. I never really thought of that before; be that I could wash away the past, he thought. What if you really could have second, maybe even third chances to make up for bad choices...bad timing...stupidity...what if? Looking ahead, he saw the exit for Ruther Mills, and, putting on his signal, merged off the interstate. His GPS told him he only had 2.4 miles to go on this part of the journey...but, in Joshua's mind, the journey ....back... had only just begun......

And, there just ahead...on the right --- the beautiful old sign, announcing

### 'Southerby Plantation'
### Established 1849
### A Retreat for Genteel Southern Ladies

Southerby Plantation was everything you would expect of a Southern Plantation...lush lawns, big 100 year old cypress trees, dripping with Spanish Moss, massive white columns supporting a wrap-around porch with welcoming chintz covered wicker rockers and swings, hanging ferns...even a wandering gaggle of chubby white geese. It was idyllic..it was *'Gone with the Wind'* in **real**, not **reel** time. Simply put..it was breathtaking. Joshua arrived at Southerby's just as morning tea was being offered on the side lawn to a group of impeccably well-dressed fading Southern belles. Pampered little ladies of a day long past, there they sat in the shade of the big old cypress tree, in their chintz covered wicker chairs, white gloves and straw hats; what stories they could tell of long ago cotillions, shy kisses stolen from a beau in the garden, of a gentler time long ago, now lost. Joshua smiled broadly at the sight of this glimpse of the past. Walking slowly to the front entrance, he spoke, nodding his head in true Southern gentleman style, acknowledging Mrs. Hattie O'Leary, the Proprietress of Southerby's standing on the front Portico. Gently taking her pre-offered hand, he grazed its aged silken skin with a touch of his lips.' Morning Miss Hattie..fine day, is it not?' Affectionately known as Miss Hattie to everyone, even though she had been married when she was much younger. Everyone knew the story... it was a scandal, you see, because Miss Hattie had run off when she was but sixteen with a boy 'of questionable lineage' - and, he had, in turn, left her - alone, unmarried and, 'in a family way' with his child. Such a scandal had never been seen in Ruther Mills before. Miss Hattie's father, the Town's Mayor, Colonel Sotherby, had 'allowed' her to come home. He found her a 'suitable husband' to hide her shame, and, he never forgave her for her 'indiscretion' but, he absolutely adored the tow-haired little boy that came with her; the Greek tragedy continued when on a summer day over 60 years ago, both of her parents, her commissioned husband and her precious little boy all perished in a boating accident on the Lake. Having no marketable skills to survive, Miss Hattie turned her beloved plantation home, Southerby Plantation into '**An Elderly Retreat for the Genteel Southern Lady**', thus affording her not only the respectability she craved, but a lucrative livelihood as well. Miss Hattie nodded her greeting, then turning quietly, they both walked back to her office. Miss Hattie's residents were not just residents to her. They, often, were remnants of her long ago past, friends of friends and such. So the tears that welled up in her aged blue eyes were real as she spoke of Miss Ellenor Rose Yon, who had just passed at the grand old age of 93 from natural causes. Speaking quietly she told Joshua Miss Ellenor had slipped ' her earthly bonds and was finally going Home to meet her Papa and Mama at that Grand Staircase in the sky.' Joshua leaned in listening carefully as talking with Miss Hattie was like slipping back to the days of mint juleps and hoop skirts. Sally- Lynn, Miss Hattie's assistant, slipped thru the side door bringing a silver tray filled with tea biscuits and mint wrapped ice tea, only acknowledging Joshua with a nod of the head as Miss Hattie was speaking of finding Miss Ellenor this morning 'looking like an Angel sent from God - all peaceful.' Raising a lace hanky to her damp eyes and inhaling quietly, Joshua waited patiently for Miss Hattie to finish, careful not to move from his

Wing chair. She sighed deeply, then turned around, reaching for the tea tray and offered him up some 'refreshment before you start your long journey home, my boy'. Joshua accepted her hospitality for it would be useless to try and rush her - things were done so differently here in the deep South. There was a measure of Honor - of respect you just could not buy...you accepted it with the same grace in which it was offered. Upon finishing with their morning tea, Miss Hattie rose gently from her chair, Joshua rising quickly in a gesture of respect. She handed him a small manila folder with the papers he would need to take Miss Ellenor on her final journey. Walking him back to the main entrance, she instructed Sally-Lynn to have Jebidiah meet Joshua at the side entrance to 'complete his trip'. Lifting her lace hanky to field off a stray tear, Miss Hattie looked deep into Joshua's eyes, taking his strong tanned hands in her frail ones, and, with a far-away look in her eye...wished him ...'God Speed My Son, on your journey '; and, with that, she turned and re-entered her office. Joshua walked back out into the mid-morning sunshine and onto the shaded Portico. Pausing momentarily, he found himself mesmerized by the sheer beauty and charm of the Mansion and its grounds. It was like he was caught in a time-warp. He could easily visualize the gentleness of this long past era...charming Southern belles in their hooped skirts and bonnets. He could almost hear the soft Southern drawl they would have possessed. This being the deep South, he thought back to the days when seeing a young man in the dappled gray uniforms of the CSA would have been the norm. In fact, if memory served him correctly, there was a family cemetery and Mausoleum on the property; and, interred were several members of the Southerby family who had served proudly for the Confederacy. He remembered back when he first began his transport business, he visited Southerby Plantation along with several other homes for the elderly in the area. It was old Jebidiah that had shown him the treasured Memorial - yes, I do remember now; because he told me the sad story of Miss Hattie's family drowning out on the Lake all those years ago. Memories..such memories we all share. We are all intertwined as God's children, he thought. He stepped off the Portico, and headed down the pave way to his van. And now, precious Lord, it is my duty, as well as my privilege, to bring another of your Flock, Home to You.

Joshua drove his van around to the side entrance. Inconspicious to the general eye, Miss Hattie had wanted it that way. She wanted her home to always be filled with life, not death; she wanted her residents to leave with reverence thru a garden filled with her beautiful flowers, thus there was no morgue. The residents remained in their own personal rooms until such time as they took their final journey. With Jebidiah's help, Miss Ellenor was carefully placed in the van, secured and covered with a lovely quilt, one that Miss Ellenor had made herself and, had embroidered her initials, ERY alongside those of her intended, RBR, III, which stood for Robert Bradford Rayburn, III, on the outside edge. Miss Hattie had said it was one of her favorites. It was one she made for her " **Chest of Hope and Dreams**" something all genteel Southern girls did to prepare for their wedding, even today. Jebidiah stepped back from the van..shaking his head, sadly.. 'Poor Missy Ell..dats quilt yonder dare she done made.. Jest nots to bes..Misser Joshua.. cause Missy Ell, wells, hers intends, dat Rayburn boy, he nots come bac from dats big ole war...so sad...so sad. '.Jebidiah went on..'Yaws nos dats Great War dey called it. Bes so sad..tsk..tsk. Yaws goin' take reel good care of Missy Ell, rights?' Joshua nodded; he was accustomed to such stories being told, as this generation seemed to be passing at an alarming rate recently. Joshua listened to old Jebidiah continue on talking about how hot it was going to be today, and with a hardy slap on the back, wished Joshua ' a goods trip home.' Such stories to be told, Joshua mused to himself as he pulled the privacy curtains on the back door of his van and closed it. And only You, dear Heavenly Father, know how long our road is before we take that final journey to Your feet, he thought. Joshua thanked Jebidiah for his help, took one last look at the beautiful grounds and slowly slipped into the driver's seat, and pulled out of the driveway. He and Miss Ellenor were headed to Montfrey Funeral Home, only 50 miles away. What a glorious day to be going Home, he thought as he started the second leg of his journey. Life can be so tenuous, so fragile at times; and yet, for Miss Ellenor, life had been a full 93 years. Perhaps, in retrospect, not all glorious. There had been trials, he was sure; ah, but what a story she would have been able to tell of all those precious 93 years. In his business, Joshua knew how fragile life, as we all know it, could be and how quickly it could slip away. Between his ministry and his transport business, he had seen entirely too many tiny white coffins closed on lives much too soon. So, I am happy for you, Miss Ellenor Rose Yon. A true Southern Lady is going ... Home. May your Homecoming be a joyous event as you join your long passed family and finally take your place in the Heavenly Father's House. God Bless You.

And so, this is what he did...with reverence and respect for those he did not know in life, but would meet in death. Miss Ellenor was on her way - home. **Home.** There was that word again. Twice in one day he thought...but this time, it didn't hurt. His cell phone jarred him back to the present - picking it up, the front wall read, Petra. Guess she was calling to see how the trip was going. He answered to hear Petra's heavy Czech accent on the other end...'Oh Josuawa, I have drown my phone'- the unmistakable sound of disappointment in her voice came thru loudly. Excuse me, what was that...you 'drown your phone, dear??' Petra wasn't crying, but sounded very distraught...finally figuring out that she had been drinking her coffee while at the kitchen sink, and had dropped her phone in the dishwater. Trying hard not to laugh at the mental picture this afforded him, Joshua told her not to worry that it was just a cell phone - it could be replaced. After calming her and assuring her that he would be home later, he disconnected the call - it was then that it occurred to him that Petra had been dropping a lot of things recently..bumping into things..probably nothing to be concerned about, he told himself - but, maybe he should say something. Mulling that thought over, he noticed the exit coming up for Montfrey. My job is nearly done, Lord. You have once again allowed me to be Your servant. And speaking to the precious cargo he had made the journey with...'I wish your journey be a good one, Miss Ellenor, Yon...you are Home.' Joshua and Miss Ellenor arrived at Montfrey Funeral Chapel and Mortuary less than an hour later. As Joshua pulled up to the side entrance, he was met by two older gentlemen in conservative dress suits. Joshua had to smile at this as he was passionate about respect..dignity for all; these being two of the main reasons he had founded his company, **A Touch of Comfort**, a number of years ago. In his role as a Minister, he often found himself helping families with their spiritual needs in the solemn transfer from life of a dearly loved one. While he tried to ease the suffering as much as he could, it was an event that happened a number of times before he founded his business that truly bothered him. On one particular occasion, he had been at a local nursing home when one of the residents had passed, and having been asked by the family to stay until the transport service arrived, he was appalled at what had happened. Two young men, in their early twenties, had come to pick up this gentleman for his final journey and they were dressed in t-shirts and blue jeans with tennis shoes. They could have been dressed to attend a high school basketball game, he thought...that is just not right, he told himself.. **not right**. So, when he finally decided to start his own company, it was **mandated** that the men would wear dark conservative business suits **WITH** a tie - and if a lady was among the group, she would also be similarly attired - this was not up for any type of discussion. This was the way it was going to be done. He would show that the end of life deserved just as much attention to detail as the beginning. It would be handled with respect, dignity and total responsibility. This was how it was with Joshua. There would be respect from the moment the team took the call - ***Respect and Dignity*** - that was Joshua's motto. So, when he began his business several years later, he literally changed the face of the transport business in Southern Louisiana, as well as the entire State of Louisiana. One of his greatest accomplishments, he felt, was that this - *his* - respectful dress code was adopted by the SFDA, the Southern Funeral Director's Association; and, for Joshua, that felt good. He **had** made a difference. So, it was on this beautiful afternoon, the life cycle of Miss Ellenor Rose Yon had come full circle. And, though Joshua never knew this Southern Lady in life, he had made her journey going **Home** a dignified one...His precious cargo, Miss Ellenor Rose Yon was on the final leg of her journey to the waiting arms of Our Heavenly Father.

# Chapter Eighteen

For the second straight night, sleep alluded Anne. She could not shut down her mind and it was most annoying. I will not get up..she told herself...and, turned over to her side only to be met by a concrete ball of immovable fur. Well, she smirked, I guess I will get up. Padding thru the hall to the kitchen, she thought..*de ja vue*. Did this last night...wonder if this is going to be the norm of things now. Glancing across the room, there it was - her laptop. Up until a few days ago, she never really paid too much attention to that modern inconvenience. Now, it was like a wound that would not heal; she kept putting a band aid on it, but it kept bleeding thru. Oh crap, she thought out loud and turned it on. Whizzing to life, she waited impatiently for it to boot. And when it did, she hesitated, then without any further thought, she shut it down and plodded back to bed.

# *Chapter Nineteen*

Elena Adams Fossey was happy in her second marriage..one that had come on the heels of one that had ended badly...very badly. She had been married to Anne's older brother, Bryan for over twenty five years - two children - good careers...and then, it happened. Her world collapsed around her and the children when she found her husband guilty of adultery.

**Adultery.** Bad word. Even worse *divorce*. Divorce in our Catholic world was the end of life. It changed everything and not for the good of anybody. But their divorce had made the War of the Roses look like a Sunday School Picnic. It divided families and, everyone was affected. Anne, Reed and Emerson were collateral damage, as well. There was this whole family 'loyalty' issue and because Bryan was his mother's favorite child - the walk on water child - Anne was caught between a rock and a hard place. If she sided with Elena, she was dead to her mother. If she sided with Bryan, she lost Elena as well as her only niece and nephew, Jenna and Christopher; and if she tried to be neutral, it was a battle of who was doing what to who the last time they talked. And, so it was for nearly twenty years, until Emerson was to be married. Emerson wanted to invite Elena, and so did Anne and Reed, but her mother played the "I won't go if **THAT** woman is invited.." so they all opted to invite the cousins and her wayward brother and his then, mistress. And even that didn't turn out well - Bryan's mistress made a scene...they left the reception and didn't even tell Anne or Reed, or even Emerson and Wright, goodbye. So, started the second family feud between Anne, her mother, Bryan and his "love". Of course, Bryan could do no wrong; so everyone looked the other way and muddled through.There were squabbles, then Bryan decided that he didn't need Anne or his mother in his life. He more or less ignored them all for years until their mother passed - and even then there was tension between all of them.. Crap, Anne thought ...there's tension between her and Bryan now. They haven't spoken since their mother's passing. The kind of tension still that has resulted in a split that even to this day stands. Then several years later, Elena's mother passed...Anne and Reed discussed it and decided that they were going to pay their respects. Elena's mother had been Anne's chaperone to the Miss South Caroline State Pageant and had always been dear to her; and, she had also been thrown in the collateral damage pile. It was only 'right' for her to go and pay her respects, and, hopefully it would work out for the best. And it did. Anne waited patiently to speak to Elena, having already spoken to one of her other sisters to make sure it would be alright. Elena turned around, saw Anne and the both of them hugged, cried and hugged some more. It was the re-start of their relationship. Anne had missed Elena terribly; she was the only sister she would ever have as she was not especially close to any of Reed's sisters, who were all much older than her. Losing Elena was a terrible loss for her, almost like a death. Now, Elena and her niece and nephew were back in her life; and, Elena would have the gift of Emerson back in hers, a fact that pleased her, as well as Rolfe, immensely. Elena had always held a soft spot in her heart for Emerson as she had been so much younger than Jenna and Christopher. She had said it was like having a baby again, but it went home with its parents and there was no 2 a.m. feeding. So when Elena saw the e-mail from Anne, she felt a bit of dread because she knew *why* she was returning a note to her so quickly. They kept in touch but not every few days..and here it was, only a day from hers. Opening Anne's e-mail, she quickly scanned through it - the simple stuff she would catch up with later- what was the reason for this? Ah, there it was — Anne had tried to contact Joshua...she knew she would. That was why she purposely left off one of the letters to his e-mail address. She wanted to give Anne more time to think about it before she contacted him...

maybe, just maybe, she wouldn't. Not that she shouldn't...it was just...well, too much time had passed. They had both moved on. Elena had been privy to the entire situation with Anne and Joshua and she just didn't want her hurt all over again. And she didn't want Joshua hurt either. But it looked as if it would be out of her hands; she sighed, and knowing she could do no different, she e-mailed Anne back...' Sorry...I inadvertently left off one of the letters..oops, you know how I type sometimes! Let me know what happens...love you much. Elena.' With that, Elena crossed herself and sighed ...' From my lips to God's ears, pray I did right..'

# Chapter Twenty

Joshua was nearing home. It had been a long, long day. The trip back was uneventful even though his mind would not afford him any down time. His mind kept traipsing back through years of memories...some good, some bad. He saw his Mother, his long past Dad...thought about the sister who died when he was just a baby himself...his big brother now losing his battle with MS...and Anne. His search for her had consumed him off and on, for the most part of 40 years. And it wasn't until the internet opened up the world to seekers that he felt he had a chance of finding her again. He had tried all of the sites he could come up with - not knowing her married name, where she lived...he couldn't even do the Classmates thing because they went to different schools. It seemed he always hit a dead end. He couldn't find her on any social site, but that didn't surprise him because she had pulled back from her outgoing ways and had, even when he last knew her, become shy and reserved. He didn't know Elena's new married name, or Elena's mother's new married name, so that hit a dead end as well. Most of the 'Group' had either passed on or moved...dead end after dead end. It wasn't until he had a friend request on Face book that Elena's name popped up as a possible mutual friend; he nearly fell off his chair in his office when he saw her name come up......OUT LOUD...***Glory Be!!*** His excitement took his breath away...then rationale took over. I have to write Elena. After a moment, he gathered his thoughts and began to ponder what his next step would be. I must pray and ask guidance. I can not walk this road alone. And with that, he reverently bent his head and humbly prayed for guidance. ' You are always there for me, Lord...I cannot do this without You.' And with that image in his mind, Joshua turned into the driveway of 17 Chapel Way, Debrussiae Parish, La.

# Chapter Twenty One

Pausing in the driveway, he went back. He remembered sitting in front of his computer, wondering how it was he had ever gotten the courage up to write Elena and ask her about Anne. He wanted to ask everything about her. He wanted to know where she was, what she was doing, how was she, who did she marry, was she happy, did she have children....the list was endless. And he knew he had to tread these waters without seeming too anxious... or inquisitive. He cautioned himself against asking too much ...but he *had* to know. Elena will see right through me..she is psychic that way. He reread the text at least a hundred times before he agreed with himself that it wasn't push or nosey ...he tried to make it sound almost like an after thought - he had 'thought about Anne just the other day. How was she? So when he received Elena's rather vague reply, he wasn't really surprised. Chain of command, he thought. Elena won't do anything without checking with Anne. Elena threw out just enough information to make him want more... but she did say that she would be in touch. So, now the waiting game begins..yet again. Tossing his keys in the console, Joshua exited his car. Now, where was Petra and her drown phone, he wondered.

# Chapter Twenty Two

Several days passed - even though things were not normal, Anne tried to pretend they were. Brennan was first to come home; then a few weeks later, Emma joined him; so she was distracted in that happy world of diapers, feedings and the no sleep issue that comes with babies. Everyone tried to help Emerson and Wright as much as they could - one baby turned your world upside down, but **TWO**...Lord help us all. Everyone took shifts and *everyone* Anne, Reed, Sara-Katherine and John, Wright's parents, were sleep deprived, smiling thru the exhaustion and the never ending succession of bottles, diapers and more bottles and diapers. Anne had been so busy she had, perhaps willed herself to put aside the turmoil her soul had been in. Plopping down at Emerson's computer in the library, she decided to check her e-mails since she had not done so since coming to help with Brennan and Emma. There it was. Elena had written her back. Surprise..because the last e-mail she had gotten from her were pictures of her and Rolfe from Italy. Reading Elena's explanation of her 'oops' brought a smile to Anne's tired being; she knew full well what Elena had done..and, she loved her all the more for it. Elena had always been protective towards her - the way a big sister would. Now with the correct e-mail address, she had the final piece of the puzzle. Again to herself, I have Joshua's full e-mail address. He has already sent me a return message on Face book ..now the ball was in her court. I can't - no I won't - reply to the Face book message, she thought.. that leaves everything we say out there for the whole world to read and wonder about. I will have to figure out an e-mail reply. What do you say to someone you loved and lost after 40 years I know, in my heart, he is still there...deep down... where I put him years and years ago. And , if I am totally honest with myself, I know that I do still love him. Now what do I do? she pondered; however her entire train of thought was lost as hearing little Emma whimper in her nursery, she quickly exited her e-mails; and, for the first time in days, she found herself humming on the way to tend to her little miracle granddaughter's needs.

Opening the nursery door, Anne quietly walked over to the antique white crib her precious little Emma was in. This was Emerson's crib, and mine before that, and my mother's - your Great Grandmother, Emma before that. It had been in their family for generations having been made by her Great Great Grandfather. Peeking over the high side rail, she saw the tiny little bundle squirming in her efforts to wake up...not fussing...just taking in this whole new world she had come into. Speaking to her softly, Emma cooed back. At only six pounds and now nearly four months old, she was barely the size of a newborn; ah, but Emma had defied the odds. In fact, she had stuck her tongue out at them; every time something else went wrong or got in her way, she found the strength to fight whatever battle was at hand. She had life-threatening surgery at only 10 days old ..at only two pounds and an amazing ten inches long, she fought her way through that - and had the scars to prove it – infections - not being able to tolerate her formula– being fed on a tube – Anne remembered falling on her knees night after night and, begging, yes **begging**, God to give Emma the will to live, the strength to continue the fight. And, every time there was a challenge, Emma rose above it. This precious little bundle would always be a miracle. Anne picked up the tiny pink blanket with its priceless cargo, and cooing while nuzzling her tiny face, reminded her how much she and everyone around her dearly loved her - and once again, thanked God for her and her brother; and, for joining their lives.Walking down the hallway from Emma's nursery, Anne saw Wright's mother, Sara-Katherine coming in through the sunroom patio doors. Since the twins' births, she and Sara-Katherine had become close friends and 'comrades in crime'. They would laugh, joyfully, because it was their joint conspiracy intention to spoil these two miracles of God's love to the absolute. Sara-Katherine didn't even stop to put down her bag or sweater before practically running to see little Emma. ' Isn't she just about the most precious little bundle of joy, you have even seen...' she drawled softly..going on... 'where is our little 'Prince Brennan', Anne?' Anne laughed softly, explaining that the little heir was still napping, and offered up the tiny Emma to Sara-Katherine's waiting arms. It was plain to see Sara-Katherine was just as smitten as anyone who came in contact with these two little darlings. There they stood in the early morning sunshine, both doting Grandmothers admiring God's handiwork. Looking at tiny little Emma, Sara-Katherine smiled as she cuddled her, whispering ..'Grand -Papa John's coming down to see you, his little Angel..' and, then to Anne.. 'He said he was going to go by the Farmer's Market to get some fresh fruits and veggies. He's going to bring lunch from the Deli for all of us.. where's Reed ..and Wright and Emerson ? ' Anne laughed and said..'Good heavens, Sara-Katherine, I could not begin to tell you where Reed might be..at least not until it is closer to lunchtime! Between the horses, the sheep and the Farm, in general, he is like the fog that covers the pasture...everywhere! As for Wright and Emerson, I sent them packing. They needed to do some errands in town and I instructed them to actually 'sit down and eat a meal' instead of grabbing something and stuffing it in their mouths. Since the 'calvary' was here, they were expendable! ' They both laughed good- naturedly. The 'Princess' Emma cooed, bringing their attention back to her; then, they both heard the whimper on the monitor from the other nursery, meaning the little 'Prince' was waking requiring attention from one of his loyal subjects. Anne winked her eye at Sara-Katherine..' Your turn, Grandma '..and, both of them smiled broadly. Sara-Katherine observed to Anne..' This is when I wish we could revise this 'Mother' model, and give all women at least three arms..one arm each for a baby, and an extra retractable one for 'whatever - whenever..' Anne added...' And, God should be a woman! ' Then, just for salvation's sake, Anne crossed herself. Together they walked down the hall to Brennan's nursery. Opening the door, they both were greeted with big baby blues eyes and an ear to ear grin. Anne looked over at Sara-Katherine, still holding Emma, and mused to the smiling little boy...'This is the only time in your life, little man, you can be completely bald, have not a tooth in your head, chubby legs and a jelly-belly..and, have every woman madly in love with you!' They all laughed...even little Emma smiled sweetly.

'Em's interviewing next week for a nanny, so I guess our time will be more limited, Sara-Katherine. I will miss this so much!' Anne said. 'Oh, me too...I don't want to give up our little ones at all. Do you suppose Wright and Emerson would notice if we 'Grand-Napped' them and skedaddled with 'em?' laughed Sara-Katherine. 'I'm thinking 'Amber-Alert' might play a factor in our crime..' Anne giggled.

# Chapter Twenty Three

Anne came home from Emerson's, relinquishing her assistance role to Sara-Katherine and John. My word will a hot shower and something cold to drink be heaven, she thought. Well maybe later. Mags and Vanna met her at the garage door demanding attention..a walk, play ball - anything. So, off they went on a late afternoon stroll. Her cell phone rang; it was Reed calling to tell her he would go on from Emerson's to the farm and feed the stock before he came home. Okay - so that gives us even more time girls. We can take a long walk if we want. They meandered down to the lake; she watched with total amusement as Vanna found several frogs and was in the midst of terrorizing the entire colony while Mags held down the fort on the bank barking her encouragement. This went on until Vanna's tongue was nearly as long as her legs and Anne made her heel - a big mistake. Vanna came, like she always did. but she was no longer a black lab as she was coated from nose to tail in the sandy muck from the lake and intent on sharing it with Anne. Vanna shook, Anne headed for cover. All the while, Mags fell in the Lake trying to get away from the one frog that would not be intimidated by that ridiculous big dog. All in all, quite a sight they must have been. Ah, but it was fun! They trudged back up the hill in the lazy afternoon sunshine dripping wet, arriving home almost simultaneously with Reed, who nearly fell over laughing at the sight of the three of them. The three of them were covered for the most part from head to toe; he reached for the garden hose and started to spray away the muck. Anne squealed, Vanna tried to eat the stream of water and Mags, well, Mags was so insulted that she was dirty, proceeded to hide under

Reed's truck. So while Reed tried, in vain, to coax her from under his truck and Vanna rolled on the mossy lawn, Anne headed upstairs for that hot shower she should have taken advantage of thirty minutes ago. Heavens, it felt good to laugh, really laugh again, she thought as the water ran dark brown down the shower drain. If reality could only be this simple.

# Chapter Twenty Four

Joshua opened the front door to be greeted by his three four footed children. The three black cocker spaniels he and Petra had rescued from a puppy mill - Lady, Tramp and Mischa - greeted him with all the noise and commotion that a visiting dignity would have received; and, Petra was not far behind, trying her best to navigate the free space around the dogs. A quick peck, questions about the trip; then he asked Petra about her phone. She said she had called the cell company and would go tomorrow afternoon on her lunch break to get a new one. She hoped they would be able to retrieve all of the info off of hers, but the rep wasn't sure how much damage had been done with the water. Well, at least, she isn't so upset any more, thought Joshua as he headed to the bedroom to change out of his suit. A shower now.. no later; he needed to go to the office and check out the day's happenings since he had not been there all day. A few phone calls needed to be returned; the central office in Landon called. There had been two other calls for removals today and three were on the schedule for tomorrow. Oh, yes, and there was a really sweet message from Miss Hattie thanking him for his coming for Miss Ellenor today. All in all, he thought, not a bad day. He looked up from his desk to see Petra bringing him a big glass of iced tea; he was suddenly struck by how pale she appeared. When he questioned if she felt okay, she shrugged and said that she had not felt too good recently, but that she had an appointment to see Dr. Hubert in a few weeks and she would address it then if she still felt poorly. He accepted that as Petra was one of those never sick a day in her life people; he attributed the tiredness with the fact her parents were elderly; and about three times a week, she made the 100 mile round trip to check on them and her mentally challenged brother, Roman. And, I am sure 'drowning' her phone today, didn't help, he thought. Besides, Petra was one of the most self-sufficient people he knew. He respected her judgement, and appreciated her input on anything he had questions about. Since immigrating here over 30 years ago from Czechoslovakia , she had taken on the role of family protector. She often would say that it had been good coming to America, because after Chernobyl, her homeland had little faith in the future. She was smart - she was funny, too. Her Czech language transfer sometimes got her into a world of trouble, but she would laugh at herself and keep on going. Just another endearing quality that made Joshua thankful she had come into his life all those years ago. He had needed someone... she had needed someone. Both coming off of bad divorces..him a loveless and frustrating one...hers a mentally abusive one. They both had needed a soft place to land. Joshua felt he had been the true winner in that one; he had found his place serving God and, he had found Petra. Things were looking up; and, for a short idyllic time period, he nearly forgot about Anne. Well, almost.

# Chapter Twenty Five

Sitting on the back deck, Anne and Reed were enjoying that soft lull that comes over the landscape as the daylight fades giving way to the tranquility of another summer's evening. In the distance, a whippoorwill made its plea for acknowledgment. One by one the stars began to shimmer as if lighting the path for the moon to follow. It was still warm from the day's heat, and the air was sweet with honeysuckle and wild roses. There was a 'comfortability' about them. One that was blended so completely into each other's lives that they often simply sat and enjoyed life.. no words necessary. Then, sometimes they rattled on about their day or what the next would bring. After nearly 40 years, it was nice how they could finish each other's sentences. Even though her doing so sometimes frustrated Reed; then sometimes they could speak what the other was thinking. Yes..it was nice. When she looked over at Reed, she felt at peace . Reed was a good man, she thought. He has put me through a lot in this marriage, but the drinking was past history now. And what he missed in Emerson's life, he is making up ten-fold with Brennan and Emma. He simply adores his little 'Princess' Emma...and, with Brennan he finally has that little man to take fishing, play ball with, take to the auction sales. He has become a Grandfather in every aspect, drinking it in like he once did Jack Daniels. He had always provided well. In fact most of their arguments back in the day were centered around his working too hard and spending too many overtime hours at his Supervisor's job. He was more available to Lofton Mills than to us, she thought; he missed so much of Emerson's life because of so many things that now don' t even seem important. But, since his early retirement at only 55, and with the twins now in their lives, he had changed. He was a more loving husband, a more willing participant in their marriage even though the passion had long been gone. His abuse of drinking had lead to being diagnosed about fifteen years ago with Diabetes 2 and with that the physical intimacy between them ended. Now, much later, he was on insulin therapy to help ward off the devastating effects of this horrendous disease. Just another thing they had in common as Anne, too, was diabetic. She was genetically disposed to the disease as both of her parents had it. Seems we do everything together these days, she mused. She missed the intimacy they once had. It had been a bone of contention between them for a long time as Reed couldn't accept it. He took it to be anybody's fault but his own. He was never good at accepting responsibility for anything he could have been remotely responsible for. But, in time, that, too changed and Reed truly became the man he was always meant to be; with no shame for having changed. Only thankfulness to have lived through it all. And, the whole time, Anne was by his side...she meant her marriage vows...'**..til death do us part** ' was carved in stone...and not up for discussion. And, so, why - *why*, now was she so intent on disturbing the calm, she wondered.

# Chapter Twenty Six

Anne heard the Grandfather clock in the hallway chime nine bells, but she just didn't want to go inside. Reed had long since deserted her for some old Western movie on the tube, leaving her to her thoughts. Conflicted as she had been over the past few days, it was suddenly clear the path she would take. She had weighed all of the pros and cons; and as usual, the cons outweighed the pros, but that just didn't matter. There was still too much to say, too much to try and explain. The time for resolution - maybe even ***absolution*** - was at hand. She must tread delicately; and, if necessary, to keep from hurting Joshua all over again, she would walk away. And with solid reserve, she vowed she *would not*, **could not** ..hurt Reed. That simply would not happen; that nagging thought she had in the back of her mind hit her hard...what if I am looking through rose colored glasses here? Could this simply be a 'Bucket List' cross off ? Thinking back, she knew Joshua had been so hurt when they were together for the last time - that elusive second chance they might have had. Yeah, a second chance; .and yet, I hurt him worse that time than the first time. In trying to protect him, she had broken, *literally* broken his heart; and, in doing so, irreparably broken hers, too. She had mapped out all of the strategy to sending him away - for his own good – she had wanted him to truly believe it was over between them so that he could leave and start over. A new job, new state, new everything. She had never intended for it to end so badly. Everything would have gone as she had planned, she thought. Yes, it would have gone just the way I planned it. Joshua was being transferred and was set to take over as a Divisional

Manager with a large retail chain several states away. This will work out. He doesn't need to know this is all a farce; but more important, he doesn't need me to complicate his life. Everything was going according to plan..that is, until that Sunday when they were standing on her front porch in the fading evening light. Kissing her gently, it was a magical moment. Anne took a deep breath, the moment of truth was upon her. She was just about to tell Joshua good-bye, really good-bye, when out of the blue, he took his hand and laying it on her expanding belly, said...'Marry me...now'. **No, Joshua** - she screamed in her head...you cannot , we cannot do this. There are so many reasons why we cannot do this. With courage Anne did not know she even possessed, she looked deep into Joshua's pleading eyes, and firmly said. . .'No.'. Then, blindly she began the whole spiel of lies - her plan to let him go; she didn't love him anymore, things had changed too much between them now, and there never again, would be a 'them'. He needed to leave to begin the next chapter of his life - the one without her. She held her breath waiting for him to challenge her, but he simply raised her hand to his lips, and with tears rimming his eyes, he walked up the front walk to his car and quietly pulled out of the driveway. Anne watched him leave - for the second time in as many years..and stood frozen on the porch for what seemed an eternity. Then taking a deep breath, she opened the front door. Her mother looked up from her reading when Anne opened the door and with a questioned look on her face, she was just about to ask Anne if everything was alright, but Anne flew past her, headed upstairs. Taking the first step on the staircase, Anne couldn't stop - the tears were much too close to spilling over. She fled to her bedroom and then, the tears came –wrenching, sobbing. The can't catch your breath kind. They flowed until there were no more. She reached for yet another tissue, then sat up straight in the bed; and with a fortitude that would have made Scarlett O'Hara proud...she announced to herself... 'I will never think of this again. It will be a piece of the past that is never re-visited.

I will lock this day - and Joshua - away inside the deepest part of my heart and only I will hold the key. Never, never again will I hurt him this way..or me....' Crossing herself, she rose from the bed, looked in the mirror at her tear stained face, and vowed to take charge of her life. And, for the most part, she had held true to that vow...until a few days ago. And now, all of the Ghosts of the Past were all around her. All because of Joshua.

# Chapter Twenty Seven

Joshua sat at his computer - he wasn't working, simply put he was trying to mind-transfer his thoughts to this hunk of modern technology to make a message appear. Lady was at his feet - napping. Tramp chewing on a rawhide bone and Mischa, heavens, there was no telling what that scamp was up to. I should be working - I have a sermon to put together. I have devotions to post on my page. I have bills to look over for the business... and, yet. here I sit, like a lovesick teenager waiting for my girl to call me back. This is ridiculous to say the least. I am a well-versed, college educated ordained minister. I counsel hundreds of people every year. I am an instrument of faith and belief to my congregation. Here I sit, reverting back to the 19 year old kid who never got over his first love. What would Petra think if she only knew what torment my mind is going thru. She would not understand why or even how Anne could still be so important to me. In her old world ways, she would probably feel betrayed...that I had somehow let her down. The very thought of hurting Petra, even if by accident, was not to his liking. What would I say, how could I possibly explain to her why finding Anne was so important to me. How could I ever make her understand. In a moment of self damnation, he prayed to be guided through this and that the outcome would be a good one. After all, he was not looking to complicate his life - especially, not outside of his marriage vows. There was just this over-whelming need to bring this full circle...to understand...and, try to explain **why** he walked away like he did. And, how forty years later, he could not, nor had he ever, forgotten her or stopped loving her. His hurt had lessened with time. He remembered calling her a few months after that last Sunday; and, he also remembered how horribly cold she had been to him. As if she could not get off the phone quick enough. He had called to see how she was..to check on her- concern like always. But she didn't want to talk - no, she didn't want to talk to **HIM**. Okay, two can play this game, he thought. So, back in those days, his answer to everything was to get drunk and forget. Think I'll call Gayle and maybe spend the night. That'll make me forget. Now looking back, he realized that was one of the stupidest decisions he had ever made.

# Chapter Twenty Eight

Anne awoke to hear raindrops pelting the patio doors in the bedroom...crap, she thought. I don't like rain. She had always called rain 'thought fodder.' And, that was just what she needed these days..a reason to think. Reed's side of the bed was empty, thus Mags had claimed the just vacated warm spot as hers. Raising her head to see what Anne was up to and realizing she hadn't really moved yet, she plopped her head down and fell back asleep. Good, thought Anne. I really don't feel like romping quite yet. She lay there in the semi-darkness listening to the rain. Wonder what Joshua is doing, she thought. She wondered again how it was he came to be a minister; why he was living in LA as the last she knew he was in Tennessee; about his wife - her name was Petra.. unusual name; she was pretty, dark hair - and apparently much taller than she was. **LOL**. Joshua used to tease her unmercifully about how height challenged she was. One of his favorite things to tease her with was that they were a *'perfect pair'*; because he could reach anything over her head and she could reach anything below his waist. She teased him about being Amazon tall and signing up for the professional basketball lottery, or, the one he dreaded the most... ' how was the weather up there'; and, he, in turn, would tease her about playing professional miniature golf or inquire of the goings on of the Pygmy Congress. They had so much fun with the differences between them. Funny, how you remember quirky things like that after all of these years.

It was Sunday and she should be getting ready for Mass. No, don't think I will today.. I hate getting wet with my clothes on. That was her justification to stay in bed, at least for the time-being.

Besides, if I get up, what will I do, she wondered. I've got bills-- the month's bills to pay; need to schedule an appointment for Mags to get groomed as it is becoming difficult to tell which end is which; need to find out from Emerson what she will need of me this week. Oh, and yeah, guess I better compose some kind of reply to Joshua - that should be my first priority, she thought. Maybe try another e- mail now that Elena has given the rest of his email address. Wonder if he is preaching today; what kind of speaker would he be. Since he was always a bit on the shy side, this truly is the other side of the coin, she mused. Joshua must have given up the Faith, as if he were in the Church, he would be a Priest, she thought. Odd...wonder what faith it was that he 'chose'. Pushing back the covers gently as not to awaken the fur ball on the other side of the bed, she walked to the patio doors and looked outside at the summer rain coming down; much heavier than before. Best go check the basement drain, she thought, because the last thing I want to be doing on a Sunday is bailing water. Slipping quietly down the basement steps, she paused on the bottom one. Closing her eyes, she remembered she needed to stand on a step to kiss Joshua. Shaking her head to clear that thought, she heard Vanna barking and hurried out to check on what her canine alarm system had encountered.

Opening the basement door, Anne looked to see what might have been the cause of Vanna's concern - nothing. Vanna was no help as she stuck her nose out the door, rain drops pelted her face and she gracefully backed up and laid back down on her bed. Well, thought Anne - one day I am going to understand what goes on in the mind of a dog. Trudging back up the steps, Anne wondered if she would ever be privy to understanding the intangible things of life...things you can not touch, cannot see. Like how much she had questioned her Faith in all things Holy that summer. Her inability to pull from that Faith made that summer even worse. And yet, now, her Faith was strong and unwavering. The power of prayer had been proven over and over the last few months with the twins – everyone she and Reed knew where praying for those dear little babies to make it...and, against all odds, their prayers had been answered. Those precious little bundles had been on every prayer list for miles around And, it didn't matter the faith preference...their names were there. **'*Pray for little Brennan and Emma-Elizabeth Mallen.*'** And, it **had** made a difference; Anne just knew it did. Especially when little Emma had life-threatening surgery at only 10 days old . She was thriving now...yes, prayer could work wonders. But wouldn't it be a little self-serving to ask God to guide me through this quandary with Joshua, she asked herself. Somehow matters of the heart did not qualify as deserving of Heavenly guidance in her thinking; but, what about matters of the Heart...those that went to the depth of your very soul, would that make the grade? You only have to ask to receive, she told herself... but...do I dare ask?

# Chapter Twenty Nine

The smell of freshly brewed coffee in the kitchen caught Anne's attention as she stepped from her shower; Oh good, she thought, Reed's home...wonder if he started breakfast yet. I think if he hasn't, I will make us some banana pancakes..that sounds yummy. Quickly drying off, she wrapped a towel around her still wet hair, donned her robe and stepped into the bedroom. She noticed the rain had picked up a bit as a slight wind was blowing it against the patio door. Great, it continues to rain - yet again on a Sunday... still thinking about Church. I'll see she told Mags who was now reclining, albeit upside down on the bed, looking at her. Feeling slightly risque, she laughed as she threw off her robe and tossed the towel over onto Mags. Talking to the happy little ball of fur wiggling out from under her impromptu prison, she glanced up in the mirror...not one to be overly concerned with her looks, she was a bit taken back by the dark circles that had suddenly appeared under her eyes. Thinking aloud, she said 'that's what dealing with newborns and the eminent lack of sleep will do to you, Mags'; to which Mags, towel hat half- on, half -off, questioningly looked at her as if trying to understand what Anne was saying. Did you know, Mags, that some people had actually said they thought me beautiful – of course that was in my younger days. Funny, because I kind of thought I was kind of cute...not beautiful by my standards. Beautiful - that was reserved for others, much prettier than I could have even been. I did have dark hair - dark green eyes - and I was tiny... do not look at me that way, you spoiled little furry mutt; but then, she went on to her captive audience, I also had a really good figure - thinking to herself, she remembered she used to laugh at herself and her figure. If she had only been 5'10. She had to laugh at Joshua when he told her she was simply ' *under-tall*'..'**under-tall**...***really***??' Comments aimed at poking fun of a news article when she had been one of the contestants in the Miss South Carolina State Pageant – all of nineteen. .her mother had point blank told her **not** to stand anywhere near the 'tall' girls..and, of course, the media picked up on her being the tiniest contestant and Helena Graham, at six foot and one inch, being the tallest. All over the newspapers it was..she laughed when she saw her mother's face after seeing the news photos of her and Helena standing back to back .. Goodness, I fit under her outstretched arms, she laughed to herself and remembering what she told her mother....' Oh, Mom..it is what it is...I had fun with it - and so did Helena!' she remembered playfully telling her mother. And her mother countering with..' My word, Anne..that girl is an Amazon!' Her figure had been perfect back then - 'perfect' .. her seamstress used to say.. While she was only a tad over five feet and one hundred pounds, the tape measure confirmed the hour-glass 36-24-36 figure. Maybe that was what got me in so much trouble, she thought. **No...** ***trusting stupidity*** ... got me in to trouble. The overwhelming need to be loved just for me, not always be the second child; it was only as an adult, had she realized how much her Father had tried to make up for her Mother not loving her the same way she did her brother. To her Father, she was his 'Princess'... and he made no attempt to hide his adoration of her. Sadly, her father passed when Anne was only in her early 20's, way too early - at 50 - from stomach cancer. But, in Anne's heart, she knew he had died from a broken heart. She had done that - that summer ... and nothing would ever convince her otherwise. And, I broke Joshua's, too. Looking back at the mirror, she saw the Anne of 'today'...the fuller figure, the finely etched laugh lines on her face, the graying hair. Was she still attractive, she wondered. I mean I did just collect my first SS check - 62- quite a milestone, my goodness, she pondered. All this seems like a lifetime ago - the days of beauty pageants and tiaras long since relegated to scrapbooks and faded memories. Good memories - like those of her and Joshua. I remember once, she thought aloud to Mags, ..'when we were on a date - it was summer - and there was a full moon – we were coming down Horseshoe Mountain Road... when for no reason, he stopped the car. I thought he was going to kiss me - but he got out of the car...sprinted over to the side of the road, bent down - now mind you, I had no idea what he was doing, that is until he came back with a hand -picked nosegay of mountain honeysuckle...'*I love you*'...was all he said and gently kissed me. That is the kind of memory a girl keeps with her forever, Mags. Yep... '*forever...and ever*'.

And yet, just a few weeks later after Joshua's graduation, they broke up...for the first time. That memory made Anne shudder. If only I could have seen what was happening; but no, I was so stubborn, so inflexible...looking back, I think it was more spoiled than anything else. Joshua had been working for a large retail chain his last year of school, and had been offered the opportunity to go into the Management Training Program. Since at that time, he didn't want to go on to college, even though he had been accepted at Auburn, so, it made perfect sense, at least to him, to jump at this opportunity. He could earn additional money for college while he was in the program..he tried to explain. Didn't matter, no I shouldn't say, that because I know Joshua *didn't want* to leave, but it was his future, hopefully would be *their* future, he thought; I just couldn't see it. ' I was furious,' Mags, absolutely furious she told the upside down puddle of fur on her bed...'and inflexible'. Please go to college first, you can still be in the training program on a part-time basis...do not let Auburn slip through your fingers. If he left to enter the program - several states away — hundreds of miles... that was '*the end of us as he knew it*', she threatened. As the day drew closer for Joshua to leave, I kept thinking, he will change his mind and choose to go to school. I just know he will...and then, things can go back to normal. He will start Auburn, and I will finish up at U-Alabama the following year. So when that Sunday finally came...'It was awful. Oh, Mags I was so angry at him, I didn't even kiss him good-bye...and I told him not to call either.' she informed the fur ball on her bed. Why is hindsight always 20-20, I wonder. Shaking the memory from her head, Anne had to ponder why all of these flashbacks were taunting her now. Was it because she had cracked Pandora's Box with *that* Face book message...or was the worse still to come. ' **Stop thinking**..' she told herself aloud.

Dressing quickly, Anne walked thru the hall to the kitchen following the smell of that delicious fresh brewed coffee. Where was Reed, she wondered. Coffee mug on the counter with warm coffee still in it, covering a hastily scribbled note - 'Gone to the farm - brood cow in labor - may need Vet...' Anne quickly dialed up Reed's cell phone and, was relieved to hear that, yes, the cow was in labor, but it did appear everything was going to work out - amazing how Mother Nature lets us humans **think** we are in charge when she really is - *all of the time*, she thought.

Pouring her a big steaming cup of dark liquid courage, she turned on the kitchen tv to her favorite radio station, then walked over and turned on her computer. Waiting for it to come to life, she noticed that the rain was lessening a bit. Good, at least the Mama Cow was in the warm dry barn and not in the field. A baby born in a stable on a Sunday...yes, that was a good reason to smile. Without any of her prior hesitation, Anne clicked her mouse on the e-mail icon and entered Joshua's e-mail address. She thought over what to say...not too much information, she cautioned herself..feel him out and see where this is going to lead. Pausing, while trying to figure out what to say. She heard the strains of a song, one that she dearly loved . Oh, how long has it been since I heard that one. She wasn't a big Elvis fan, but this one... oh, this one came at a time in her life when it seemed it had been written with her and Joshua in mind. Listening carefully, she fell back to that wonderful time when things were right between them, just before everything went wrong. And then, without thinking, she began to sing along.. *'Memories...pressed between the pages of my mind... Memories sweetened through the ages, just like wine... Quiet thoughts come floating down and settle softly*

***to the ground, like pools of autumn leaves around my feet....*** The song ended...but Anne was still lost in that faraway world of yesterday. Slipping back to reality, Anne realized that she had not written a single word; ok, she said out loud.. 'Get with the program and do this.'.. Basic stuff - she told him Elena had left off one of the screen letters and so this was her second try at an e- mail. Let's make this easier, she thought. I'll give him my home telephone number..even my cell number. That's totally selfish of me, because I **want** to hear his voice. I want to talk to him - ***again.*** The last time I talked with him I was so mean, she recalled. Only a few days before that last call, she had run into one of the 'Group' wives, one of his Mother's friends, and asking about how Joshua was doing, she was rather taken back when Mrs. Glochenous had made a point of telling her how wonderful he was doing. There was a wonderful new girl in his life; one that truly 'cared' about Joshua..an obvious dig at me, she thought; and, according to the information she had, it might even lead to marriage! From that moment on in the conversation, Anne could only hear her heart beating, and after a few more minutes excused herself and left the store quickly - to lick her wounds, as is often said. And luck would have it, just a few days later, Joshua called. Still reeling from the hurt, she, once again, vowed to lock him away and throw away the key. Maybe, this time it is ***final***, she thought when she hung up the phone. Why does this keep happening over and over...and, here I sit willing another chapter to be written. Another hurt, maybe...oh well... Anne thought, maybe the third time's the charm. But what possible expectations could either of them have this time. Maybe, it was good to be doing this... maybe we can each heal this time. Or maybe, this will be the final chapter. Re-reading the e-mail for the tenth time, she finally gave up; ... that would have to do ... after all, what do you say after 40 years? Inhaling, Anne hit '**send**' – no turning back now. Looking out the front window, Anne saw the rain had stopped. Best go to Mass - need to confess my sins and pray for guidance, 'cause I have a feeling I am really going to need it.

# Chapter Thirty

Making the finishing touches on his sermon, he tucked his head and asked that the hand of the Lord be on him today - to inspire his congregation with all that is good with the world. Looking at his desk calendar, Joshua realized that tomorrow would be Carey's birthday. Where had the time gone, he pondered ...Carey was going to be 40. And yet, it seemed like only yesterday he had looked into that nursery window and saw the product of his decision to get drunk and spend the night with Gayle. I am a Father now...the mere thought simply blew him away. The tiny little bundle wiggled in his blue blanket and let out a squall - that's **my** boy, he thought with all the pride he could muster. At least, I **think** he's my boy. **No**, that is of no consequence now...my name is on his birth certificate, so he **IS** my son. **Hello**... back to now, he instructed his brain; then, thinking back to last week when he and Carey were in Carter's Electronics getting some electrical supplies for a project at Church, he noticed Carey looking at a new stereo system for his truck. I should get him that. He'll probably just give it to Marissa, his daughter, Joshua's granddaughter. Laughing to himself, he thought... *that might just work*...**everybody's** happy and I'm out two hundred bucks. **LOL.**

**PING. PING**

**Messages waiting - 'You have Mail" ...**

When did we become a society that allowed our machines to talk to us, to dictate our lives, he wondered; turning around and looking at the screen, he ran through the new e- mails.Wonder if anything is here I need to answer. Then, his eyes caught an address, he didn't recognize. Could that be what I have been waiting for *..forever* it seems... Lord, give Your servant, strength, he prayed. Joshua inhaled deeply and, finding some inner strength, willed his hand to move the mouse to the appointed e-mail and hit read. He quickly scanned the first sentence of what Anne had written..re-reading it again...**again...*again*.** She wrote carefully, he noted, not giving out too much information, but appearing pleased that he had, indeed, wanted to contact her. Sometimes Anne was a hard read...especially that last summer. For someone he once knew almost as well as he knew himself, he thought, she holds back a lot...***but***... gives you the impression that she is being open. She reminds me of a wounded bird....wanting to trust the hand that is offered, but, afraid that it was ***that very*** hand that caused its hurt in the first place. This is going to be a challenge - will she even believe me when I tell her I have been searching for her for *years*..will she be wary as to why...does she know, I wonder, that I still love her, even now...or will she think I am just playing her... to get back at her... for - whatever. I will write her later... when I have had time to compose my thoughts. There is too much to write. We ***need*** to talk...not write***...but talk***. Dare I use one of those numbers to call her; she gave them to me, she must want me to use one or both. Oh, do I ever want to hear her voice again...that soft Southern drawl...that sweet laugh. What about her husband; will he understand or does he even know . I mean, I am not telling Petra for fear I would hurt her. I have told her a little about the special relationship that Anne and I had...but that was years ago. I remember telling her once when we were talking about the past...that I had my heart badly broken before; to which Petra had asked innocently..'..by Gayil, the #1 wife, no??' ......'no'... I had answered before thinking. Oh, well, too late now..' ..by Anne - but that's a long story and all in the past.' Petra did not ask, and I did not offer any additional information. Okay ..back to Anne... what kind of marriage does she have, I wonder. This is nonsense, I have her number, call her, you idiot. It was only then, that after

four tries, he heard Petra' s voice, calling his name..'Josuawa , ya need leave for church.'

His sermon in his pocket, Joshua sprinted the short distance to the Sanctuary. The parking lot was already filled with numerous cars...and on a rainy Sunday. Thank goodness, his congregation was not made up of fair weather Christians. **His** congregation. He always felt a little embarrassed to say that. They were his friends, his colleagues, his neighbors... but, on Sunday, he took on a different role altogether. He became their spiritual guide, their mentor...that was a heavy load to shoulder, but one Joshua did with pride and joy in his heart. He was so thankful that he had been able to hand his troubled life over to the Lord and be saved...and he was more than willing to unashamedly share his story with any and all who would listen. He was not your typical minister - because when Joshua spoke of being lost, he knew what he was talking about...drugs, alcohol, divorce, single parenting, the list went on and on. But, it had all changed that Autumn day over twenty years ago when he had contemplated suicide at the Mississippi River Junction and chose to follow the Lord instead. Thinking of all the bad decisions he had made in his life, Joshua knew that was the best one he had ever made. And, after reading Anne's e-mail, he felt he had done the right thing in persevering in his search of her. Another good decision, he thought. I'm on a roll, Lord..... Praise be.

# Chapter Thirty One

A lazy summer afternoon - Sunday - still lightly raining...what else was needed to make this a day to just kick back and veg? Be a big old couch potato and eat too much, watch too much tv or read an entire book. Sometimes a little self indulgence was a good thing... it renewed the senses. Well, that's the musings of someone who is wanting validation for being lazy, Anne thought. Lounging in her big comfy chair in the family room, she looked up from her book. Good thing she didn't want to move as there was her big old cat, Bear sitting on the left arm snoozed out. Raisin, his sister, on the right arm, stretched out like a lizard, and Penelope, **'the I adopt you, not you me stray'**, a beautiful hodge-podge yellow, black, tan and white, was at her feet. And, of course, sweet Mags was on the ottoman - half- on half- off. The telephone rang waking Reed from 'watching' yet another re-run episode of **'Bonanza'** and thru sleepy eyes, he read the caller ID out loud – ...'Do we know anyone in Louisiana?' he asked. Looking up from her book, Anne replied that it was probably just a telemarketer and to ignore it. After four rings, the answering machine cut in - and... click - nothing. Satisfied that she had been right in her assessment, everyone went back to what they were doing before the intrusion. Meanwhile, in Louisiana on the other end of the line, Joshua sighed as he returned the receiver to its cradle.

# Chapter Thirty Two

The morning service had gone well. Despite the dismal weather, the congregation was in a receptive mood. Joshua's sermons were simple but heartfelt... he was not the fire and brimstone - salvation now or not, type minister. No, he believed that people **needed** to know - more importantly - **honestly believe** - that regardless of the mistakes they had made - God forgives all. All, if only you ask Him ... Go to Him, He does not judge... He knows all of your human failings.. and, He forgives. Look at me... **IF** He could forgive such a sinner as I, then there is hope for you, as well.

Returning home, Petra and Joshua ate a light lunch...excusing himself to go to his office to work, Joshua entered the office and quietly closed the door. Looking at the pile of papers in the **"IN"** box versus the pile in the **"OUT"** box, Joshua had to pause...why is the **"IN "** always larger than the **"OUT"**, he mused. Sitting down and pulling up to the desk, he looked at the desk phone. She should be home on a Sunday afternoon...especially one that is as wet as this one is. Remember she always said she hated to get wet with her clothes on. To which he smiled broadly at that memory. Don't even go there, he thought. Shaking his head to erase the pleasant memory of a hot summer day, being caught in the rain, and cut-off shorts and a wet t-shirt, Joshua reached across the leather top desk mat and picked up the phone ; he didn't even have to look up the number as he had already memorized both of them. I'll try the home number first..he thought.. Hearing it ring... he took a deep breath and waited...

Well, at least I heard her voice....Joshua mused..and, it was the same one I remembered...the same one that had a tinge of happiness in it. *' Hi, sorry we missed your call...leave your name and a brief message and we'll call you back ... Have a great day!* She can't call me back because she doesn't even know I called, he thought. Maybe I should try some other time of the day...she didn't say any time was better, just gave me her numbers. Guess I could call her cell phone, but then she said that she rarely, if ever, uses it unless she is away from home. And while contemplating his next move, all three dogs began to announce the arrival of someone in the driveway. Standing up from his desk to go and answer the door, he hesitated at the computer, then reached over and turned it off. No need to worry with that... for now.

# Chapter Thirty Three

M onday dawned absolutely perfect...bright sunshine, bluer than blue skies, no clouds, and everything looked fresh and renewed after yesterday's rain. Anne looked out the kitchen window at her garden in the back yard. The Impatiens were spilling over their containers giving the impression of huge balls of colored yarn on the ground...the hanging spider plants had outdone themselves as there were so many babies on them, it was a nursery in the truest sense. The wind had blown down a few pine tree limbs - I'll take care of that later, she thought. Walking outside, she checked the koi pond to make sure the spill filter had done its job and not allowed the pond to overfill. All is right in my world she thought. A quick call to Emerson - yes, the babies were fine, everybody is doing ok and she was going to take a shower and maybe even slip in a quick nap while the babies were down...we'll talk later. Reed was off to the registered bull sale in Columbia and would not be home until later tonight. I have the entire day to myself, she thought. Oh my word, when was the last time that happened? Hearing the phone ring, she hurried back inside – why is it I never pick up the portable when I go outside... oh, no, I would much rather break my freaking neck running to get the phone than to have it in my pocket, she laughed at herself! Peeking quickly at the caller ID on what was the fourth ring, she saw' Louisiana' and thought, oh bother, I probably just answered a telemarketer and, now I will have to either hang up or listen to some spiel about life insurance, or buying something from some organization that didn't even have an office in South Carolina... too late now. She answered ' Hello' and waited for a reply on the other end. Nothing at first, then…a very masculine voice returned her 'Hello' only a mere millisecond must have passed but it seem like an eternity..'Anne?…It's Joshua'.

Hold onto the phone, do not drop the phone…better yet, hold onto the counter, do not fall…breathe. Inhale….breathe, dammit, breathe. Anne heard her mind's instructions loud and clear, and yet, nothing was coming out of her mouth…and then as if on auto-pilot, '**Joshua…*is that really you?***' she heard herself ask. Why was the room spinning, she wondered…oh dear heavens, what now.

# Chapter Thirty Four

And so it began - again. That first phone call lasted two hours... and, it would have lasted longer but Joshua had to finally answer a business call - since he said he had already allowed it to go to voice mail three times, maybe it was time to say good bye for today... to walk back thru the door to reality and return to their respective worlds. So with promises to call again...perhaps they could talk again tomorrow... he would text her to see if she would be available... and, with that, they said good-bye. Anne returned the receiver to its cradle and sat down hard on the sofa. What just happened here? Am I reading too much into this or, ...no, not after all this time. I am being silly, she thought. And on the other end, Joshua completed the business call; pleased with himself, he leaned back in his chair, then getting up quickly, left his office and nearly fell over Mischa in his eagerness to leave on a transport. Time to think, he thought...time to think.

The rest of the day for Anne was weird. She couldn't keep her mind on anything for long. Being alone only made it worse...do I stop this now, she wondered...or, do I see it through to...whatever. Memories kept tugging her back - back ...how is it I remember all of these things and yet have a hard time remembering what I had for lunch two days ago. And yet, some memories she just could not pull back regardless of how she tried. Her illness had done that to her – a migraine let go too far, leading into meningitis. And, luckily, she did not have a stroke. Medical wonder, she was told. But it had left her... wounded... both her soul and her physical stamina. Retire...that was the doctors' advice. Selected memory retrieval is difficult to deal with. You don't need to work...

go home...heal. So, she had done what the doctors told her to do. Some long term memory is lost forever - and yet, some may come back if it is jogged by something or someone. Do not get frustrated as there is nothing you can do to retrieve it... and yet, I remember everything there is to remember about that whole damn summer. That is just plain cruel. And with that, she put her head in her hands, and cried... really cried for everything that she had lost so long ago.

# Chapter Thirty Five

It is often said that the heart can be a cruel master... that it allows one to love, to truly love and just as easily, it can vanish. The first time Joshua walked out of Anne's life she said he had chosen his job over her; and, while that wounded her ego, she wouldn't let herself admit that she could have been wrong in issuing ultimatums for their future. So, after a few weeks of waiting for him to call, even though she had told him not to, she picked up the pieces and went back to life - before Joshua. So be it, her pride told her...he made his bed, let him sleep in it. Maybe it was the surface anger that allowed her to think about dating again... maybe, it was because she missed Joshua so much and refused to admit it to herself, why else would she have allowed Trae into her life. Treavor Michael Howard, III. He was everything - *everything* Joshua wasn't. 'Trae' was blonde, the rugged outdoors type, employed with a construction firm because he could not think of being anywhere near the Corporate world. They met by chance - through mutual friends - the first couple of dates were okay. Looking back Anne should have seen his motives. But all she could see was that Trae seemed to dote on her. What ever she wanted, he was more than willing to do. She was the center of his world, or so it appeared. He introduced her to his big boisterous middle class family - there were seven siblings, five girls, two boys with him, the baby. The large family rather intimated her at first, but they, also, appeared to take her to their hearts, so she started to let down her guard. She told herself she was not going to get involved with anyone – anytime soon. Her heart was still healing and she would not fall into the age old syndrome of a rebound romance. And, it didn't hinder her plan to take it slow...because everyone, well, at least it seemed like everyone, didn't really like Trae...everyone was a bit skeptic of him and how they had come to meet in the first place. They certainly did not run in the same circles, so it was a bit odd when a casual friend introduced them at a football game; and, Trae had called her the next day asking her on a date. She hadn't even given him her phone number, she thought; it was only much later, much later that she had discovered, quite by accident, that he had taken a dare ... a dare that Anne, rich, spoiled Anne wouldn't go out with him if he asked; but by the time Anne found that little tidbit of information out, her heart had been so badly wounded that one more stab just didn't matter. But she thought, I really did kind of like him; and, he keeps me from thinking about Joshua. Joshua...I can't reach out to him...he is lost to me forever by my own design. So, why not go out on a date, she asked herself. They began to date and all too quickly, they were a couple...not serious, but not dating anyone else, either. It went on that way for a while, then everything changed after the accident; 'the accident that changed my life forever' ... they had gone out on a Saturday afternoon to get a burger and fries. While sitting in her car at an intersection waiting for the red light to change, they never saw the pickup truck headed straight for them, not slowing down, the driver too drunk to even think about breaking. He hit them going nearly 40 mph; and, to make matters even worse, Anne's car was a convertible. So the truck not only hit them dead center, but jumped up onto the back of the car. Sitting in the passenger seat, Anne was lucky she was not killed. As it was, she was badly injured, but Trae walked away without a scratch. But it was the way Trae took care of her, never leaving her side...even at the hospital, sleeping in the chair...that was when Anne fell hopelessly in love with him. And, that would be the first step on the road to devastation. After her recovery, Trae seemed to be always there; and, before too much longer, he had asked her to marry him. Still blinded by his devotion, Anne said yes. She should have known something was amiss when Trae asked her Dad if he could marry her and her Dad refused...simply refused. Anne was furious upon learning that her

Dad had put a kink in her happily-ever after. In trying to explain to her why he had said no, the only thing Anne could grasp was that he didn't want her to be happy. Then, he totally surprised her when he countered with....' I said no, **BECAUSE** I want you to be happy, Anne...' With that, Father and daughter hit an impasse. Oh, why am I rehashing all of this again...she wondered as she raised her head from the cradle of her tear stained sleeves. Have I not gone over this so many times as to be able to know each word said...or screamed...or all the doors that were slammed. What a fool I was to think that my Dad had anything but my best interest at heart. Why couldn't I see Trae for the gold digger he was... no, for the **bastard** he was. How can I still hate him so much all of these years later...I still shake when I think of him...how he stalked me for years after that summer...how he would call and hang up the phone...how I would look up in a store, and see him just yards away from me, waiting... just waiting... staring... and, I never told anyone of the horror he put me through. And, now, decades later, I still get sick to my stomach when I think of it. Okay, enough is enough...thought Anne. Shaking her head, Anne picked up her keys, and headed out the back door. Slamming the door of her Lexus, she turned the ignition and pulled out of the garage. Mindlessly she drove to where she knew she had a captive audience. Crouching down on the mossy grass, she touched the hard granite stone...'Hi - Daddy, it's me... Can we talk?'

# Chapter Thirty Six

Joshua was in a good mood as he pulled out of the driveway headed to the office in Landon... business was not too bad for this time of the year. It is just so freaking hot this time of the day, he thought as he cranked up the ac and eased his van onto the Expressway. Thinking back to the just ended conversation with Anne...he thought..she sounded good...didn't she? I can't believe we talked for hours...but then we always could talk, about anything. She even loved to talk sports..laughing to himself. A girl that likes sports..now that's a keeper. Petra didn't like sports - well, with her European background, the poor woman thought soccer was a sport! She would look at football, and with her eyes rolling to the top of her head, in her heavy Czech accent... ' it'z makes no sense ta hold ball and run downs lawn..' she would say...' much better ta kicks ball...get it there soon...' to which Joshua would laugh and just shoo her away to continue cheering on his beloved college Alma Mater, Auburn, or the New York Giants. And even today, he found out that Anne loved the New Orleans Saints... and, her Alma Mater, Alabama. Not 'Bama , he would groan... and, they would both laugh. They talked about their kids, his two boys and her one girl.. now, all in their 30's -- but, his boys were much older than Emerson . He was a grandfather long before her.. his oldest being nearly sixteen... yeah, grand kids are great, they both agreed. They talked about their marriages... he was on his second, the first ended in divorce after seventeen years, he told her. When asked about hers, she hesitated and said hers was good - and, that she and Reed were closing in on 39 years, having married in '73; when did he get married the first time she asked...and he said '72.

She got kind of quiet after that, he recalled ..oh well, it's been a lot to take in...**RED LIGHT...*RED LIGHT*...** better keep my mind on the road, Joshua chastised himself, and with that, he turned the radio on and went be-bopping down the road, singing to Percy Sledge's ...' ***When a man loves a woman..***'

# Chapter Thirty Seven

Sitting on the cool grass, Anne plucked a few stray weeds from around the granite headstone ...brushing off some wayward dirt, she felt a calmness wash over her. It's always so peaceful here, she thought. And beautiful...up on this hill. What I wouldn't give to have you back Dad – you were always such a good listener... and, you didn't agree with me unless you agreed with me. I always liked that about you...well, **most** of the time I did, she thought . Why couldn't I see what you tried so hard to show me about Trae, Daddy? Why couldn't I see what a jerk he was? And, why, please tell me why I was such a jerk to you? I know I have said it a thousand times, Daddy, but I am so sorry for letting you down... for making you ashamed of me. I know you were even though you never said so. And, I know I broke your heart...I loved you so much, and yet, I was the one that hurt you the most. Maybe, some day when we are together again ...maybe then I can tell you - face to face - how truly remorseful I am even to this day. I talked with Joshua today, Daddy. **Did you hear me....Joshua**. He called me...I don't know why now ... what could be the reason...it's been so long, too long. The past is eating at me again...and , I don't think I am going to be strong enough this time to survive it.. Daddy , Joshua told me he was on his second marriage. I did the math, Daddy... he must have gotten married right after he left that summer. I don't understand that one. How could he have found someone else? He was supposed to come back home, Daddy . He was supposed to come back ... to me. I wanted him to ... but I didn't ask him to ... but he didn't...he got married instead.....' Quickly wiping the tears falling down her cheek, Anne looked away. Feeling as though her heart was going to literally break, Anne stood up...then knelt back down, pressing her fingers to her lips, she kissed them and in turn, gently laid that kiss on the marker, beside the stray tear that ran down her cheek and fell to the ground.

# Chapter Thirty Eight

That night Joshua would come to Anne in her dreams...not the curly haired Joshua of her youth, but the mature Joshua as he was today. He simply reached out his hand, and taking it, they walked down a country lane in the dappled sunshine of late summer. No words were spoken, no mapped out path. And for the first time in weeks, Anne slept.

While deep in the southern bayou country of Louisiana, Joshua tossed fitfully - finally giving up, he plodded down the hall to his study. Flipping the lights on to illuminate the darkness, he swept his hand over his head, chuckling to himself - used to be hair up there, now just a perfect bald head.. Wonder what changes Anne has experienced, he thought. There are no pictures on Face book of her. We all change, he thought, but I hope her eyes haven't - her eyes, those deep green eyes, *no*, I don't want them to change. Stretching his full 6'3" frame on the sofa in his office, he closed his eyes, remembering ...***remembering...***until sleep finally took over.

And, so as it would happen just a few weeks after their re-connection Joshua would be in the area to attend a conference of the SFDA, the Southern Funeral Director's Association as a liaison for Transport Services. The conference was set for a Thursday and Friday, with workshops on both days and the final conference on Saturday morning. Joshua called Anne to tell her he would be coming to the area - the dates, times, etc. and, wanted to know if there would be anyway possible they could meet and have lunch...dinner...whatever time they could mutually agree on. The delegation would be staying at Hinton House; he had planned to check in the Wednesday evening before. Anne checked her calendar; what if he could come a bit earlier for registration and they could have lunch there at the Hotel. The Hotel had two restaurants; one was **Eve's Garden**, a favorite of hers for many years. She and a group of her friends would meet there occasionally to catch up on their lives. So, he said he would plan on being at the Hotel by 1 that Wednesday; so, on both of their calendars, they penciled in lunch. To clear the fog from forty years, Anne thought, it's going to take more than a hour...or two.

Joshua was antsy as traffic had been backed up on the Interstate for a good while. Looking at his watch, for the umpteenth time in the last few minutes, it was totally obvious that he was going to be late for a **very** important date. He had only ten minutes to go forty miles...and, traffic was moving at a snail's pace. Okay, **what do I do** ...do I call and cancel.. *no, not an option*...do I call and beg her to stay put that *I am coming*. Good, traffic is at least picking up; better call.. she could freak out and think I'm not coming. Hitting re-dial on his phone, she finally answered just before it going to voice mail....'Anne...I'm running late...there's been a traffic snarl for hours. I'm only about fifteen minutes away.'...catching his breath. Anne quickly answered...'Slow down ....it's okay...I'm not at the restaurant yet anyway. I will wait on you if I get there first...*promise*...' And as it was, Joshua got there before Anne anyway. She had come through downtown - at lunch time, nevertheless - and, his was a straight shot off of Interstate. So when she pulled up, it was she that was all of five minutes late. She took a quick peek in the mirror - her cell phone rang – it was Emerson - **great timing, sweet pea**, Anne thought. She listened to her daughter's request to run by CVS and pick something up for her before she left town..'.bye, Mom's got to go Baby...later...' - hanging up the phone, she just realized...I haven't got a clue as to what Joshua is driving. Oh well, here goes. Getting out of her car, she turned to close her door and when she looked back up... *there...**there*** he stood. Huge smile on his face...arms outstretched...' *I believe I know you*...' he said with a laugh. She walked into his arms - and he proceeded to hug her so hard that she almost couldn't breathe.. ' My word, have I waited for this day. You still fit in my arms...just like old times..' she heard him say over the brass band playing in her ear. They walked arm-in-arm across the parking lot and entering the hotel, she lead him off to the entrance of **Eve's Garden**. A huge wrought iron garden gate opened up to expose the majesty that made this quaint little restaurant a favorite of all who dined here. Hanging ferns, huge baskets of brightly colored geraniums and impatiens, tall ficus trees filtering the sun from underneath the massive beams of a lattice work ceiling, appearing to be open to the outside, but cleverly designed to only look that way. Wrought iron glass topped tables with oversized gingham covered wing chairs nestled up to them...flowers everywhere...**but** the real conversation piece - and, it never failed to get noticed – was a massive Red Delicious Apple Tree (all be it fake) loaded with the 'forbidden fruit' ... thus the **Eve's Garden** tie in. Joshua chuckled at the site of the tree, whispering in Anne's ear, 'Are you **sure** this is the place we **should be** ...?' The young girl at the reservations desk recognized Anne; spoke and asked if she wanted her usual table. Anne smiled sweetly at the girl, calling her by her name...'No, actually Serena, I .. no, *we* would like something further out on the lanai, if possible.' Anne instructed. To which Serena was all too happy to lead them both to the more private dining area. Holding her chair, Joshua leaned down and kissed her cheek, a gesture that brought a flush to Anne's face... but a pleased feeling to her soul... he **really** is still *MY* sweet Joshua, she thought.

So, for the next three and one half hours...**yes, three and one half hours**....Joshua and Anne 'ate' lunch, in that their lunches took a back seat to everything else. Once Joshua had seated himself, he reached across the table and took Anne's hand in his, and that is the way it stayed...only letting go if absolutely necessary. They laughed, they reminisced, they were serious at some points, and others, quiet.They reconnected. They talked of their marriages, of their children, grand children..there was almost nothing that was off - limits. And then, suddenly without any prior warning, Joshua crossed that *forbidden* line..'Anne...I *need* to apologize to you...for so many things...I...' and, before he could go any further, Anne looked at him with a puzzled look on her face... **'You need to apologize to me???** I think it is the other way around; it is I, who has so much to apologize for...' Not wanting to look at him for fear of breaking down, Anne tucked her head to try and hide the tears rimming her eyes....' Joshua, I would *give* anything to be able to go back and do it all...*again*...I don't know if I could have made it any better, but I do know I would told you - the whole messy story – and maybe, **I would not have hurt you the way I did...I never...never** meant to do that to you...' her voice trailed off. Joshua looked at her feeling her pain. 'Anne...look at me...please...' he pleaded...'..I do not know if things would have worked out for us. We were so very young at the time. But I do know, that *if* I had to do all over again, I would not have walked away. I would have fought to stay and, who knows, maybe that would have been wrong, too. But I would not have left without a '*why*'... because I knew you were lying to me. I just didn't know at the time what got into you ...you blew me out of the water when you said you didn't love me anymore, because I knew you did. Maybe, maybe some day, will you tell me *why*? But all of that just doesn't matter any more...because here we are nearly forty years later...and **I still love you just as much** today as I did when we parted ways. ' Anne?...**did you hear me?'** Quiet. Quiet. Anne's face seemed to pale with his last statement. Re-gaining her composure, her voice was firm when she said. 'And, I you...I don't think I ever stopped loving you. It's just that I have had you locked away, tucked in a faraway corner of my heart for so long, I am almost afraid to open the door - again... we are...married to different.. ..we can't hurt......' her voice trailed off as the emotion of the moment was getting the better of her, then continuing... ' Joshua, we are opening up a Pandora's Box... and nothing, nothing good can come of this...too many people **can** and **will** be hurt...and, it is not my intention, and I know it is not yours, to hurt anyone, so that we can be together...I fear that both of us will wind up ...trying to re-capture the past. The pieces of our past are cataloged now to be just that ... Pieces of the Past. We must respect that. We both know that nothing is ever carved in stone, so I suppose, if we truly believe in **Karma**, someday, somehow, we will be together. It's just ... **when and if** ... is the issue. ' Joshua took a deep breath and said.. 'Anne ...I have something to ask you...' Anne looked up through tearing eyes as Joshua continued...'Anne...this may sound ridiculous... but I need to know.. will you marry me?' Joshua watched the emotion fill Anne's face - the tears were so close to spilling, he held his breath. Anne looked at him, her eyes softening as she spoke...' Oh, Joshua...that is the **second** time you have asked me that '... her voice wavering with emotion, ' did you not hear a word I just said..' she laughingly asked him. And, Joshua countered...'Yes, I heard every word, Anne. Now, **will you marry me?** ' So, it was sitting there under a canopy of flowers and sunshine, forty years after the first proposal that Anne looked up at Joshua and, realized time had not changed the fact he was still **her** Joshua. And this time, with her heart almost exploding inside her chest, Anne said... **'Yes... a thousand times ... Yes'**.

# Chapter Thirty Nine

Why is it when we are young we do not think of what the future can hold for us. We do not think of the mundane things – we live each day and assume there will always be another day, tomorrow... ' Ten foot tall and bulletproof ' used to be what you felt you were and yet, nobody was ever or, is completely safe from hurt, disappointment, tragedies. It all comes with getting older, growing up. Anne was in a melancholy mood on this cool Autumn day. She had seen Joshua a few weeks past as he was in the area for a couple of hours. They had met at a local sandwich shop and chatted for much too short a time before he had to get back to Louisiana. They had continued their daily chats. The more they talked, the closer they became again. I guess I didn't think we would ever talk - much less reconnect this way. It has been good, she thought. Joshua had been a mainstay in my life for so long - so long ago – and she had missed not having him there. She just did not believe he would ever fall back into that special place. Wonder if he feels that way or if he wishes - maybe, that he had not found me..again. He said that it didn't matter how long it would take, if he had not found me when he did, his search would simply have continued until...one day, he hoped, he would. And Joshua always, even as a kid, meant what he said.

Meanwhile, in Louisiana, it was raining - **hard**. This hard pelting rain; it is entirely too warm for this time of year, thought Joshua as he left the main office in Landon. Great, no jacket, no umbrella... guess I'll make a dash for it and get soaked in the process. Rainy days... Joshua reflected, as he stood under the door's canopy. Anne never liked the rain. For one thing, she didn't like 'getting wet with her clothes on..' That particular thought took him back to a memory when they had gotten caught in a sudden thunderstorm and they were drenched by the time they found cover in an old wood shed. For him, it was magical. Well, maybe not 'magical' as one would say...as they both were soaking wet, to the point of dripping. He nearly laughed out loud when he remembered how Anne was standing there next to him trying to wring out her long hair and muttering to herself - ' like a drown rat, I am...' - ' but a beautiful drown rat ' he heard himself say. To which Anne gave him **THAT** look. The one that says, 'have you completely lost your mind?' They waited out the quick shower, and then trudged across the fields back to her house...an empty house, if memory served him correct...best not go there, he warned himself. I remember her changing into dry clothes..a t-shirt and shorts...best put that image back in the memory bank, he chastised himself. And with that, he made the mad dash to his car.

Quickly slamming the door against the elements, he turned the ignition and as the engine whirred to life, he turned up the radio...'... **BEEP BEEP BEEP...' '...ATTENTION...THIS IS AN ALERT...THIS IS NOT A TEST...THIS IS AN ALERT... THE NATIONAL WEATHER SERVICE HAS ISSUED A TORNADO WATCH FOR** .... ' Joshua turned up the volume to hear it appeared parts of lower Louisiana and Mississippi were included as this storm was intensifying rapidly. That was one of the bad things about living in the deep south, as you always had the chance for catastrophic weather. Cold fronts dipping down from the North hit the much warmer air of the South, and it was like the War between the States all over. Deadly tornados had hit only a few weeks ago in Oklahoma and, again in Alabama leaving unbelievable devastation. In fact, his company had been called to transport a family of three back to Mississippi for burial. It was always so heart wrenching to be witness to the wrath of Mother Nature. She wasn't choosy...an elementary school or quiet neighborhood. Didn't matter. Best get home and batten down the hatches he thought. The dogs will be nervous as he knew as they tend to sense these weather changes quicker than us humans. And Petra, where was she today? Driving thru the pelting rain, he kept a careful eye on the ever darkening skies in his windshield. Looks like I'm heading right in to it, he thought.

# Chapter Forty

Anne flipped on the kitchen tv to catch the tail end of a news item about a deadly tornado outbreak in the deep South. While that, in itself, is devastating it unnerved her – what part of the South - *where* – *when* – she frantically turned the tv over to the Weather Channel - nothing - what about CNN - wait...wait...there it is...OMG it hit Mississippi, ...no, wait... also Louisiana...where in .... she heard something about the lower Bayou...Commentator saying that New Orleans had been spared...but the corner of Louisiana was hit, the tornados moving on to lower Mississippi , grazing Alabama.. *'what area of Louisiana'* she heard herself say out loud....what Landis...no, Landon...*OMG* ... that is where Joshua's main office is...panic took over. Reaching for her cell phone, she quickly dialed the number only to read the text that 'service was not available in this area'. She tried several more times only to receive the same message. Keeping her eye on the tv, and hitting redial every few seconds, she discovered that most of the devastation had been in rural areas, the tornados touching down, but not traveling far on the ground. And because it was the more rural areas, it appeared there was no loss of life...*no loss of life*...she replayed that over and over in her head. Thank you, Lord. Meanwhile, cell phone reception was still dead.

Joshua drove on through the pelting rain into what appeared the crux of the storm. His speed slowed almost to a crawl as he carefully watched the road, but his main attention was on the huge black cluster of clouds in front of him...lightning...yeah, and he could feel the ground shiver with each boom of thunder. Boy, am I testing fate to be driving into this...no funnel clouds, but there is the hail... and, I am watching, Lord. This storm is really moving...**fast**. And then, it all but stopped raining...what? ***Quiet***... oh no, ***QUIET***...looking quickly into his rear view mirror, he could see what he had just driven through barreling South. Grabbing his cell phone, he dialed the house...and amazingly, Petra answered the phone...'**Hello**...' Joshua screamed into the phone - ' **are you okay**..' 'Yess, but it haz rained very much...but we r fine...where r ya, Josuawa.....why r ya yellin?' Taking a deep breath, he explained that he just left the office and that there was a tornado watch ...' and, why do you not have the radio on, Petra...' Petra replied to his questions surprisingly calm '...zee lights went gone wid storm... zee dogs and me, we r in front room...I read, til no powers...den, we vait outs storm..we r fine, Josuawa...we r fine.' Joshua took a deep breath - 'I'll be home in ......' and, with that his cell phone went dead.

Okay, enough is enough...how will I find out if Joshua is okay, Anne worried. Of course, he is okay, the reporter said no fatalities. And most of the pictures that were now streaming thru the tv were of trees down, some scattered wooden farm structures, and some road damages due to the wind swept rain...creeks were overflowing from the dumped 3 inches of rain in the span of an hour. But it did appear, while what had happened was bad, it was not the devastation it could have been. ***Aargh,*** but I can not get through, Anne thought.

Once Joshua realized that Petra was okay, his mind flashed to Anne. **OMG** if she sees this on tv, she will be frantic. Grabbing his phone, he frantically tried to get a signal. Must have knocked out the main cell tower, he thought. My word, it could be days before that is fixed. No, I can not wait that long. Seeing a Mobile station up ahead, he quickly pulled in, parked and went inside to see if there was a land line phone he could use. Approaching the service counter, everyone's eyes were drilled to the news report of the tornados that had pushed thru just minutes ago, only thirty miles from where they stood. Asking if there was a land line he could use since his cell phone was useless, the cashier quickly handed him the phone...'Calling home, hey Mister?' And, without any hesitation, Joshua answered....'Yes...thanks...'

With her eyes still drilled to the tv, Anne jumped when the phone on the counter rang. I can't talk to anyone right now. Looking at the caller ID, she was a bit puzzled to see ' Mobile Two-Four-One' show up. Answering it...there was a momentary pause on the other end and then, 'Anne - it's Joshua...I'm okay – I knew you would worry and I had to call and let you know everything is fine.. Anne??...are you there?' Pause – Anne crossed herself before answering..' Yes...yes...oh thank you so much. I couldn't get through, the cell service is evidently down...are you sure you are okay...is the damage bad?' '.. I'm not sure of the damage yet... but it appears everyone is - okay... I will call you as soon as I know more...by the way, I love you...' ' You are safe...that is *all* I need to know... ' Anne said. And with a smile in his voice, Joshua countered, ' ***ALL ?? ?*** ' Walking out of the service station, Joshua looked up beyond the gas pump canopy to the southern skies now a brilliant shade of blue, and saw what he was looking for. A rainbow... God's promise that he is always looking over us.

After that - there was a change in their relationship; suddenly, it wasn't so cavalier. It was more serious...even more necessary than before. And it was then, that Anne decided Joshua was too important in her life to take another day for granted. Wait, she thought ... had Joshua told her he loved her before they hung up the phone...or had she just willed it so in her mind. She had purposely let him go once, for his sake, she thought. And the time before, well that was just stupidity for not being able to see the future. There would be no third time...at least not from her. I will always have him in my life - from now on - they would just have to figure out exactly how that was going to work..but, before I can even hope for that to happen... I must stop procrastinating It is time - the moment of truth - her own Armageddon, if you will. And so, she promised herself that she would tell Joshua everything. Because it was now obvious Joshua would never ask.

# Chapter Forty One

Joshua's sermon that Sunday after the tornado outbreak was on *"Rebuilding"*. Walking purposely to the pulpit, Joshua picked up his worn Bible, and holding the treasured Book in his hands, stepped down to the floor of the sanctuary, and began speaking. ' After a storm, we can pick up the scattered pieces of buildings...we can rebuild bigger and even better than before... but, can you rebuild your relationship with the Lord if you do not believe He is always there for you, even in the darkest hour, He will shelter you..' And so, Joshua related his story of the horrific storm the area had just seen...he told them of his fear...of his concerns for his family...in his words, his mortal concerns...because in his heart, Joshua knew, beyond a shadow of a doubt, that the Lord would be with him...' ... if He brings you to it, He will bring you through it.'

Genuflecting, Anne quickly crossed herself, and slipped into the pew beside Reed's aunt. Bussing her on the cheek, she touched the elderly woman's sleeve in a tender gesture of genuine respect. Looking up to the altar, she gazed at the huge hanging wooden cross with its Crown of Thorns, gleaming in the morning sunlight. On one side of the altar was a beautiful recreation of Michelangelo's *'Pieta'*; and on the other, a life size Nativity of Mary and the Holy Child. She was always struck by the poignancy of the Triad - it told the life of Jesus through the eyes of the Holy Mother - and in such a reverent manner. Birth, Death on the Cross, The Blessed Holy Mother holding her sacrificed son - the Son of God. Settling in, she looked over her guide for today's service..."*Forgiveness*". Forgiveness - her mind slipped back to Joshua. Embarrassed that she had thought of him in this Holy place, she closed her eyes and fingering her Grandmother's Rosary, offered a small prayer. The organ processional announced Father Murphy and the accompanying altar boys. The congregation rose and after a Prayer of Welcome, the Abbey's choir began the blessing. The beautiful music resounded throughout the Sanctuary setting the tone for morning service. Father Murphy ascended the steps to the Pulpit. Looking out over his congregation, he quietly began speaking. '**Forgiveness.** What a beautiful word. We are taught in the Holy Bible that Forgiveness is next to Godliness. Our most precious Lord, Jesus Christ, dying on the Cross was able to forgive those that were to take his life; and, in dying, He forgave us our sins. And, we, in turn, must willingly forgive those that harm us; but just as important, we must forgive ourselves. We can not harbor ill will or hatred. We will face many trials in our lives, but we must turn to Christ. Allow Him to enter our hearts...to show us the way. We must trust that *if* the Lord brings us to it, He will bring us through it...' Anne listened intently to the words, taking each one to heart... trying hard to believe that maybe, just maybe she could **forgive**. And in doing so, would it wash clean the hate she had harbored inside of her wounded soul for so many years – long enough to even...*forgive* herself. A fact she still did not believe she was capable of.

# Chapter Forty Two

Leaving morning services, Joshua thought of yesterday. He thought of how in all of the fear and confusion, while truly concerned for the safety of Petra and the pups, he was also worried about Anne. He needed to reassure her that he was fine. I suppose nothing ever really changes, he thought. I have always wanted to protect her, to keep her safe from harm. So, why should it be any different now? But, shaking his head, the **one** time I **needed** to protect her the most, I couldn't ...*she pushed me away*. Looking back, I suppose I could have stood my ground, and yet, maybe, it was for the best. I do not know if we could have made it. Maybe we were too young or maybe, it simply wasn't meant to be then...but what about **now**. Are we, or will we ever be on the same page. And yesterday, I told her I loved her. It just came out so easy, I didn't even think about it. That's what happens when you speak the truth - from your heart. And the truth is so easy to remember..isn't it. Oh dear Lord, please help Your servant - I know not what to do. Feeling that long ago familiar pang of guilt in his stomach, Joshua bowed his head and prayed. Prayed for guidance on this new and uncharted road.

Driving back home, Anne glanced down at her phone. There was an hour time difference between them. She would be leaving church just when his would be beginning. Anne hoped she would be able to talk with Joshua for a bit today – to tell him about her church service and the revelation she had felt with Father Murphy's sermon. *But,* she also knew with it being

Sunday, it would be unlikely; especially if he had additional services or afternoon obligations. Well, maybe tomorrow.. that would probably be better. Pulling into the garage, she turned her phone off.

# Chapter Forty Three

Autumn's beauty quickly gave way to the starkness of the coming winter. The trees had shed their leaves, days were shorter; it was as though for a while, Mother Nature had gone to sleep. Anne and Joshua continued to talk daily. It was so amazing as they never seem to tire of chatting with one another. They were able to lean on one another even by phone and, could laugh at even the most ridiculous things. In so many ways, they were reverting back to their old ways, in that they were happy just to be. Their families were so important to the both of them. Joshua voiced his concerns about Petra's paleness..her dropping things; she had recently destroyed her laptop by spilling a glass of water on it. He had encouraged her to address all of this with her Doctor ; she had tests run, there was an underlying issue with her blood, but nothing he felt to explain away any of his concerns. And, Anne, in turn, was thankful to have Joshua's input with regard to the twins. To voice her concerns about Reed's health and his inability to handle.... no to **want** to handle, his diabetes. And, she voiced her fear of the Parkinson's that ran in Reed's family. The stuff that every days are made of. That's what they had...normalcy. And yet, in so many ways, there was nothing, **absolutely** nothing normal about any of it.

Christmas was fast approaching. The holidays were Anne's favorite time of the year. It was such a joyous time. And, this year, they would have the twins. They would be too little to remember any of it, but everybody else would. People always seemed to be in a better frame of mind; if only you could make the holiday spirit last all year, she thought. She found herself busy with all of the holiday goings on. The shopping for gifts, the baking, decorating. And, Joshua, of course, was equally busy with his transport business as well as his ministry. But they always had time for one another. It might only be a few minutes in their day, but it was assured if at all possible, they would talk. In her mind, she kept telling herself each time they talked, I will tell Joshua...just not yet...not during the holidays..and, not over the phone. This would require a face-to-face where she could try and make him understand why she did the things she did all those years ago.

Sitting at her desk addressing Christmas cards, Anne heard her phone beep indicating a new text message had just been received. Picking it up, she was delighted to see Joshua was on a transport call and would have some free time to chat. Dialing up his number, his voice seemed especially cheerful. Joshua soon explained the cause of his better than usual mood. He would have the opportunity to come home in a couple of weeks and wanted to know if they could plan to have lunch. Seems his brother,Will was not doing well on his new medication, and so, he thought, why not come home for the holidays and cheer him up a bit. Because Petra's parents were elderly, she would not be coming. He had planned to be at Will's for at least a few days. The two of them had always been close, especially after their father passed when Joshua was very young; and, not having a strong family unit in place with their alcoholic mother, Will took on the role of being a Father to son, more so than brother to brother due to the ten year age difference. He was pleased that Will's Doctor had pretty much told Will to get his house in order – even though it was painful, the truth was the best. Will had never listened before, but yesterday when they talked, he said Will mentioned that he and Grace, his wife of nearly fifty years, had been to the attorney's office and had finalized their wills...*their* wills, Joshua noted to Anne. Joshua's work with his ministry had taken him to being involved with **HOPE** - a group dedicated to end of life issues; so, in Joshua's mind, it was good that Will had at least listened this time. They chatted on - and upon hanging up, Anne realized with Joshua coming back home -- this could be her chance to follow through on Father Murphy's sermon; her chance to forgive herself. And tell Joshua the whole story...face to face.

The call a few days later changed everything. Joshua had been complaining for sometime with his shoulder. He had injured his rotor cuff and had it repaired years ago, but with his transport service, he just seemed to keep aggravating the old injury. It finally came to the point, on that Tuesday, after the transport of a 300 pound deceased gentleman, he could no longer put off the surgery. Thus, the Christmas trip was put on hold. Anne was concerned that he had, once again, re-injured it, but was glad that he had finally agreed to have the surgery. This would be the second time for Joshua to go through this ordeal, and it was an ordeal. Reed had shoulder surgery a couple years back and it was horrible for him. There was such intense pain, the physical therapy nearly killed him, and still has only limited use of his arm. She knew first hand what Joshua was looking at...but then, so did Joshua. He knew he would be out of commission for several weeks, if not months, and he was not a happy camper. Joshua had never been one to be still. He was like that robotic bunny from the battery ads ... moving, constantly on the go. But reality had hit - maybe a little too hard because he finally realized he could not continue on his current diet of 2 Advil and 2 Alleve twice a day with a side order of Celebrex thrown in for good measure.

As the date for the surgery approached, it dawned on Anne that Joshua would not be able – maybe for days – to communicate how the surgery had gone, or how he was doing. If everything had gone alright. Uneasy with that thought, she wondered how that was going to work. Asking Joshua the next time she talked with him, she was relieved - even a bit surprised - to find out Joshua had taken care of that, too. He had called Will - explained everything to him - and, asked him, if anything were to happen, to call her immediately. No questions asked. Sensing the urgency of Joshua's request, Will agreed. Everything would be fine, but just in case you need him, Will is there for you. Thank you Anne mouthed to herself...and then out loud ... "Joshua - give me Will's number - you know, just in case.

# Chapter Forty Four

Pins and needles...that is what is said when you are nervous about something. Oh, and another good one...Cat on a hot tin roof. Yeah, but that one only brings a visual of Elizabeth Taylor in her silk slip ranting at her alcoholic husband. That is not the visual I want in my mind, Anne laughed to herself. Haven't heard anything yet, so that must be a good sign. Joshua said Will would call if anything were wrong .. so no news is good news. Busying herself with her morning chores, she kept glancing over at the microwave, my heavens time is moving slow this morning. But there is an hour difference between us, and no surgery ever begins when it is scheduled to. Reed was scheduled for an 11:30 a.m. procedure with his shoulder, and they didn't even take him back to the prep area until 1 p.m ; and the surgery, intended to be about an hour, took over four due to the extensive damage Reed had. In fact, the Orthopedic Surgeon later told them, he nearly stitched his shoulder back up because he didn't think he could repair it. It was his Intern working with him that insisted they try. Guess that proves Doctors sometimes are at a loss, too, she thought.

Looking out the front window, she noticed the overcast sky had just let go of the first snowflakes indicating the start of the expected weekend storm. A prediction for snow in South Carolina tends to catch your attention...and this was no exception. A rare, not totally uncommon event, but one to actually get excited about. The forerunners were wee and almost difficult to discern from rain, but then they were quickly replaced with big puffy cotton ball snowflakes - now falling gently, pretty, so pretty. Mesmerized by the quickly changing landscape, she didn't hear the phone at first, but when she did, it froze her to the spot. Joshua said Will would only call if necessary ...answer the phone ... it doesn't have to be Will, her head told her. In fact, the caller ID said BPF&S. Picking up the receiver and gingerly answering, 'Hello'... there was a slight pause on the other end and, then Will's measured voice ...'Anne....this is Will ... I know you well ... enough to know you were worried... but Joshua is fine ... the surgery went off... without a hitch...and .... he should be ... released later this afternoon.... if there are.... no complications........ with the anesthesia........ you know, ....he often..... has a bad reaction to that...but it..... looks like........ everything is fine...' Anne crossed herself and took a deep breath, completely taken back with Will's struggling to talk with her. Thanking Will for his concern; then re-gaining her thoughts, she asked how he was doing; and again, in measured tones, he said okay, but that it was a hard transition to make. She told him she was sorry that he had taken ill and wished him well. Anne thought quickly in her mind, this was why Joshua wanted so desperately to come home during the holidays. Will is fading fast. Since conversation was difficult for him, she did not want to make him talk any more than necessary. So, they only spoke for a minute more, and as they were ending the call, there was this long pause on Will's end.. Thinking that his breathing was the problem, Anne waited patiently for him to continue speaking...'Anne...don't hurt him, ....***please***...not again...I don't think.... he could take it ...again..' Gathering her wits about her, Anne answered in a firm and steady voice, 'I won't...I promise.' Hanging up the phone, Anne vowed she would do everything she could to keep that promise.

# Chapter Forty Five

That very afternoon when Joshua was released from the hospital, he called Anne from home to let her know he had been released and everything had gone well. She was glad, if a bit surprised to hear from him. Happy that everything had gone as planned, they talked for a few more minutes. She told him Will had called; he called in on an ID of BPF&S ... what was that, she asked. Joshua thought for a minute and, then explained that was the initials for the commercial side of the farm - Butler Plantation Farm and Stables. Getting back to Will, Joshua thought; Petra must have called him with an update, because I haven't talked with him yet, he thought. I thought he was just supposed to call if something went wrong; and in his mind, he knew then that Will must have had an ulterior motive for calling. I'll talk with him later, he thought. Promising Anne to abide by the Doctor's orders, Joshua hung up the phone and collapsed in his recliner.

It would be a few days before they would talk again – Anne knew the torment he was going through and sincerely wished there was something she could have done to ease his suffering. She texted him wishing him a speedy recovery, good thoughts and such. Careful not to put anything that could have been misconstrued if Petra were to check his phone for him. He doesn't need that, she thought. She had seen her Reed battle the incessant pain, the inability to get comfortable - to sleep..and, she knew Joshua was mirroring that. Anne worried with Joshua's history of addiction, the heavy duty pain medications would undo what the Lord had done. Reed had nearly become addicted and he hated to take any kind of pill; so her concern was a honest one. Coming back to reality, she thought - should go let the dogs out; they can play in the snow for a while. Need to clear my head anyway. So, off all three of them went. The recent storm had given them only an inch of snow, just enough to be pretty, but not cause havoc with anyone who had to travel. While snow for their area was not the norm, every once in a while, Mother Nature would let them know what it would be like if they were up North. With the temps quickly returning to seasonal, this beautiful white stuff won't last long, she thought. But the dogs are having a ball! Watching them romp and spin around chasing anything that moved was a real mood enhancer. Getting them back into the garage is going to be a real challenge. Toweling them off in the driveway might help she thought... No, Alpo treats are the way to go. So, with a little bit of bribery, the two came in.

Back upstairs in the hallway, she heard the familiar beep from her cell phone informing her she had a message...quickly taking off her coat, she walked to the counter and picking up her phone, she saw the message was from Whitney - a friend she had helped with her wedding this past Fall...they had become quite close over the last few years...despite their age differences..my goodness, she thought, Whitney was almost young enough to be her daughter - that is if she had her when she was fifteen! Whitney had lost her mother many years ago and looked at Anne as a close friend but also a surrogate mother, - one who filled in that special spot. In fact, it was when Whitney was trying on wedding gowns, the sales consultant had asked ..' What does your mother think? ' looking over at Anne . So there was a running joke between them that Whitney was the child she gave up for adoption; and, while Whitney had no idea as Anne laughed at that statement each time it was said, it really did make her feel a bit uncomfortable. Returning Whitney's call, they chatted happily about the past week's work, about the weekend storm; and made plans to get together soon. Anne was also doing the interior design work for Whitney's new home; to date, they only had about two more rooms to go. Saying goodbye, they promised to touch base the

coming week and see what their schedules would allow. Hanging up the phone, she smiled. Whitney is such a sweet girl - she just can't make decisions! Thinking in cell phone lingo...she smiled to herself - **LOL.**

She heard the basement door close, indicating Reed had just returned; coming to the foot of the steps, he called her name - and, then told her he was off to the Farm to check on the livestock and the horses and would be home later. The roads are clear so if she wanted, they could go out to grab a bite and she wouldn't have to cook tonight. Ok...see you later.No more had she closed the basement door, than her phone beeped again.. She was surprised when Joshua's number came up. That must mean he is feeling better. Dialing his number, she was anxious to talk with him to see how everything was going; when he answered, she quickly sensed from his voice how tired he sounded. While he assured her he was, indeed, feeling better, it had been a tough few days. They talked on for a few minutes, then Anne cut it short knowing that he needed his rest much more than using his limited strength to talk with her. Hanging up the phone, she shuddered when she thought about how tired Joshua sounded...almost like Will, she thought. No, **not** like Will...she countered.

# Chapter Forty Six

Refusing to allow his surgery to keep him down for long, Joshua was up and on the go just a couple weeks into recovery. Against his doctor's wishes, but with vague promises not to do too much, Joshua was once again on the go. Maybe he would even start making short trips - back in the pulpit this Sunday, he thought. Talking with Anne, she could not help but scold him. Recovery means time spent **recovering**, Joshua; not working..at whatever. Same old Joshua, she thought. Can not sit still. Perpetual motion... plenty of time to rest when I die. Heard that a thousand times. Joshua countered with the inactivity was driving him bonkers. And, besides, he explained to Anne, he really wasn't doing **That** much; he had only co-piloted a few transport calls, and spent most of the day in his office doing the paperwork he absolutely hated or filling in for the dispatcher, when necessary. 'Shuffling papers...**IS NOT WORK**.' he laughed to Anne. Anne gently reminded him that this was the second go-around on this surgery; and getting his attention, she added..' You know, **third chances are rare**, right, Joshua?' ' Point taken..Anne ' he said seriously. Hanging up the phone, Anne had to smile as she didn't want to admit it to herself, but deep inside, she was truly happy that things were slowly returning to before.

# Chapter Forty Seven

Winter's chill was letting go and the first signs of the coming spring were peeking through. The nights were warmer, the skies bluer...even the birds seemed to be celebrating making it through another winter. Joshua's shoulder healed, making it through physical therapy and proudly telling Anne that he didn't even threaten to bodily harm his therapists - well, **only** once. To which Anne laughed whole heartedly; remembering her Reed coming in from an afternoon PT session ...telling her in all seriousness...'...that is the only 100# woman I have ever known who can send cold shivers up and down my spine when I see her coming...and, that is **not** a good thing..' as he laughed at himself. And Joshua agreed completely. Now that Joshua was nearly back to his old schedule, they again were back to almost daily calls. It didn't matter whether it was a fifteen minute commute to the PT office, or a quick trip to the store...it didn't matter, they would catch up on the day to that point and promise to talk later. With one particular call, Anne could sense that Joshua really needed to talk. Sometimes pulling Joshua out of his self imposed shell could be difficult, but in just talking with him, he finally opened up of his concern for Will. He was fading so fast. When he had talked with him after the surgery, Joshua picked up on the halting speech, the struggle to finish a sentence. He sensed Will's frustration and, knowing Joshua the way she did, Anne knew that he was bothered that he could not be there to help him more. As exasperating as Will was sometimes, Joshua felt guilt for the inability to help. Will so often treated Joshua as if he was three years old, a fact that annoyed Joshua more than he could say. His answer was always the same...yell, stomp away in anger. Maturity, on either side, was the only answer to that problem but it was something neither one of them seemed to possess at times. Anne remembered when she had talked with Will after Joshua's surgery; how frail he sounded.. how he had struggled to finish sentences; but, what she remembered most was that he had begged her not to hurt Joshua again. Wonder if Joshua knows ...she thought.. about Will's plea .

Driving out on Route 68 to a SFDA Director's meeting - short for Southern Funeral Director's Association - after ending the last call with Anne, Joshua took his Blu Tooth out of his ear - need some time to reflect, he thought. Calls can wait for a few minutes. Thinking back to his conversation yesterday with Will, he was glad he had opened up to Anne about Will. I really need to go see him and soon. ' Lord ' he said out loud, ' he is my only family...it is going to hurt so much to let him go. I know he will be in Your loving care...and out of pain...but, he is all I have left of my childhood. I don't have Anne' - and, at that moment, being completely honest with himself, 'I probably never will. Make his journey an easy one, dear Lord. He is suffering so much...and, forgive me for losing my temper with him once again...he knows all the right buttons to push. He always has. It is up to me to make what ever time is remaining...and only You know that... good for the both of us. I need to make peace so when You finally call him Home, I am ready.' Then thinking to himself, I see so much death in my line of work; but, it is always different when its family. Another memory flashed before his eyes. I remember the last time I saw Anne. No, not the last lunch we had a few weeks back. The time, the last time, before she was lost to me for years. It was Mom's funeral...back **Home**. The family was leaving the chapel. I was the last one in the limo, and I looked up to see her and her Mom leaving the service; and, I didn't even get to acknowledge her being there, he thought. That was Anne's doing ... I know. She didn't want me to be uncomfortable or for things to be awkward between us. She saw Gayle, I know she did ... she had to. So, out of respect for me, for what had been between us, she stayed back - out of sight. That was Anne; and, she wasn't even "my Anne" then, he thought. His GPS beeping with voice acknowledgment that he had reached his destination, pulled Joshua back into the world of the living; and now, he would go sit in a meeting for hours discussing the dead.

# Chapter Forty Eight

Winter had finally relinquished her hold, giving way to one of the most beautiful springs or maybe it just seems that way, Anne thought. Spring is always so welcome, more so than any other season because all is new and things are slowly returning to ...what .. normal. What is normal, anymore, she thought. But at the very least, the hated overseas wars were ending; our servicemen are coming home; the economy, well that still sucks, but it does appear to be re-bounding. Her family was well, happy and well; the twins were growing like garden weeds; Emerson and Wright had weathered a bad spell in their marriage and seemed to be, once again, on solid ground; she and Reed were content with their lives ... trying to spend more time with one another instead of going off on their own so much. Yes, all was good - at least it appeared - for the moment. Never take anything for granted, her Mother used to warn her as it can all change in an instant. A fact her Mother knew for certain. Dad had taken ill so suddenly; no one could have ever imagined that almost a year to the day of him becoming ill, he was gone. He was my hero, Anne thought... he was made of steel... bulletproof. She thought of all the stories she had been told as a child of his exploits during WWII; - he was an Army-Air Force Pilot and flew over 45 combat missions in the European Theater; he was shot in both legs; his plane went down behind enemy lines somewhere in France...but he survived..and he came home a war hero - medals, ten in all . **War Hero** - a title he downplayed anytime it was spoken. He survived WWII, enemy bullets, being shot down; he survived a broken back in a train accident in the late 50's, being in ICU for nearly five months with 11 steel rods in his back; he walked away from so many automobile and motorcycle accidents, it had to make you wonder if he was like a junk yard cat - maybe he did have nine lives. So nobody could possibly envision the cruelty of him being sick - no terminal. **TERMINAL**. That word sent Anne's world into a tail spin the first time the Doctors had used it; and, could still send cold shivers up and down her spine, even today. Daddy wasn't going to ...*die*...he said so himself.; he would beat this thing called *cancer*. Do not worry. So, Anne put blinders on. She and Trae were planning their wedding, even though her parents, especially Daddy, were not thrilled.

'Fine' - her mind told her; they don't want to help me with this. I'll do it myself. I can pay for my own wedding. Looking back, Anne thought, I had to be the most spoiled Princess on Earth, chastising herself, what now nearly forty years later. How could I have continued on with wedding plans... my beloved Daddy was dying...*no*, even he said he wasn't dying. So on I blindly went.. s*tupid*..*stupid* girl. Mother eased her disapproval enough to start helping me with the details. After all, I was their only daughter, she couldn't just ignore that. So in a way, the wedding plans took on a kind of happiness; a restrained happiness, at best. There were those **'doubting Thomases'** who were convinced Anne was making an enormous mistake. And Joshua was one of those in that group. He told Anne later when he met Trae for the first time, he remembered thinking he is so wrong for her, so wrong. But seeing Anne apparently happy, he didn't voice his concerns. However, on a weekend trip home, he had cornered Trae – before he left going back to Tennessee, then his home, explaining – no warning- that would be a much better word – to the much smaller man, in clearly understandable terms, Trae had better be **good** to Anne...or he would answer to him. A fact that Anne did not know for a long time afterwards. Joshua told her once that summer he truly hoped to run into Trae 'just one more time' to which she never questioned why. But years later, when Joshua, the Minister, told her what the **'before'** Joshua should have done with that '

piece of crap' the first and only time he met him, Anne had to pause. Looking at Joshua, she wondered when he had morphed into her fake Uncle Gino from Chicago.

Re -entering the world of now...Anne jumped when Mags started barking at the doorbell, bouncing up and down like a rubber ball; answering the door, Anne graciously thanked the UPS delivery man, and taking the package out of his hand, closed the door much to Mags' displeasure as she did not get to be petted ..' Get over it,' Anne said with a laugh. To which the disgruntled ball of fur jumped back up on the sofa and sighed loudly. Realizing the package was formula for the twins, she sat it down on the counter and made a mental note to call Emerson and let her know it was here. Em often had packages sent here because she never knew if anyone would be there to accept them at her home during working hours. Guess she forgot about the Nanny being there today because of a schedule change. Oh well, gives me an excuse to go see my darlings, she thought. '***Cherish, is the word I use to describe*** ...' hearing **The Association's** oldie come on the kitchen tv, took Anne back to where she had been - only moments before the UPS man – back to that day when she finally saw Trae for the man he was...or maybe, the man he wasn't.

# Chapter Forty Nine

This meeting is going to go on forever....Joshua internally moaned; and, we haven't even gotten half way. A quick peruse of the meeting agenda, told Joshua that a 20 minute recess was just ahead. Good, I can stretch my legs...he thought. Finally outside in the hotel lobby, Joshua was able to admit to himself his shoulder was hurting - a little, nothing I can't take, he thought. Walk around and get the kinks out. Walking out to the hotel garden area, he noticed a wedding was just starting; not wanting to disturb the proceeding, he stood quietly on the lanai taking in the wonderful smell of all of the beautiful flowers brought in for the ceremony and listening he could just hear the beginnings of the ceremony. I shouldn't be privy to this, he thought. But, he appeared unable to move; he remembered another wedding.. his first. He and Gayle were married quietly at City Hall, their only guest being the unborn, Carey. That should have told me something, he smirked. Then the second, to Petra...that was an event - what it took over 2 hours to become man and wife. And Anne - her "first" wedding didn't even happen...Praise be. Wonder what her wedding to Reed was like. The organist brought him back to reality and with that, Joshua hurried back to the meeting, already underway.

Meanwhile, Anne was in the throes of memories, too. Weddings are supposed to make everyone happy...thought Anne. We were nearly there, maybe once we are married, everyone will see how happy we are; and, they will see that they were all wrong. I know they will. Deep in Anne's soul, however, she was having doubts.. serious doubts. Not just the cold feet kind. ***Doubts***. But her resolve was resolute...I will marry Trae. So with only a few weeks to go, the invitations, so many plans already made - it's going to happen, thought Anne. I just wish Daddy wasn't ill...that would make it perfect; and in her mind, Anne thought, I did think it was going to be perfect. My gown was beautiful - the gown I had used for my Coronation as South Carolina's Region I Magnolia Princess... my veil, handsewn by her mother, the beautiful diamond tiara from my coronation...all patiently waiting in the guest bedroom; and then, what was it, two weeks before the appointed date, my photographer was killed in a hit and run in front of the *very* church we were to be married in. **Shock. Sadness**. Bill had not only been a family friend for years, but also the photographer Anne had used her crown year; now he was - gone. And, on a rational in the moment thought, how do you get a photographer on such short notice, she wondered. Maybe **this is a sign**; things hadn't been good with her and Trae for some time. Maybe this would be a good thing; it would be perfectly understandable, as she would have to find another photographer... to just postpone it for a bit. Would that ever make **everyone** in her life happy, she thought; and maybe me, too. So with that frame of mind, she called Trae, told him they needed to talk; before she told Trae, she told her parents. Daddy's face ...yeah, I remember seeing Daddy's face; you could tell, he was pleased, but out of respect for her feelings, did not overdo it. She remembered telling him...' Go ahead and smile, Daddy, I know you are happy about this..' all the while thinking she was a bit pleased herself, but don't let on, she cautioned herself. 'I do not, under any circumstances, want to hear..." I told you so " ... from... **ANYBODY** ' she explained to her parents, all the while smirking a bit inside.

Trae was absolutely furious...so what if they didn't have a professional photographer. Pictures are pictures..anyone can take pictures.' Besides, you..we'll save a lot of money if we don't have to use some 'fancy-spancy' picture taker. This is no reason to cancel the wedding', he fumed. Anne calmed him as best she could, all the while a bit concerned about how quickly he became enraged about this change of plans. It was a postponement, Trae... *just for a while*. Anne tried to make him understand that a girl's wedding was the *one* day all girls dreamed of from ..well from infancy. It was *'their'* day..their moment to shine. It was more than just a *'day'*. However, the more he ranted and raged, the more Anne was convinced maybe a little more time would do them both good. She had never seen this side of Trae before and, quite frankly, Anne did not like it at all. He was acting like they were on an some unbreakable time schedule. One that had to adhered to at all costs. Anne couldn't understand why a simple postponement would be that upsetting. After all, their chosen Photographer had just been killed, for Heavens sake. Have a little more sympathy. Trae was ...*what* was the word...acting... **insane?** Anne was slowly, but surely beginning to see and to understand what everyone else had seen for months. There was a crack in the foundation of her *'Happily Ever After.'*.

Coming back to reality, Anne shook her head; not wanting to think what had just popped in her mind could possibly be true. Trae had always been interested in our Family Tree, the money being of greater interest than anything else. I should have seen the warning signs much earlier than I did. There was the day I caught him in the Library reading, *no memorizing* my Trust Statement. I would not sign a Pre-Nup like Daddy had wanted me to; and, Trae was very pleased about that. He agreed that there was no need for that. What was mine would also be Trae's with our marriage. The trust my Grandfather had set up for me when I was born would be coming due on my 25th birthday. In just a few years, I would be a very wealthy woman in my own right. And Trae knew that and, once, I remember, now he even made mention of the fact that we 'would be rolling in the dough' and 'not have to look to your stuffy old family for anything..' I didn't like Trae talking like that, but I had to remind myself, my world of privilege was not like the blue collar one Trae had grown up in. Now what forty years later, I hate to admit this, even to myself, because I never even thought of it at the time. What if Trae had *planned* all along to marry me - or marry the money - any way he could. Could he have already known - *no he could not have known* - but could he have had a fail-safe plan in place for insurance? If that was, in fact, the case, he might have felt my postponing the wedding could be the beginning of his own house of cards coming down. *No way could he have been that smart.*

# Chapter Fifty

Driving back home from the meeting, Joshua stretched his tired neck and shoulders as best he could. Boy, what I wouldn't give for a neck rub, he thought. Yeah, Anne gave good back rubs, he thought wickedly. When he had seen her a few weeks back, as they were leaving the restaurant, he mentioned his neck and shoulders were so tired from his trip. Reaching up on tiptoe, Anne gently pulled his shoulders down and began to slowly knead the tiredness out of his body; moaning softly to himself, what I wouldn't give for us to rewind back to the days of... us. She had always, almost intuitively known what he needed - even back then. He had always appreciated her, he told himself, maybe **too** much. For in the back of his mind, the entire time they dated, his deepest fear was losing her. He wanted to do everything he could to keep that from happening...and yet, it did.

Pulling into the driveway, he noticed Petra's car was gone. Odd, he thought, it's almost six; she is almost always home from work by this time. Putting the key into the lock, he heard the familiar canine greetings and before he could even close the door, he was attacked by all three of them, each wanting to out do the other for his attention. Finally freeing himself and managing to maneuver his way to the kitchen, he noticed the bright pink neon note under the equally neon green frog paperweight. 'Joshua - I had a Doctor's visit ...will be back soon.' Strange - Petra hadn't mentioned a Doctor's visit this morning at breakfast; guess she just forgot. Looking over at the calendar, he noted that there wasn't any memo on it either. Again -- odd; Petra is so organized. She even puts grocery shopping down on the calendar. Quit being paranoid, he scolded himself. Opening the fridge door, he perused the possibilities for dinner and, not seeing anything he was intent on fixing, he thought..we'll just go get something when she gets home; Petra doesn't like to cook anyway. Content with that game plan, he meandered off to check messages in his office and, he thought, maybe a quick shower, too.

With her head throbbing, Anne pulled herself back to reality; opening the medicine chest, she took down the bottle of **Advil**, and shook out the bright green pills into her hands. How easily it would have been to have to have stopped all the nonsense that summer and just had a bottle of **Advil** for dinner. No, I could never do that; that would condemn my soul to eternal damnation. Even Joshua would not have been able to save me from that, she thought. Needless to say, what would it have done to my parents; Daddy already sick..no, I did not even contemplate that solution, she thought. Getting a glass of water, she gulped down the pills and hoped the pain would go away. Some pain never goes away she thought philosophically. Never...you just push it aside...tuck it away. But, something simple and unexpected can always take you back to it; not wanting to admit it to herself, but knowing it to be true, that is exactly what Joshua has done, she thought. He has brought all of the pain back.

The happy sounds of Lady, Tramp and Mischa brought Joshua out of his power nap. Must be Petra, he thought; and, listening, he heard the front door close softly, then the front closet door. Following the happy sounds of the pups barking, he fully expected to hear Petra's knock on the door, but when it didn't come, he went looking for her. Finding her standing in their bedroom, he quietly walked up to her. Turning around, he noticed her eyes were rimmed with tears threatening to spill at any moment, ' Petra... what is wrong...' he asked softly. Falling into his arms, she simply said...' Josuawa, Ja.(I).. Jestem chory (I'm sick)...I sick ' Joshua held onto her trembling body as he processed the proclamation... what. What do you mean '**sick**???'...Petra is never sick, he told himself. Waiting patiently for her to compose herself, his mind went wild; first Will, now Petra. My whole world is falling apart before my eyes; and, I am helpless. Little did Joshua know this was only the beginning of the unthinkable.

Within a matter of days, it all became so clear...the headaches, the paleness, the clumsiness. Petra tried to give Joshua as much of the basic information she had been told today. There would be a more intensive meeting in a few days but what she knew was it was a rare blood disorder; while it was incurable, it was not an automatic death sentence. It could be slowed with medication, blood transfusions would be needed; intensive testing to figure out the best way to begin treatment.. but the bottom line: it was ultimately fatal. Petra had it ...her parents had it...her brother didn't...all in different stages ..but, how... was it genetic...in a way, it was. It all stems from the nuclear accident at Chernobyl. Even though that was years ago, they were exposed..all of them; and, it takes years for the damage to mutate. Her parents were more at a risk than she and her brother right now due to their advanced years; they probably would not see the New Year. With that statement, Petra once again collapsed into Joshua's arms...' Ja (I) must like rock.. be dare ...what, Josuawa....Ja see dem home to God... they not suffer...and Roman...he isze younger to ja, he will leve out ja, fer sure... isz bad dat he whil be lonely...jestem zmeezonyoh (I'm tired) , how say do widzenia ( goodbye) Josuawa? Ja not say do widzenia – you - Josuawa ....Ja wil be not here fer you...' The last words being muffled as Joshua felt Petra's face bury in his chest. Calming Petra down, he finally convinced her to take the sedative the Doctor had given her and, waited until the peacefulness of sleep had taken over before he even contemplated leaving their bedroom. Still reeling from the information that had just been thrown at him, Joshua found himself on his knees in the sanctuary...not even remembering how he got there. ' How many times have I come to You, my precious Savior..how many times have I asked for Your guidance and You have never let me down. **Please**, I *beg* of You, help me...help us all...get through this with grace and dignity. That is all I ask, because I know Your plan is already in place. *I beg of You - do not let me waiver in my duty to You*. It is with Your love and guidance, we - Petra and I - will make it through this. Give her the strength...and me, to see her through this final chapter.. **Amen.**'

Rising off of his knees, Joshua realized his cell phone was beeping a voice mail. Answering it, he heard Anne's voice on the other end. His mind was still racing and sorting through what Petra had told him; oh my word, how will I do this. I don't know where to even begin. She will understand my fears, she will try to help, I know she will. But, the truth is, I simply can't talk with her - or *anyone* right now. Standing there in the dimming light of the day, Joshua hung his head; then, turned off his phone. How do I possibly tell the woman I love and have loved for so many years, that the **other** woman I love is dying. Maybe..tomorrow.

The next few days were a blur of Doctor's visits, consultations, tests, more tests. The disease ... Hemochromatosis - Thalassemia - Major - words that Joshua could not even pronounce kept being repeated over and over by the medical staff; but, the common denominator in all of it was - genetic. This was a rare blood disorder that seemed to be more prevalent in families of Eastern European - Mediterranean cultures. Words like - Auto Somal Recessive Trait - Alpha Thalassemia - X-link – causes mental retardation. Joshua's attention was caught ... Roman ... mental retardation. The list went on and one until Joshua thought his head would explode. While this disease could be treated with blood transfusions and other medications, it would eventually be fatal. Anybody who had this disease was particularly susceptible to any type of infection. Something as simple as a cold could be a death sentence. A cold could cause respiratory failure, kidney failure, pneumonia..the list was endless ... Joshua held tight to Petra's hand as she listened to all of this. She listened intently, took it all in; she knew it was up to her to try and understand what she would have to tell her parents and her brother. A thought flashed quickly across Joshua' s mind. That is why Roman has always been a bit 'slow'. Why couldn't someone, somewhere have seen this in the cards? All the pieces were there, but, they were not looking in the right place. Looking at Petra, Joshua saw the deep circles under her eyes, the paleness that had worried him for sometime; it was all there, and yet, nobody saw it.

The medical staff kept talking and talking, but Joshua had passed the point of even listening; he only saw their mouths move as if they were mimes. He bowed his head and offered his thoughts to the Father. We will get through this, won't we, Lord? Your plan is already worked out..now we must walk down this path with faith and reassurance in Your love. When he raised his head, he saw a tear roll down Petra's cheek. She looked at Joshua ; with the courage only a dying person can have, said to him.. ' Josauwa... we must leve now..have still much work to do..and, there isz little time, Ja fear..' . The bottom line was **black and white**...and, there was nothing anyone could do to make it go away.

Several days went by and Anne was getting a bit concerned as she had left Joshua a voice mail and several texts with no reply. He's busy, she thought. Finally, her phone beeped while she was at Miller's, a local nursery and plant outlet. It was a text from Joshua. 'Call if you can, need to talk...love you'. Oh, I hope nothing has happened to Will, she thought. Calling his number, the call went to voice mail; how can that be, she wondered. I just got his text. Leaving her number and before she could even put the phone back in her pocket, it rang. She heard Joshua's voice on the other end, but it just didn't sound right, she thought. They talked on for a few minutes and finally she asked if something was wrong. ' Petra is sick...very sick, Anne. Will is not doing well either..I'm waiting for the other shoe to fall because bad things always come in threes.' Joshua told her. She wondered what she could do to ease his worry; offering to do anything, but knowing they were hundreds of miles apart, made even the gesture seem inconsequential. Joshua didn't seem to want to talk about either of them or their situations..so, she let it go for now. He is processing.. that is Joshua...once, he has done that, he will tell me. They talked on for a few more minutes; Joshua got a business call, thus they said good-bye for now. He promised to call her later when he had a bit more time..but before he hung up..' Anne.. I am so glad you are there..you are my rock. Please let me apologize for not getting back to you sooner. I didn't mean to worry you. It's just there's been a lot going on for the last few days..but, I will keep you posted from here on out.. And, know that whatever happens, or when it happens, that I do so love you..*very -- very* much..'

They went back to the comfort of talking nearly every day. Joshua's spirits seemed to improve, but he really had not elaborated on Petra's illness . He would talk a bit more about Will. And so it was about ten days later, her phone buzzed while she was working in the yard; looking at the caller ID, she saw Joshua's number come up. Oh good, he read my mind, she thought. Answering, Joshua didn't even say Hello...simply...'Anne ...Will just died.' Silence... what could she say...' I am so sorry, Joshua...is there anything I can do? ' They talked on a little while longer...final plans had been in place for a good while; he would be coming home to preach the service, Since Will was being cremated, the service would be sometime later - probably towards the end of spring. Before hanging up, Anne asked him how Petra was doing; there was a pause on the other end, but Joshua confirmed, that she was, indeed, doing better. Anne had to wonder - 'better ?'

Hanging up the phone, her heart broke for Joshua... he has lost Will ... what a horrible feeling that is, she thought. Having lost first her Father, then, her Mother a few years back, Anne knew first hand how it was to lose someone you love. You ache inside. You rationalize how they are better off - with the Lord - the whole thing. But in the cold hard daylight, the truth was it just plain hurt. And only time would ease that ache. Time did help with her mother's death. And it did with her Daddy's, too. But the other deep hurt, the other loss - no, time didn't - hadn't eased that one a bit. And up until a few months ago, it had been safely locked away. And Petra...she knew of Joshua's concerns in the past for her health, but had never contemplated that it could be anything serious. The fact that Joshua wouldn't - maybe he couldn't - talk about it. What on earth could an otherwise healthy woman of 56 be sick with? Her mind raced down some of the possibilities. Joshua must be in his own private Hell, she thought..and, I can't help him...at all.

# Chapter Fifty One

Soon, they were again back to the every day chat thing. Even though, Anne thought, Joshua seems distracted. Well, of course, he's distracted.. There's Petra....his brother, his surrogate Father, he just passed. She tried to emphasize with him, to ease his pain...she tugged him into conversations that were about anything - anything to take his mind off of what he was going through. Yet, each time she asked him of how Petra was doing, he would answer okay; never offering any additional information. Not wanting to pry, Anne would let it go. Joshua, she thought to herself, what is going on? Why are you being so evasive with me about her. You will tell me in time, I know, but I wish you would let me help you.

Will's service was planned for the middle part of May. Joshua would be coming in about a week before and would stay for a few weeks afterwards to help with the Estate and whatever else Grace, Will's widow, would need him to do. He didn't know how Grace was going to manage the farm by herself, but thought, she's been doing it by herself for a good while...no question she was capable in that area. And she would never - *ever* - think of selling the farm; it had been in her family for generations. She and Will loved it just as much as all those generations before them; but what would happen to it after she passed, he wondered. She was an only child; and, she and Will didn't have any children. Guess I better talk with her about that - and he made a mental note to do so.

Calling Anne, he informed her of the arrangements, and what his plans would be. There was no question, he wanted to see her.

He would let her know of future plans as the time neared. He thought to himself, I'll stay at the farm with Grace...maybe in the Carriage House. If I did that I could work when I want and not bother anyone. But what I really want - no, **need** to - is to talk with Anne - privately. Not in some busy restaurant or coffee shop. How do I approach that without it looking like what it would look like. However, somehow, that didn't matter; he needed to talk with Anne, to be with her - alone. I need to hold her...just hold her. I need to tell her about Petra and how when I found she was so sick, I felt like I had been punched dead center in the stomach. Was it guilt, I wondered. I had found Anne by then; was I being punished for that? And why would Petra be the scapegoat? Was it fear of the unknown? Could I possibly tell her without sounding like an ogre that the thoughts of us possibly truly being able to be together keep pounding in my head. Am I a bad person for even pondering that...after all, my wife is fighting for her life. I know God has a plan for all of us and I, as one of His layman voices, must abide by His decisions. When He closes a window, He opens a door. Is that what this is..an Open Door ? I need to pour out my heart to her and feel her healing love enfold me. I should write a romance novel, he smirked to himself. Yeah. I need her 'to enfold me'. He envisioned a Greek God, hair blowing in the wind, engulfing the willing maiden to his chest; laughing out loud at his sudden silliness, he went back to work in his office.

Good, Anne thought; Joshua is coming home to be with Grace. If anyone can mellow Joshua out it will be Grace. She had met Grace a number of years back when she and Will came home for Joshua's high school graduation. They were a striking pair. Will, dark, oh so tall, with a boyish charm and a killer good looks, and Grace, equally tall, porcelain skin, blonde hair and a look that screamed 'ice queen' only to completely blow that theory out of the water as soon as she opened her mouth and that sweet deep Southern drawl became evident. To Anne, Grace was the epitome of what her name said...'*Grace* '. In fact, she reminded you of the exquisite, Grace Kelly. She was so beautiful; but it was her eyes that drew you in. Her eyes were an intriguing blue..not baby, not sea blue - but pale, like cool iced water.. like wolf eyes. They were mesmerizing; and Grace always, always was smiling. She was one of the sweetest people Anne had ever met. Will once said that Grace was an enigma in the truest sense; because she was gorgeous, rich, with a pedigree that would choke any heraldry buff ...so, she should be a snob. And yet, she was one of the least pretentious people on earth. She loved getting her hands dirty with her prized Arabians; she loved country cooking; she loved the hard work on the farm; and yet, she had a closet full of designer clothes ... names like **Christian Dior, Givenchy, Chanel** for when she had to be the Lady of the Manor at some social event or gala. And, on any given day at the farm, Joshua told Anne once, you could find Grace in her jeans, check shirt, and Wellies. The real kicker to it all, however, was that she *always,* **_always_** had on her Mother's pearls. She was **never** without them. But **_that_** was Grace.

So, Joshua was finally coming **Home**. Maybe in some way, **home** is where he truly needs to be now. Sometimes, just being back to where your life was simpler without trials and worries can make the world seem a better place. Maybe, just maybe, Joshua will find some semblance of peace here. Coming back to the home, the 'stable' home of Will and Grace, Joshua had known since he was a kid of fifteen. That was Anne's wish for him. He needs to begin the healing process. Even Anne could not have possibly imagined **_how much_** Joshua really did need to come **home**

# Chapter Fifty Two

Spring had definitely arrived...tulips, daffodils...the bright colors of the earth awaking from its winter sleep. The winds were warmer, the days longer. It was good to be alive on a beautiful day like today, Anne thought. And yet, in only a few days we will be celebrating the life of William Carson Breckenridge, aka Will, while entombing his ashes in the family Mausoleum at the Farm he so loved. And she would see Joshua. That made the day seem even better. Then, maybe whatever Joshua was struggling with, she could help ease his pain.

Joshua was making the final preparations for returning home. His mind was torn in so many different directions these days. Surprisingly once they had the diagnosis of what was going on with Petra, things appeared to improve. Her parents did not appear to be having any health issues. The medicines she was on did seem to renew her strength, so much that after only a few weeks, her color improved, her balance improved and she was once more back at work. He did not like leaving Petra, but knew she could not accompany him because of her parents. He didn't think with her current health situation, she should be subjected to the long road trip even if that had not been an issue. I suppose we could fly; then she could come back the same day, but even that didn't seem practical. And, if he knew anything about Petra, her practicality was forever in place. They had said their Good-byes the night before he left...'..Please be so careful, Josuawa ...it be a long trip, not tire over... no over tire, you ... and ring me when you there...and, give Grase my love...' So, it was on that beautiful spring day, warm wind blowing from the Gulf, he slammed the trunk of his car and left Debrussiae Parish, Louisiana with his GPS set for **'Home**.' In only fourteen hours, I will be Home. Pulling out of the driveway, he felt his shoulder twinge - ever so slightly - as if apologizing for the fact it had been the reason he did not get to say good-bye to Will. He ran back through his memory to the last time they had talked, just a few days before.. he died. He re-ran the entire conversation in his head; did he know I wonder that last time...he seemed so at peace. I hadn't told him about Petra's illness as I didn't want him to worry about her. He asked about her and I lied, Lord. I lied to him and told him she was fine. Fine. In hindsight, I know it was the right thing to do, but it still bothers me that I lied to him. He asked me about Anne. In all of the craziness of learning about Petra's illness, I had not talked with her like we had been. I said we had not talked in a few days, again a lie; he questioned if everything was alright. Again, I lied, saying I had really been tied up with the church what with Easter just a few weeks back ..the transport business .. but no, there was nothing wrong between us. In thinking back what Anne had told him about his call to her concerning his surgery, he finally asked Will why he had called her since everything had gone alright. He waited for Will to catch his breath; Will told him that it was important for him ... for him, Will...to talk with her. To let her know that he knew she was back in Joshua's life, and try to understand why after all this time, they were once again... together. Then Will said what Joshua already knew in his heart..' I told her ... asked her ... not to hurt you ... again, Joshua ... not like before. ' Joshua was touched by his big brother's concern for him, and said ' I'm a big boy now, bro...I'll be fine.' Only to have Will counter.. ' That is...true...but, I won't....I won't be here...to pick up....the pieces this time...' That confession brought a lump to Joshua's throat he just could not swallow.

# *Chapter Fifty Three*

Joshua texted Anne that he was on the road, coming **Home**; he would be free to talk if her schedule would allow it – for what about fourteen hours, plus or minus, so, there was hope they could talk at some point during his trip. Anne was at the Dentist's office when Joshua's text hit her phone. She didn't know it until she left the office because she had turned her phone off; thus, it was over an hour later before she even had the opportunity to try and reach him. Sometimes cell service is so undependable - as service areas could be sporadic at best; so on the third try, her call went through. Oh great, voice mail...okay, buddy, tag, you're it. Throwing the phone back down into the console, she pulled her car out of the parking lot and into traffic. Thank goodness...the traffic is light. I'll be home in just a few minutes and I can brush my teeth and get this funky taste out of my mouth. She was nearing home when Joshua finally returned her call. He had been talking to his office and, then there was another call, and another...and finally, he could return hers. It was good to hear her voice, he thought... ' Why do you sound a bit muffled ?? ' he asked. ' Only because I had novocaine to fill a cavity. So, you're saying my speech is like Elmer Fudd, right?' She teased him...he laughed. Good, she hadn't heard that in a while. There was talk of how the trip was going, when he expected to reach the farm; and, then Anne asked what he knew she would..'Are you okay, Joshua...*really* okay? ' Pause. ' For the most part, I am... we'll talk when I get to the farm...K? ' Don't push, Anne...he'll tell you - he always does. By then, Anne was home, and knowing that she would probably lose signal, told him to call her when he got to the Farm.

# Chapter Fifty Four

Once Anne was in the house, she quickly went to her bedroom to change back to her comfy sweats.. ' What, you don't think enough of me to greet me at the door, you lazy ball of fur ?'... she teased Mags, who looked up from her spot on the end of the bed with sleepy eyes as if to say..' You been gone..??? ' Quickly brushing her teeth and changing, Anne padded back down the hall..checking out the fridge. What's for dinner, tonight, ole girl? Wonder if Reed laid anything out he wanted. Seeing the hamburger thawing on the shelf, she thought...umm, what taco salad, or maybe spaghetti. I'll see if the novocaine wears off enough to even allow me to eat dinner before I decide..might be just Jewish Penicillium, aka Chicken Noodle Soup, for me. With that she turned on the kettle to make some hot tea hoping that would make her numb face feel a bit better. Hearing her phone ring, she found her purse on the sofa where she had tossed it. Looking at caller ID, wonder why Joshua is calling me again. Answering, his voice strong – he said he simply ' got lonely and wanted to hear her voice.' 'You only talked to me - what like five minutes ago,' she teased. ' What's five minutes between buddies? ' he laughed. They chatted on for a few more minutes and agreed, once more that he would let her know when he arrived at the farm. Turning on the kitchen tv, she listened to the daily news round-up, catching the weather for the next few days– good it was, at least going to be nice for Will's service, she thought. Sipping her hot tea, she was thrown back to forgotten memories when a Renee's Bridal commercial hit the air. Looking at the screen, there was the beautiful young bride, all aglow in her white tulle gown, veil flowing behind her. Glancing down at her left hand where her Grandmother's diamond antique wedding band rested along side her own band and diamond engagement ring, she thought back to hers and Reed's wedding. It was so beautiful. Simple. Elegant. In April. It was relatively small, only about a hundred and fifty people there. Most of them family and close friends; and Bryan gave me away. The church was beautiful. There were lilacs..lots and lots of lilacs in big white wicker baskets... my favorite white, lavender and pink lilacs everywhere. She closed her eyes and could still make out that wonderful sweet smell. Opening her eyes, back to the ad on the tv screen, she blinked. Of course, my beautiful memory has to be pushed aside; there was the groom...blonde..of course, he's blonde..of course. And with that image in her mind, back came all the unwanted memories of her first *'almost wedding'*...what was I thinking, trying to marry Trae? He showed his true colors only a month after postponing - no, by then **cancelling** - the wedding. He was being a total jerk by then; there was no denying in her mind, she had made the right decision. Trae, just wouldn't let it go..he kept at it. He kept the argument, the disagreement about postponing, then cancelling, the wedding on the table every time they would talk; he wanted it re-scheduled as soon as possible..on and on. But it was something he said one night when we were out with some friends at a restaurant, that really made me uneasy. She thought back - all I said was..I wasn't feeling too good; something about the smell of the foods made my stomach uneasy ... and, there in the restaurant, was only making me feel worse. That is when he looked at me, kind of funny; I will always remember what he said to me...no, what he raised his voice and said to me...' You better hurry up and marry me, little Miss Perfect...you might just find you're going to 'need' me to marry you.. or better yet, pay me off not to..' and laughed. I had no idea what he was talking about; and, from the puzzled looks on Tim's and Arianna's faces, they didn't either. I remember looking at Trae as he was laughing, but nobody else was. 'What? Am I the only one that thinks that's funny?' he asked. However, it would only be a few days later that Trae's cryptic comment made sense. The news even I couldn't believe...I was four months pregnant with our child.

# Chapter Fifty Five

Anne closed her eyes and trembling went back to that spring day when her world came crashing down...and Trae was of no help. Since it was going to be her afternoon off at the office where she was working for the summer, she called her ob-gyn's office earlier that morning to see if they had an opening...why, they asked. Because she simply had not been feeling well. Complaining of headaches, but not migraines. And she had felt poorly for a number of days, now; not getting into the fact her mother had encouraged her to make an appointment - herself thinking Anne was probably in the throes of simple depression..what with the wedding being cancelled - and then her Dad was going downhill almost every day. It would certainly be easy to see how this could be affecting her life. Yes...there was one cancellation for 1:15. Anne took it and thinking back; I thought the Dr. would tell me I was run-down, maybe give me some vitamins and send me on my way. Yeah; that would have been the perfect outcome to that, wouldn't it..she sneered to herself. Entering the medical office doors on her way to Dr. Moore's office, Anne held the door for a very pregnant lady coming through. Oh my word, she looks totally miserable, Anne thought. The woman acknowledged her gesture with a tired smile and said with a laugh to Anne...' I will be so glad when this little soccer player gets here...he's such a kicker!' Anne laughed . Wonder when was the last time she saw her feet. Closing the door behind her, Anne registered at the desk, sat down, picked up a magazine and settled in to wait. You always have to wait, she thought to herself; only to hear her name called. Amazing...I only just sat down, she said to the nurse. After all of the preliminaries of weight, temperature, urine, the nurse escorted Anne to an examination room. No need to undress as she was only being seen for general malaise..headaches. So sit down in one of the chairs and wait. When Dr. Moore came in, he greeted her and listened patiently to what had been her reason for wanting to see him; then the bottom fell out of her world. Anne was absolutely incredulous when told all of her symptoms would go away ...what in about five months or so. How could Doc know exactly how long her symptoms would last. He smiled at Anne, took her hand and offered his congratulations. W hat do you and Trae want..a boy or a girl? A boy or girl? A boy or girl what? What? she thought; then, it hit her like a lightning bolt. My God, I can't be pregnant..Trae always used protection, he told her so. There must be some mistake..she heard herself say out loud. No, no mistake; if calculations are correct, you guys will be blessed with this new life by the end of summer. Not sure I would use the word 'blessing' she thought to herself. She quickly re-gained her composure, and making a follow-up appointment, left the office. Sitting in her car, she was incapable of moving. Now what..she wondered. Trae has been an ass since I cancelled the wedding. Oh my God, she thought..the comment he made just the other night..no way he could have known. But the words kept ringing in her head...' ..have to marry me...or pay me off.' Now what? Well, I'll go by his job site and tell him... have no idea, no idea how he will take this unexpected news, that is *if* it is 'unexpected news' to him. Anne pulled on to the construction job site. Trae's boss saw her and with his walkie talkie, she overheard him radio ...' ...Hey, Trae, that good looking cutie you been trying to get to marry you, just pulled on the lot. You just might wanna come down and see her before one of these other hard hats hit on her...' and with that tipped his hard hat at Anne telling her Trae would be down, all the while, opening her car door for her. Anne sat there for just a minute more, then seeing Trae, she exited the car; smiling and thanking Hanson for his gesture. Trae grinned at Hanson – and then, taking Anne's arm, he planted a big 'for show' kiss on her lips as all of the hard hats on the rafters roared their approval. 'And to what do I owe this visit...' he asked when he finally let her go. Pulling back to keep her thoughts straight in her head, Anne wondered how she had ever thought she wanted to marry this man..everything about him, now simply repulsed her. I am a snob, she thought. What good did I ever see in this...what do I want to call him...no, better not call him **THAT,** she thought. Was this the place or the time to tell Trae this news..what will he do..she fretted. This will give him even more reason to push for a wedding...a wedding that now, she did not want, under any circumstances. Not at all ..but, now she needed. Calmly, she told him she had been to her doctor - about the headaches and such. Good that will lead into it, she thought. He asked what she had found out; she paused. Well, here goes nothing. Well, according to Dr. Moore, this will all go away in about five months. Searching Trae's face for any indication that he knew what she was talking about; she picked up on a slight smile, but he kept his composure waiting for her to explain. She took a deep breath...' Trae, I'm four months pregnant with our child...' she heard someone say; but, she could have sworn it wasn't her voice that had said it. There he stood in the afternoon sun with his mouth wide open... acting dumbfounded. And then it started... there was no way she could possibly be pregnant because he had used protection. And, then he confirmed her suspicions when he said to her..' And wasn't it just the other night I told you – you might need to marry me ? And it continued. With the question that was a dagger to Anne's already fragile heart...'Are you sure it's mine ? ' Trae sneered at her. Anne remembered thinking...You bastard, you know it's yours...I'm going to be sick. Not even giving Trae a second to recoup his faux pas, she swung around and slapped his face so hard she nearly fell down; which Trae did falling backwards as he tripped over some metal rods on the ground behind him. The hard hats on the rafters thoroughly enjoyed that scene as they whoopped it up acknowledging the entertainment going on below them. One yelled out... 'Got you a real spitfire, ain't ya, Trae.. yeah, man, make her mad, why don't ya??' And all the others behind him were laughing heartily at the sight of Trae, spread-eagled on the ground trying to disentangle himself from the rods. Anne turned around opening the car door, and attempted to get in, but Trae was already there in front of her. She looked at him..and remaining calm, she looked dead into his eyes..and, with a steady and calm voice said..' I have no intention of marrying you, even if you begged me to... you want no part of this..fine. I can do this on my own. And, furthermore, you can go straight to hell..and in case, you were wondering...I would give all of my inheritance away **before** I gave you a single penny. That ship has sailed. You will gain nothing from me. **Nothing.**' Trae caught the door...and stammering, he continued his barrage...'... If that *REALLY* is my kid, I'll marry you.. but if it ain't....I...won't... have it..if it ain't mine...and you will have to pay me to keep quiet, Missy..' Anne could not believe the venom spewing from Trae's mouth. ' Oh, please Trae, get a life. I don't need you for anything... you know this child is yours, and you, dumb ass that you are, just let the 'Golden Goose' slip away..so crawl back under that rock you call home, and leave me ..us..alone.' Anne screamed at him. And I was going to marry him ...what a fool I was..am. Looking back in the rear view, as she exited the lot, she laughed out loud as she saw Trae bend over to pick up his hard hat that had gone sailing across the lot when she slapped him; he non-chalantly dusted it off and shrugging his shoulders to his jeering co-workers, headed back to the construction site. I am an idiot, a total freaking idiot. So with tears streaming down her face, she headed for home... **home**...oh what, am I going to do? This is going to kill my parents. What can I do? Pulling into the driveway, she was thankful that her parents were evidently out. That will give me more time. The wall phone was ringing as she entered the sun porch, and with no caller ID – yeah this was the 70's - she thought...she blindly picked it up to hear Trae falling all over himself trying to apologize for his behavior...he was scared...oh yeah, His cash cow had just died. Like she wasn't scared...good one, Trae. He rattled on and on...and finally he 'offered ' to marry her so she could keep her 'good' name ..my former fiancee 'offered' to marry me. Processing that fact angered Anne so much she slammed the phone down as hard as

she could. The phone rang again...' **Go to hell** ' she heard herself say; and with that stormed off to her bedroom.

Boy, did I ever make a mess of things from there, she thought as all of the long ago past screamed for her attention. I remember throwing myself on my four poster bed and, angry as I was, simply could not cry. I kept hearing the phone ring and just kept ignoring it until finally on the like 10th time, I picked it up and screamed ..'***Stop calling me!*** ' to which my mother answered, 'Anne, are you alright, honey? We just wanted you to know we were going to pick up subs on the way home...are you sure you're alright?' Anne covered quickly saying that she and Trae had a fight and he would not leave her alone. She was fine..see you all soon.Anne, back in the present...thought out loud...'Yeah, we had a fight alright..more like WWWIII; the battle lines were drawn, and thinking back she laughed about what her solution could have been. Shame I didn't have an Uncle **'*in the business*'** in Chicago. I could have called him ..' I have a bit of a problem, Uncle Gino...do you think you could help me out ? ' And laughing out loud at her next thought, that of Joshua telling her what he had wanted to do 'with' Trae when they had talked at **Eve's Garden**. Great minds think alike. Ha. Thinking of Trae possibly swimming with the fishes in Lake Michigan did not really bother her. My word, I am crazy she thought. Literally laughing out loud of her present day solution to a long ago problem, she thought - that would have solved at least one problem. However, the biggest one remained and was growing inside of her. I held that secret for nearly a month. I wouldn't talk with Trae, and even now, wished that I had not relented on that front. Finally, I bundled up my courage and told my mother. She didn't rant - or cry - she just asked me where we went from there. I wanted an abortion - a taboo word in my Catholic world ... you know, PRO-LIFE, hell, damnation and all that; but, even I knew that wasn't going to happen as I was nearly five months along. I could see the hurt in her eyes, but she didn't express it. She said she would talk to Daddy; we would figure something out. The 'something' we figured out included Joshua. Thinking back, it wasn't the best of game plans, but then hindsight is always 20/20. Joshua came home shortly after all of this happened. After the craziness began, and being Joshua, he was willing to do anything to help. He was still living in Tennessee, so it was decided I would go there - he would be there to help me with anything I needed. I could get an apartment. but most importantly, I could get **away** from Trae, away from home...have the baby there. We still did not know where exactly this new little innocent life was going to fit into this plan, but, it seemed for the moment, we **had** a plan. Once everything was figured out, come back home...like nothing had ever happened. We had a plan... didn't say it was a **good** plan or even that it was going to work. And it all fell through because only a few weeks after leaving home for Tennessee, I was back home, mainly because I just couldn't cope with the loneliness. Almost as soon as I had returned home, Joshua was back here. That was **that** Sunday, when he asked me to marry him... and I couldn't - I just couldn't do that to him. I would be putting his career at risk; needless to say, we would have kept the baby; and Joshua would have been fine with that..I knew. But I wouldn't have been. Because by that time I had made up my mind; I would put the baby up for adoption because if I didn't, Trae would never - **ever**- leave me alone. And, if I hadn't known it before, I knew it for sure now...Trae was **insane**..certifiably **insane.** .

The rest of the story - what Joshua never knew was the torment Trae put me through those last few weeks...and, for **years** afterwards. He was a stalker in the truest sense. He threatened me. Told me he would kill me. He would tell me in gruesome details how he would cut the baby from my still warm dead body - his sister could help him, she was a nurse, remember...even if it wasn't his..he would sneer..'I can do away with 'it'' in one breath; and, then in the next, that he would go to the ends of the earth to prove he was the father, continuing to rant of his 'rights' - he would take me to court to get his child. Or, better yet, get rid of me before he had to go to court and steal his child. He could get 'rid' of my family, too; those snobs that didn't like him from the get-go, he would sneer. He was, simply put, insane. Having to deal with his rantings and ravings was totally taking a toll on me. In the short span of a few weeks, I had come to terms with what I had to do. I would allow this child to be adopted; that way Trae would never know, or would I, where he/she would go. But, more importantly, Trae would never get his hands on this innocent little pawn who did not have a voice of its own. I knew Trae would never leave me alone; he would torment me forever and even more so if I tried to do this on my own. The last time I spoke to him face to face, he threatened to run me off the road, and make it look like an accident killing both of 'his problems' with one fell swoop; that was the conversation my Daddy accidently overheard. He approached me and asked me how long this had been going on; I tried to lie to him and said that Trae was simply angry - that he wouldn't hurt me. And so, as if I didn't have enough to be worried about, I was totally afraid since my Daddy was so ill, he would take it upon himself to become the now infamous fake Uncle Gino and 'handle' the situation.

With all that had been going on, I think, back now and believe in all sincerity that was truly one of my biggest fears. This man, this despicable worm, had hurt his little girl; well, it could be taken care of...no questions asked. So with all of that stomping around in my head, was it any wonder that I would deliver prematurely? But it didn't stop there – oh, heavens no. Trae came to the hospital; his sister, the nurse, sneaked him in thru the employee entrance and got him to my room. That is, after stopping by the nursery to see his "son". Could this get any worse? Yes, it could; under pressure from my family, in the weeks leading up to my giving birth, my family wanted me to keep the baby. Maybe Bryan and his wife, Elena could adopt it ( a fact Elena later told me had never been presented to them. She said she would have been glad to do this, but even then, wondered if it would be a good idea as Trae was so unstable); or, we could find someone else in the family circle that would help. Mother had relatives in Mississippi; aunts, uncles, cousins - we could do a private adoption. I know they were just trying to help, but what none of them could see was that it would be a recipe for disaster. And, I even gave it serious thought. Maybe we could do this; but even though that little bundle came home with me; it only took two telephone calls later, to confirm it was a **huge** mistake. 'Watch where you go in that pretty little car of yours, Princess. I can take it out in a heartbeat with my truck... steal that baby and nobody will ever find us again. You'll be dead, you know, no witnesses....ha ha ha ha ha'. So, it was with a heavy heart, and against my family's wishes, the necessary papers were signed ; and, on a beautiful clear pre -Autumn day, a ' **before'** just husband and wife, became a '**Family'** of three. As cruel as it sounds even today, I innocently thought **... I was free....Free** . How **wrong** could one person possibly be? .

GET your life in order, I told myself.. **get your life in order**. And maybe, just maybe... Joshua. No, I quickly remembered by that time Joshua was already lost to me. Remember what Mrs. Glochenous had said - Joshua had moved on...he was thinking marriage with someone **ELSE**. Happiness with someone else. Let it go..put it away, put Joshua away. Find a place deep in your heart and lock him away **once and for all**. And, so I did. I accepted the first date with Reed. I *told* myself I had moved on.

Life was slowly, ever so slowly returning to normal. Anne finished school and began looking for employment. She didn't want to teach as being around children right now was not what she wanted to do; at least, not at the moment. Even being around Jenna and Christopher hurt - or Reed's nieces and nephews...it just hurt. She interviewed for a job and began working as a Paralegal with an Attorney. She was dealing with the constant threat of Trae showing up; but, she was determined to keep it all to herself. She would trust no one with that information. She watched as her beloved Father began losing his battle with the Big C. She watched this Hero of a man - well over 6 feet and 250 pounds, dwindle down to a mere shadow of himself. She watched his valiant efforts at humor when the chemo took his hair - and then, his strength. She watched as his mind started to fade..at least, *if* there is a God in Heaven, he won't remember that horrible summer, she thought to herself. It broke her heart to see him struggle with simple daily tasks - like feeding himself. She thought she would collapse in a blubbering heap on one particular afternoon; her Father had been admitted to the hospital a few days before; she would make arrangements each day to go and feed him lunch. As luck would have it, she was late on this particular afternoon by about twenty minutes, thus he had finished his lunchtime meal before she arrived. She walked past the nurses' station where she heard the group laughing at something that they had seen/read somewhere -- ' loafing' she thought as she went by. Walking into his hospital room she would find her Father sitting up in his bed, trying to feed himself – ice cream running down his face, the food from his lunch covered his bed and hospital gown. But he literally beamed when he saw her and motioned her to come and eat with him... which Anne did. But, upon leaving his room, she called her boss and told him what had happened. He told her he would back her up in whatever way she needed...so, with his blessing of *'Go-For-It"* in her pocket, **before** she left the hospital that day, **every** nurse, aide, orderly, janitor or candy-striper who had the misfortune to be on that floor at the time - as well as the Administrator of the Hospital - knew of what had happened in her Father's room.. and ***THAT IT WOULD NEVER HAPPEN AGAIN ...OR ELSE...*** there would be a major lawsuit filed for negligence and it would - she **promised** with enough anger in her voice to make the point ring true – bring the entire establishment to its knees. And, it never happened again. But it didn't matter, because only a month after that incident, her beloved Father passed at 3:29 p.m. on a Wednesday. Anne went to pick up her Mother for the trip to the Hospital that evening ; it was her Mother who told her he had died that afternoon peacefully in his sleep...with only her there. Anne felt a dagger go deep into her very heart..down..down..down where Joshua now resided. She couldn't move.. cry ...then, her tormented soul reminded her at that moment.... 'I never got to say 'Good-Bye'.

The funeral was held on a beautiful Sunday afternoon nearly two weeks after his death. It was cool, but the sky was bright blue and cloudless. The service was attended by most of the small tight-knit community - her Father was a native son, having never left the area of his childhood home. The service had been delayed as he was an organ donor, so all that had to be finalized - finding compatible donors and such - before his body could be released for cremation. The burial was private - just immediate family members and one very special invited guest .. her Dad's Golden Retriever, Sam.

Sitting in the Chapel listening to her Father's final service, Anne wondered if Joshua even knew of her Father's death..or his illness. She had wanted to call him, or something...but didn't - for a lot of reasons. Little did she know that while she and her family were listening to his service, Joshua was less than five miles away. He had come home to take his mother to see Will as he had just been diagnosed with MS. Joshua's mother knew of Raleigh's illness and eventual death. And, she knew Anne's married name - even where her parents had moved after Raleigh got sick - but, she never told Joshua, even when he point blank asked her once. When the final **'Amen'** was said...Joshua was all of ten minutes away.

So it was in the span of only a few months, Anne had lost all three of her most beloved treasures...her first born child, her one true love, Joshua and finally, her beloved champion of life, her Father. And so it was just shortly after his death, she found herself at his grave, talking to him...a habit she would use many times over in the following years; he was still her confidant, he just couldn't protect her anymore. It was up to her now - and, she was alone. She would bring flowers and talk...cry...scream...whatever she felt she needed at that moment. It wasn't until nearly three years later that she knew the craziness was going to stop - **right then**, when on a sunny Saturday afternoon, she was getting in her car leaving the cemetery to look up and see Trae at the end of the property ...watching her. *'Enough'* ..she whispered to herself. Driving to the end of the driveway, she wheeled her car out of the parking lot

and headed straight for the Police Department. Since Trae didn't seem to get the message to leave her alone and was incessant in his abuse, Anne finally got up enough nerve to get an **Order of Protection**..then, and only then, did the stalking and abuse stop.

Anne left the Police Station with a copy of the **Order of Protection** in her hand and a smile on her face. Thanks to an old friend's help, one who just happened to be on the force, things were going to change. Feeling the last rays of the afternoon sunshine on her face, she found herself smiling as she drove straight to her Daddy's grave. 'I did it...I did it..thanks Daddy for showing me what I needed to do...' She blew him a kiss, drove home to her new husband. And, for the first time in nearly three years, slept with both eyes closed.

# Chapter Fifty Six

**M**ight as well get it all out, purge once and for all, thought Anne. I really need to be able to tell Joshua all of this so he'll know - **why** I would not marry him. I remember when he asked me to marry him...my heart almost stopped. How could I impose all of this craziness on him. If we married, we would become a family. I knew Joshua would take this child to his heart and that it would never be an issue. Knowing Trae as I did, I knew there would be nothing normal in Joshua and me becoming a family of three. It would not work, I would always feel guilty...guilty for bringing all of this trouble into his life. He was an up and coming executive even then, this might damage his career..or worse, it might damage us. I could not take the chance of Trae showing up with the insanity I knew he possessed, and have all of us become the headline story on the 6 o'clock news. I knew he was capable of almost anything his perverted mind could envision. No, send Joshua away to safety...do whatever you have to do to convince Joshua - tell him you don't love him anymore..you never did... *LIE*..do whatever you have to - get Joshua out of the line of fire. Trae will get tired of this stupid game and leave me alone. And, if he doesn't, well it will only be me, and maybe him that gets hurt. The plan worked with regards to Joshua, but Trae -- well it took a bit more convincing - legal convincing - the kind that - ***you could do time -*** and an **Order of Protection** ...convincing to make him leave me alone.

And, I thought I had it made – I also need to tell Joshua that the crazy bastard went by my mother's new house sometime back - what maybe 15 years ago...according to her, he was in the area and wanted to 'check' on me...oh good grief, get a grip. When I found out about that, I nearly went ballistic. With the help of a that same friend in the Police Department, I found out where the nut case was; calling on an untraceable line, I asked if he forgot there was an **Order of Protection** out on him...and it does not expire...actually, I think it does, but I was praying he didn't know that. I told him that if he ever so much as looked in my direction again, I would go to what ever legal extremes that were available to have him put away in prison for what ever trumped up charge I could come up with; and, I told him that if he ever decided to visit my elderly mother again, I had told her to shoot him on sight. He was a danger to her. According to him, he just wanted to find 'his son' and 'make it up to him' and 'me' —I laughed in his ear - but I wanted to spit in his face. My final words to him were plain and simple... ' **I think I told you once before when this all began, you snake, go and crawl back under the rock you came out from under - and, if God is willing, you will fall straight into the fires of Hell. And, hopefully, be damned for eternity. Of that I can only hope.**' Trae called out my name one last time...to which my reply was ' **Go to Hell!** ' and slammed down the receiver to the desk phone – **hard**; so hard , that, in fact, I broke my little finger. **Crap**. It just never ends.

Oh, and while we are getting all of this out and purging my soul, I get a call from the attorney's office that handled the adoption; accordingly to records, the child - what now in his late twenties - was looking for his biological mother to 'fill in some blanks in medical history'. I told the attorney's intern that all of the medical information I had to give was given at the time of adoption. I had nothing to offer. There is a request for a visit.. I am told. ' No' - I heard myself say. Will this never end, I thought at the time. But, I relented, and did, in fact, meet this young man sometime later. My heart literally fell to the floor, when being seated at the restaurant we had agreed to meet at, I was absolutely dumbfounded as this young man was a perfect clone of Trae. Does it ever quit, Lord? We talked for about an hour; he told me of his life having been adopted by a Presbyterian minister and his wife, who already had a daughter, age 3 and wanted another child. The wife was unable to have any additional children due to uterine cancer a year after their daughter was born. He said his parents had been strict, but loving and supportive. They had divorced about 10 years ago with his Dad remarrying a much younger woman and now he had half siblings - a boy and a girl, ages 6 and 8. He and his father were no longer close; he was currently living with his mother and grandmother while attending college classes towards a degree in Marketing. The next statements floored Anne – he had been involved with a girl several years ago - and he had a child by her, a boy, now 5. Anne's mind raced with thoughts...*'like father, like son'* being the first..and then, it hit her...I am a Grandmother - again. He said he didn't see him but once a month as his mother lived in a different city. His sister was married and lived in Maryland with her husband and son - his nephew. He said he had been looking for me since he found out, quite by accident, that he was adopted. He wanted to meet and get to know his 'real' mother. He wanted the one thing from me that I could not give him, as he said...his 'real' mother. Anne thought I heard those words - 'real' – and I looked at this clone of Trae sitting across the table from me. Then as gently as I could, held his gaze and told this young man, I was his **birth** mother; his **real** mother was the one who raised him, who opened her heart to love him, kissed his hurts. I was sorry that he had not had a happy childhood ...there are no guarantees. He had wanted a 'Happy Ever After' reunion from me, and I couldn't give that to him. If anyone knew there were no 'Happy Ever Afters', it had to be me. He never asked about his father except why his name had not been on the birth certificate. I said there were reasons..and did not elaborate - **at all**. He said he had placed ads in the local newspapers for years to try and find me – or anyone that could tell him more about 'him'..and, that he had all but given up until three years ago when because he was of age, the adoption files would allow him to look into previous 'closed' adoption records/files; and, he could look into the county/city records . Anne quickly thought - what is it with all this need to find me all of a sudden. Maybe I should have left the country instead of staying put...first Joshua - now Todd.

It is true what they say about hindsight - 20/20. As much as it pained me to listen to all this young man wanted to tell me, I felt he was trying so hard to be the son...as he put it 'that I would want him now' .. to which I told him the truth that it was never an issue of whether 'I wanted you or not' - it was the rationale that I could not 'keep' you or 'raise you'. Do I dare tell him the gory details, I wondered. No.. somethings are better left unsaid. I told him the age old explanation – young, alone, single parent raising a child. This would allow him to have the kind of life he deserved . Why is it a lie seems to sound better than the truth sometimes? In allowing you to be adopted, I gave the ultimate gift not only to you, but to the two people who wanted you to become a member of their family. I never requested any information about you because when I signed the papers relinquishing custody, you were no longer mine. I told him when I said good-bye to him all those years ago, I sang the same lullaby to him that day that my Grandmother sang to me in my nursery. Anne paused returning to the moment ...the same one I sing today to Brennan and Emma. Then closing her eyes, she sang out loud the old English lullaby...'
***I pray you'll be alright, and make it through the storm, find shelter safe and warm to keep you from all harm, let this be my prayer when storms clouds gather near , I'll keep you in my thoughts, I'll hold you in my heart, til you're in my arms again.'*** I kissed your tiny little head, said a prayer of hope for you to have a good life. My one wish was you would always be safe from harm. I wondered, from time to time, especially on your birthday... if that really happened for you; I always lit a candle in the church on that day for you. When we finally said good-bye, I knew he wanted more from me than I was capable, even then, of giving to him. In letting him go, again, I hoped I had saved him from any additional hurts. I could not tell him that his very own father had wanted to do away with him - and me. And, I could not entertain the thought of having this young

man in my life, now. What if Trae were to somehow find out about him; find out he had been in touch with me. I could not expose this young man - even, now a pawn - to that craziness. So, with that rationale, I let Todd go back to his life ...with no invitation to become a part of mine..with no further contact. I know that may sound cruel, but the fear is that Trae is out there, *still*...could I risk his wrath once again. **No.** This is for the best...maybe this time, this time, it will be the end of the story. Crossing herself and offering up her prayer, she uttered....'God Speed, Todd...may you find the happiness you so seek. '

It wasn't until she had returned home that she found it...in the pocket of her jacket, she pulled out a small piece of blue paper. Thinking it a left over grocery list or something like it, she nearly threw it away; but upon opening the folded note, she had to catch her breath; it read....' Mrs. Ebersol, if you are reading this, I know I can not call you Mom.. Mother...but, at some point in our lives, I do hope we can be friends...if you ever need me, for any reason, please call me..I am, and always will be your son...256-673-8141..I will never change that number, because I will never forget you. Until 'someday'...Todd. Anne felt her shoulders fold...her spirit nearly evaporate. Somehow, someway ...maybe I **can** do that Todd, just not while your father is still out there - somewhere. Maybe. So, taking a deep breath, Anne went to her closet and pulled down an antique hand-made oak chest. It had been her Mother's, before that, her Grandmother's and even before that, her Great-Grandmother's. Story had it that it was a wedding gift for her Great-Grandmother from her father- Anne's Great-Great Grandfather. The richness of the wood intrigued her and always had...but inside is what really mattered to Anne. Among the many treasures, there were her father's war medals; the six-pence she and generations before her had worn on their wedding days in their shoes for luck; the lace hankie her mother had made her for her first Communion; her pink crocheted baby booties, made by her maternal Grandmother; Her diamond tiara from all those years ago; Emerson's Christening Gown, a lock of her hair and her first tooth; one diamond stud earring..the one Joshua put in her ear all those years ago; the withered, but now preserved, bouquet of honeysuckle Joshua had given her the first time he told her he loved her; Reed's first love letter to her; all of these pieces of the past she had saved all of these years. So, with a heavy heart, she added the small piece of blue paper to these treasures...putting it with the tiny lock of blonde hair she took from Todd on the day she let him go. Closing the box, she let go of the tightly held in emotions, feeling the hot tears roll down her face. Will I ever find any peace, she wondered in between sobs.

Finally, re-entering reality and sighing deeply, Anne thought - that is it...all of it... Joshua will understand, like Joshua always does. I wonder ...will it, could it change anything by spilling all of this out. In all fairness, Joshua needs to know the whole story. But, at what cost and what good could possibly come of it now. No..Joshua needs to know; hopefully he can forgive me for hurting him the way I did. Surprisingly, I do feel better. But, Father Murphy was wrong...maybe others might be able to find the courage to forget and forgive...but ... *me...no ...I will never forgive myself.* AND, crossing herself, dropping to her knees...'*Lord help me...* I *WILL NEVER EVER- EVER FORGET.*'

# Chapter Fifty Seven

Satisfied that she had finally been able to purge her memory of all of the hurt, the long time guilt; and that she finally had the courage to tell Joshua the rest of the story. Anne was pleased when her cell phone rang and looking at the caller ID, yes it was Joshua.

Joshua pulled into the long paved driveway of the farm; don't know why they insist on calling this a 'farm'. It is a Plantation Estate at the very least, but before he headed to the main house, he stopped. Taking in the beauty of the centuries old estate, he was moved by the calmness...the peacefulness. No wonder Will loved it so much here. Seeing the beautiful Arabians grazing contentedly in the field only deepened his sense of tranquility; you could lose yourself here, he thought. Picking up his phone, checking for service, he first called home; Petra was at church. It was Monday, he forgot. Leaving her a message and telling her he was here.. fine and going to collapse into bed after a much needed hot shower, he ended the call. He then dialed Anne's number...hearing it ring... then her voice ...'Anne...I'm at the farm...' They talked on for a few more minutes - him giving into exhaustion, and begging off to find that hot shower and hitting those cool bed sheets for some well needed sleep. There was the main house - just up ahead - lights on waiting for his arrival. Having heard his car coming up the driveway, Grace was waiting for him with a smile and eyes that showed her deep appreciation for him coming. Joshua was always happy to see Grace. She had been Will's wife for nearly fifty years...the true love of his life; and a sister and surrogate mother to him. A tall, statuesque blonde with beautiful blue eyes, she was the opposite of Will in every possible way, except height. Will was tall, 6'8, but, Grace held her own at 6'1. Joshua used to tease them if they ever had kids, they had to have at least five..a professional basketball coach's dream. Will and Grace would have made great parents, but, it just wasn't meant to be. They had tried for years, suffered through the nightmare of miscarriages, etc; and at one point, looked into the adoption route. Ultimately, they decided that if they couldn't have children of their own, they would offer their farm to inner city kids each spring and summer and have the joy of kids around at least for a few months of the year. And, the kids so enjoyed the big openness of the farm and all of the animals. Over the years, many of the kids they 'adopted' came back to see them; and, brought their own kids with them. It was good for everyone. Turning off the ignition, Joshua came back to the moment; seeing Grace's warm smile awaiting him, he quickly exited the car; they chatted on for a few minutes, then knowing that he must be exhausted from the drive, she told him to go on to the Carriage House. Are you sure you don't want to stay here in the main house ...she paused. When Joshua shook his head, saying that he had always loved the little cottage and, that he would be able to work there without bothering anyone with his late hours. She nodded her understanding; and, said she would have Mrs. "C" send a tray over with a late dinner – they could talk tomorrow . ' Good night, Joshua...thank you so much...' Grace said, and with that she re-entered her ancestral home and closed the centuries old oak door behind her.

# Chapter Fifty Eight

Tired as he was, sleep alluded Joshua. Reaching over to the bedside table, great...two a.m. He hit the '**on**' button on the clock/radio beside his bed..maybe some music will settle my restlessness. Only to be met with a 60's tune. '***Why am I losing sleep over you. Re-living precious moments we knew, so many days have gone by, and still I'm so lonely, I guess there's just no getting over you and there's nothing I can do, but spend all of my time, out of my mind, over you. Within the prison walls of my mind, there's still a part of you left behind, and though it hurts, I'll get by without your lovin', but, I guess there's just no getting over you and there's nothing I can do..but spend all of my time, out of my mind...over you.***' Yeah, someone in that group...what was it Gap something..***The Union Gap***... that's what it was. Yeah, they knew heartache. Reaching over and slapping his hand on the '**off** 'button; that was a super idea, old man, yeah. That helped sooo much...and, with that he picked up his pillow and pulled it hard down over his head.

The next few days for Joshua and Grace were filled with final preparations for Will's service. There was still so much to do. The service would be in the Family Chapel located on the farm with the burial being private in the family Mausoleum...on a small hill overlooking the farm's lower pasture. Grace said she would take Joshua there later ...if he wanted. The service, itself, would be invitation only, as it looked like there were simply too many people to fit in the small Chapel. And having the service in the Chapel was what Will had wanted. Never one to allow a problem to exist, Grace simply planned a reception for the entire community her family had embraced over two hundred years ago when her Great-Great-Grandfather built Butler Plantation. It had been one of the few that survived unscathed from The War Between the States. Flowers, Caterers, musicians, wait staff, valets; they were all checked off the list one by one. Will and Grace's Minister would give the Eulogy; Joshua would give the sermon. Finally pulling back from the library desk where they had diligently worked for hours, Grace looked over at Joshua. He is so tired – mentally and physically from all of this. And, he will have to do this, yet again, with Petra, her parents. Joshua had told Grace all about Petra and her family's illnesses; and had asked her not to tell Will... as there was no need for him to worry. He knew Will would... he always did with anything ...anything that involved his baby brother. Joshua raised his head to look out of the tall library windows to the front lawn where some wayward sheep grazed. My word, thought Grace...look at the deep circles under his eyes...he needs a break. Gently touching Joshua's arm, she looked deep into those troubled eyes...'Joshua.. why don't you take a break...why don't you call Anne and maybe the two of you could have lunch... here if you like...or...' before she could even finish her sentence, Joshua had stopped her... ' I called her this morning - we're going to meet at **The Bistro** around two.' ' Good...you need a break...' Grace smiled at him. She could not imagine having had to do all of this alone. She stood up and stretched her long lean body before leaving the library and its peace and jumbled papers to Joshua.

Sitting there with the late morning sunshine streaming in from the tall library windows, Joshua leaned back into the soft worn leather of his wing chair. It calmed his soul as he gazed at the farm's sheep grazing peacefully outside of his window - they were simply allowed to wander at will. God's lambs of choice, he thought...peacefully going about their day without a thought to tomorrow. Tomorrow..and what will tomorrow hold for me...for Grace...he thought. He was pleased with all he and Grace had been able to accomplish these last few days. While Will had planned

who he wanted to speak at his service in the Chapel, and that he wanted to be entombed into the family Mausoleum, that is all he would do. He told Joshua, with a wink, he would ' leave the rest to Grace.. as she'll change it anyway..' to which Grace would roll her eyes and simply smile.

So waking up early this morning, it is entirely too early to be making any phone calls, he thought. Must wait until *at least* breakfast time; with that plan in mind, he had called Anne and asked if her schedule would allow them to have lunch. Not a noon lunch she had said, but what about a late one, say around two. So she picked **The Bistro** – a new Italian Restaurant/Coffee/ Internet shop, apparently all the rage. The coffee and scones were to "die for" according to Reed's youngest sister, Lacey. So it was set...looking at his watch and realizing that it was nearly twelve now, he would have to get a move on. Thinking back to early thoughts of wishing he could be with Anne...**alone**...he fully understood that would not be a good idea. Too close to her, and he might not be able to walk back through the door to reality. And, for all his doubts, he knew Anne well enough to know that she would never..*no* , **never**..put either of them in a compromising position of choices. He stretched his frame to its full height, and ambled out into the foyer. Taking in all of the old Southern charm of this beautiful house, he took the side entrance and walked the short distance to the Carriage House. He liked the fact that he was staying in the quaint little cottage. It was private, but with full access to the main house if he needed anything. Ducking his head to enter the porch entrance, he thought of what the next few days – weeks – were going to be like. There would be little time for pleasure. The attorneys were coming in a week; and, he and Grace still had a lot of preparation before their arrival. I really shouldn't be going anywhere, I *need* to stay here...**no**, I really **need** to see Anne. So, with that rationale in his head, he grabbed his car keys and walked to the garage.

He and Anne pulled into **The Bistro** parking lot almost at the same time. To himself, he laughed at that - why does that make me laugh? Maybe I just **need** to laugh, he thought. Funny thing, she hadn't seen him yet. She was out of her car and walking toward the front entrance before he could even find a parking space. Finally maneuvering his car into a space, he grabbed his cap and headed off to the entrance. Pulling open the huge ornately carved door, he was once, again, taken back by the mere sight of her. With her back to him, she was evidently checking their reservations with the front attendant and did not even know he was there. He called her cell phone, and when she answered, she heard him say...'Turn around '..to which she whirled around to see him standing there almost in front of her; and then - for just a few precious seconds, time stood still. What needed to happen, did...it wasn't planned... it simply happened.. She walked into his outstretched arms, he touched her cheek, she reached for his hand. Then raised up on her tip-toes. Joshua lowered his head, coming on level with Anne. Barely grazing each other's lips...the kiss began as an innocent buss for memories long past. What began innocently enough as a soft remembrance of all those many years ago, ignited quickly to escalate to a passion tht surprised both of them. The kiss they shared spanned one of nearly forty years of yearning to which neither would have readily admitted just months ago. With the skilled ease of knowing each other, the kiss deepened into their very souls interrupting all rational thoughts of current obligations - soft, yet urgent - tasting of each other as if refilling an empty tank. Tender bites of the lower lip; suddenly feelings were raw and exposed. Exploration of ground so well mapped in their mind, was now rewinding to so long ago. Breathing became difficult, standing nearly impossible - and yet, there was no indication either would let go of the moment for fear it was just an illusion - a wanted to have, but can't have dream. A fluttering of eyelashes, then a moment when eyes opened, if ever so slowly, throwing them both back to reality. And, yet, no embarrassment from either of the moment they had just shared. It would have been useless, anyway, because they both understood without a single word, the past was in charge now; destinies, maybe *even* life as they both knew it, would - nor, could ever be the same again. And, they **had**

**truly** been in their own private world, for no one in the front café of **The Bistro** was even vaguely aware of what had just occurred in the Foyer, as they as they mindlessly continued to sip their lattes and check the Internet.

# Chapter Fifty Nine

And so, it was on that warm day in the middle of spring, Joshua and Anne relived the Past, talked about the Present, and, wondered about the Future. Anne's sister-in-law, Lanthe, had told her to ask for one of the red leather booths in an alcove away from the hustle and noise of the late lunch crowd. **The Bistro** was everything 'Lan' had told her it was..and so much more. The entire establishment had an Italian Renaissance charm to it. Entering the enormous front doors, your attention was first drawn to a three tier water fountain working its way down the interior massive stone walls covered with wisteria. To the right, the maze then opened to the latticed iron work banisters that would take you to one of the three dining levels. The cavern-like openness of the room allowed sunshine to pour in through ingenious cut-outs in the third floor ceiling. There were massive - and, that didn't even adequately describe the size of the wooden chandeliers hanging from the rafters. They appeared to have huge pillar candles with melted wax falling down their sides..but you knew they were electric ...clever, thought Anne. Grapevines were scattered throughout the decor, giving you the feeling you might have to pick a cluster of grapes for your wine, that is if, you wanted to. Anne chuckled at that thought. If you wanted just to enjoy your coffee and the Internet cafe , you went to the left of the front offset; you would be seated at high pub tables, with wine bottle candles and plenty of well-lit available areas to work, play or entertain yourself with the laptops set up for use. ***But***, if you wanted the full dining experience, you would be ushered past the hustle of the Internet section to the main dining areas. There were wrought iron tables and comfy chairs; or if you preferred, the small red leather booths Lan had suggested, which were set off from the main dining area for more intimate dining. Off to one side of the towering room, was an aged wall of oak wood behind tempered glass doors that must have housed hundreds of bottles of wine – and, once you were seated, your server would tell you - ' the wine is chilled to the perfect temperature for your enjoyment .' Upon being seated , you were handed a *three* page list of all the wines that were available for your **'enjoyment'** as well as the food menu about the size of a bed pillow; huge silver carafes gleamed on the polished tiled counters with an old world etching encased in an ornate frame on a mini easel, no less. These were placed under each of the carafes depicting what the particular brew of coffee each held; but the true *piece d'resistance*' was a massive wooden two- tier pie safe like structure that took up the entire wall and held all of the day's offerings of scones, muffins, huge iced cupcakes, cookies , fresh fruit pies - the list was endless. Pick your own or wait for your server and order from their menu of panini sandwiches, cannolies - sweet or with Italian sauces. The menu was a nightmare aimed at **Weight Watchers**. Taking in the uniqueness of this wonderful venue, Anne and Joshua were amazed at what they had walked in to. The parking lot and outside tan limestone rock simplicity certainly did not prepare you for what was on the inside. With the afternoon sunshine pouring in, the old world windows with their alternate stained glass and iron etchings gave off a pattern of grape leaves on the tiled tables in the center of the room. Having been escorted by their server, they slipped into the booth; Joshua leaned in to Anne – ' I kind of wanted to be closer to you...do you think anyone would notice if we **both** sat on one side of the booth??' Looking around at all of the other couples seated enjoying their own personal feasts, Anne replied, ' I have a feeling no one, except our server, even knows we are here!' as her face flushed a very becoming pink. And with that, Joshua exited his side of the booth to join her. Taking in all of the ambience of the room, Joshua leaned into Anne and with a huge smile on his face whispered ... ' Remind me to always let you pick where we go to eat..first, **Eve's Garden** and, now this. I did not know places like this even existed - much less this close to home... *Amazing.* ' Their server greeted them, took their order and exited returning in just a few minutes with their iced lattes along with warm butter melt scones. With a smile at seeing the seating arrangement had changed, she smiled and informed Anne and Joshua that '... their Cheese-Mushroom Cannolies would be forthcoming. ' They looked at their food; it was Joshua that laughed first...' ...do you think we will **actually** eat the food this time..I mean our track record for **actually** eating is pretty poor...' Anne had to agree in that food always took a back seat anytime they were together – there was so much to say..to catch up on..to try and make sense of. It felt good for both them to simply be together...but, baring their souls...getting all of the hurt out ...answering long over due questions, that was what they both had needed for much too long. Anne was the first to begin the walk back down Memory Lane. She took a deep breath, leaning into Joshua for support, and, then, began her confessional. Hesitant at first, she would pause to catch her courage up with where she was in the past; each time she did, Joshua simply held her hand a little tighter. Finally, after what seemed an eternity for Anne, she had bared her soul... there it was - all of it. Joshua was, at first furious, not at Anne, but that he had not known the full hell she had gone through after he left. He was furious at himself for not realizing it before now, he said. Then the question he knew he had to ask her...'Anne..why didn't you accept my marriage offer...we could have tried ...no, we would have tried to do everything to make it work..' his voice almost pleading with her to explain. There it was..taking a deep breathe, Anne began the rest of the explanation she had waited forty years for. 'Joshua...By the time I came back from Tennessee, all Hell had broken loose...it was plain to see that Trae was certifiably insane..he threatened me, you - Mother and Daddy... even his unborn child. Then, out of the blue, you came back that weekend. Trae had found out I had gone to Tennessee; he called the house when he knew Mother and Daddy were out. He was and had been 'watching' the house noting all of our comings and goings, and, he was livid. Ranting that you would **not** have what belonged to him...you would not have **his** child..you would not have me..oh, yeah, you **could** have me, and, in the next breathe, you couldn't have me because he would kill me first...and, it went on until I hung up the phone. You came in the sun porch door almost at the moment I hung up the phone; do you, by chance, remember, you asked why I was upset. I think I told you that Bryan had called wanting to know how I was... and, talking to him had just made me sad...you know the hormone thing. I think you accepted not giving it too much thought. After just talking with Trae, **no**, after being yelled at by Trae, I knew that you were going to be collateral damage in all of this craziness. I thought if I could make you believe there was no future for us, you would - you would leave and at least, I could, somehow, make sure you were safe. I had it all planned, right down to telling you I simply didn't love you anymore - at least, not enough to plan any kind of future with you. Then, you blew me out of the water when you asked me to marry you. I didn't see that one coming....we had never discussed marriage...at least, not seriously...so, all of what you saw after your proposal, was an act. I thought you wouldn't accept what I had said, and argue with me..deny what I had said as being truthful. But then, you... you kissed my hand ...and simply turned and walked away... that hurt more than telling you I didn't love you anymore. That is what broke my heart...you simply walked away...I was crushed. I knew I had done the right thing, but that didn't make the hurt any less painful.' Joshua sat there numb from what she had just said. Then, finding his voice, he told her ' ...You said '**No**' and, that is all I heard - my head took over, because my heart stopped beating. There is no way I can tell you how bad that hurt; I left wondering why you were lying to me..wondering if I would ever see you again..ever hold you again...it was like I was bleeding and I couldn't stop it. All the way back to Tennessee..and, for days, weeks afterwards.. the pain... the horrible gut wrenching pain held on..I can't even tell you today - forty years later - how bad it was.' Regaining his composure, he added...' All the pieces were there, I just didn't connect the dots. Why didn't you tell me...

we would have figured out something to stop him. Let me get this straight in my head...there was **no** restraining order, **what** where you thinking...' he asked Anne...'...and, it didn't stop for three years.....***THREE freaking years???***' he said with a stunned look on his face. Continuing his questions....'...did you even tell Reed. Pray, why not...you mean you kept all of this to yourself. ***You told no one***?' he heard himself ask incredulously. The moment the words came out of his mouth, he wished he could take them back. Anne's face blanched snow-white. Taking a ragged breath, Anne, in a voice so fragile he had to lean in to hear her.. ' I told Daddy...when I visited his grave..' Joshua saw her shoulders fall, but, then she straightened and with tears threatening to fall, she went on.. 'After the adoption went through, Daddy seemed to give up...in the matter of about two months, he was gone. I thought of calling you after he passed...just to let you know... but, Mother said your Mother had said she would let you know. She evidently called shortly after Dad's passing; and, said that she would not be able to attend the services as she had plans to go out of town for a short while. I thought after you didn't come or call; well, things were left so badly between us. I did my best to understand but, it really hurt you stayed away..' Joshua pulled back from the table. Not letting go of her hand; he then shook his head in disbelief. Anne could see the controlled anger on his face; and, the fact that he was nearly cutting the blood flow off to her hand was another good indication that something ...***something*** was terribly wrong. ' I can't believe she did that - she really was a piece of work...if I had only known..' Joshua said. Looking at the puzzled look on Anne's face, Joshua finally started to speak...'Anne...my Anne...the last weekend we were together, I sensed that you were pulling away from me and I wasn't sure as to why...it wasn't that I believed you when you said you didn't love me anymore..it was just that you didn't seem to need me...you were determined to do all of this on your own. And while I truly admired and respected that, I wanted to be there...your rock...your...anything. Just there. I sensed your Dad was not well...but, I did not know about the cancer. That whole summer had been hard on everyone. I thought a lot of what I saw was that with him. I never knew he was that ill. The weekend of your Dad's service, I was home; I had come home to go with Mother to Will and Grace's as he had just been diagnosed with MS. We went to spend the weekend at the farm. I didn't know your Dad had died. I was home...what, maybe ten miles away. I was there..and Mother knew ...she knew. I have to ask, something... did she know who you married...where you where...please tell me...I have to know..' Anne was quiet for a moment...then, answering cautiously ...' She had to know, Joshua...she sent a gift to my bridal shower; and, was invited to, but did not come, later, to my wedding to Reed. She had to know. '*Damn..**damn**...she knew...and, I had asked her point blank if she knew where you were...where your parents had moved to..what your married name was...she knew... **Damn it to Hell**... she knew.' Joshua, the man, **not** the minister heard himself say out loud...loud enough to garner the attention of a couple seated a table away. Watching Joshua, Anne felt like she had just sucker punched him in the stomach. 'I did not know... you... did not know' she stammered...' ...I think that was one reason, now that I think back..I was so surprised when you said you had such a hard time 'finding' me; other than you not knowing my married name. I just thought your Mother would have told you...' Their conversation was interrupted by their server bringing their lunch. For the next few minutes, they were quiet. Joshua held tight to Anne's hand... ' I am inclined to believe that somewhere an unknown force was working against us. No one would believe this. Even I don't believe this; and, my word, I was a part of it...' ' But...there is more..' Anne hesitated...' the rest of the story...the part that, even now, I have problems dealing with...even more so...more so, than that summer.' Then, Anne gave him the epilogue, if you will, with the latest in the never ending saga that was her life. She told him about agreeing to meet her son years later. She felt she just couldn't continue or even encourage that relationship as he was not only a clone of Trae, but, that was no assurance that Trae would not re-surface. She told him she felt serious remorse for that; even with confessions and prayers, she would probably be eternally damned for that decision.

To which Joshua took the hand he had been holding, caressed it slightly, then pressed it to his lips. ' I fear **not** for your soul, Anne; I fear the salvation of those who have so deeply hurt... you...myself, included..'

Then, it was Joshua's turn at confessional. Anne listened intently while he poured his heart out over losing Will. How he so wished he had postponed the shoulder surgery and come home. He would have at least been able to say 'Goodbye' ; he wondered what the future would hold for Grace. He talked on about how self-sufficient Grace was..and, how well run the farm was. She would be financially solvent, and would never have to worry for money, but it would be hard as she and Will had been together for so long. He paused...Anne took the opportunity to ask the question she truly wanted an answer to.. how was it you came to join the ministry? Did I have anything to do with that? And, why the Episcopal faith and not our Catholic one. He could have become a Priest, probably being much higher up in the Church hierarchy by now. He told her about how it all had played out ..of his failed attempt at suicide and finding the Lord instead. Anne nearly choked on her tea when he said the word 'suicide' – her mouth agape, Anne heard herself repeating...**'*suicide*'** - 'Joshua, how could that be - you, no I do not believe you could have fallen that low to even think ..oh, Joshua..' Anne said, her voice breaking with emotion. He told her about how badly she had hurt him with their last telephone conversation. In fact so much so, while it did not excuse his own behavior, it was the catalyst for his first marriage. A failed one that started with an unplanned, at least for him, pregnancy. He told her the marriage was doomed from the start. **Tell him, tell him**...Anne heard her inner voice screaming. 'Joshua.. that last conversation we had. I thought you had already moved on and you just needed closure - to get me out of your head...Mrs. Glochneous had told me that you had moved on with another girl - you were going to marry her.. I thought you were lost to me..forever..so I **HAD** to make you think there was nothing to come home for..' Anne said. Joshua's face paled before her eyes. Closing his eyes, he said ..'I hadn't moved on, I needed you...I called ...I wanted us back...I wanted to have a life with you...I hadn't moved on, because I just could not give up on the possibility of an 'us'. Mrs. G didn't have a clue as to what was going on..unless Mother was behind it...' and, he continued, ' Yes, I did marry Gayle several months after that last conversation; but, not because I was over you... but mainly, as you know, she was pregnant with Carey..and, I thought about everything that had happened with you and Trae...and, I knew that if I didn't take responsibility for my actions, albeit stupid , as they were, then, I was not any better than that scum bag who treated you so badly. And, in talking with you that day, I truly....I thought you were over me. By the time I finally admitted the marriage was doomed, you were already married. I was going to stick it out – I loved Carey so much...I couldn't let go and walk away. I didn't know who you married, and at that time, didn't want to know... because you were lost to me - for good, I thought.' And, then he finally told her about Petra. It pained him so much to talk about what lay ahead for her - for them. She could feel his pain...see the hurt in his eyes... no one should have to deal with so much all at once, she thought. But, if anyone can, it will be Joshua...he had a strength about him that was like steel.' My dear dear Joshua.' Anne started.. 'I will be there for whatever you may need whenever you need it. Just ask. Regardless of when, where...or worse, what it may look like to those that may not understand. I will be there...*promise made*...**promise to be kept**.' Now, that all the secrets of each of their Pandora's Boxes had been emptied, they both found a new inner peace. They talked for hours; going into detail of each of their lives. The 'other' parts that had dropped between the cracks with what was their own ' Peyton Place' . After everything that had transpired over that one long summer so many years ago, the rest of their lives seem to pale in comparison. By the time they finished, the sun was slowly dipping in the Western sky. They had to stop and laugh, and apologize to their server - the wait staff was preparing for the dinner crowd when they finally rose to leave. Straightening up, Joshua explained to their server as he was handing her the bill folder...' Want to thank you so for your kind tolerance of us, old folks...we had a lot of catching up to do .. Forty years, in fact. And, that pretty lady there...well, long ago, we were engaged once..and I let her get away..' winking at the server who gave a broad '**been there, done that**' grin back at him.

Catching Anne's arm, he extended her wrap around her shoulders, bent down and gave her a light peck on her cheek. ' Will's service is Thursday a week at 1 p.m at the farm; why don't you and Reed come and plan to spend at least the night, and maybe even stay a few days. There's plenty of room and it would please Grace immensely if you would accept her offer...' Anne was touched by the open gracious generosity Grace had extended. Then telling Joshua... ' I spoke with Reed, no..he's not coming...he didn't know Will...he said he would go if I wanted him to...but, he won't be coming with me. I'll come down next Thursday morning to help Grace with any last minute things. So, I'll see you both around 10, if that's alright. I'm sure we'll talk before then...' With that Anne reached for Joshua's hand, and, together they walked out to the parking lot. Joshua hugged Anne, bussed the top of her head... just like he used to do, thought Anne. Then, they separated with him striding to his car and she to hers. They had finally caught up with their pasts. All the hurts, questions and what-ifs had been answered. While everything else had been discussed, they never mentioned the kiss they had shared - there really wasn't any reason to.

The days quickly passed until the Thursday morning of the service. Anne had packed an overnight bag the evening before, filled her gas tank, and left all kinds of instructions for Reed. He had left earlier going to a registered Charolais stock Auction in Camden. He had told her to drive carefully, to call him when she arrived.. normal stuff..and then, Reed hugged her tight to his chest and with his mouth close to her ear, said...'Anne, I know you've been struggling these last few months. All the old memories have been dredged up with Joshua coming back into your life. I don't know how to help you.... but, I am here to try in any way I can.. I really hope everything goes alright. Stay at the farm as long as you need to. Forty years is a long time to try and catch up on. I'll be here when you get back..' And with that being said, Reed kissed her, touched his hand to her cheek and held her just a little bit longer.

Anne threw her two small bags in the back seat of her car, slammed the door. She sat there for a few minutes just thinking. My word, I have done too much thinking these last few months. So many what if's - could have beens – maybes..hindsight is said to be 20/20, but I don't know that we could have - or even should have - done anything different. It all played out the way it was meant to, I suppose. **Karma** - the way things are supposed to be. Joshua is happy with his life - his wife; and I have Reed, and, I do so love him. The babies are here, safe, sound and growing... our lives are the way they were supposed to be...at least, now they are. Was Thomas Wolfe right in saying.. 'You can't go home again..' I wonder. But, I'm not trying to go home again. I've been here all along...and Joshua...he is home, too. It's just that 'his' home and 'my' home are worlds apart. Yet, why is it I feel he has never really left my world..and, for him, I never left his. I wonder if there is any solution to this. Joshua and I started out as friends. Now, some forty years later, we must figure out how to go back to being friends - **just friends**. Will there ever be an 'us'..who knows..so many things would have to change for that to happen. What am I to do...I still love him so much; and, there is no doubt that he still loves me. Shaking her head to clear her thoughts, she pulled out of the garage, picking up her phone to call Joshua. No, it can wait. I am sure he and Grace have their hands full this morning. Besides, I'll be at the farm in little over an hour.

In actuality, things at the farm were running like clockwork. Grace was efficient and had seen to every minor detail. How does she do it, Joshua asked himself. She just lost her husband and she has in the matter of a few days, organized this right down to who sat where in the Chapel. The wait staff was busily occupying themselves with last minute duties. The flowers had just been delivered and were being distributed between the Chapel and the main house; the caterers had taken over the kitchen, and in doing so, ruffled the feathers of Mrs. Campbell, "Mrs. C." , the Housekeeper; the lower side yard had been roped off for vehicles; even the horses were acknowledging the goings-on as they eased their graceful heads over the board fences in the hope that someone – surely someone in **all** of these people - had a carrot and a nose rub on their agenda. Joshua laughed at the sight of one of the new foals trying to figure out how to get his head back through the fence he had just stuck it through. Little boy, you're going to find out we all need help sometime. With that thought stuck in his head, Joshua raised his eyes to the deep blue skies and, quietly thanked his Lord for getting him this far. Now, just guide me with Your loving hand for a little while longer, he pleaded.

Grace had taken a momentary break, and walking out onto the big shaded front Portico saw Joshua standing there. Looking at the direction his head was turned, she saw the little foal with its head between the fence supports. Walking over to where Joshua stood, she looped her arm into his, and laughing lightly said..'It is truly amazing how much trouble those little guys can get themselves into.' Both of them took a big sigh of relief when the little guy finally escaped from his self imposed prison and went off like a kite in the wind looking for his Mother. Taking in the calm of the moment, Joshua leaned into Grace, patted her hand with a gesture of 'we'll get through this..with grace and dignity, like always..' Grace appeared to understand the gesture, and looking at Joshua, said...' Won't be long now... a few more hours...I miss him so much already, Joshua...he was so full of life; he didn't deserve this...I know he is looking down at us and wondering why all the fuss... and, he's probably chuckling at all of the commotion..' Grace 's attention was caught by one of the caterers who needed to speak with her; so off she went to downplay the latest 'what's wrong in the kitchen, now' problem, leaving Joshua to his thoughts. I bet Will's thinking ahead to a lot of things, Grace....Joshua thought. I know I am thinking ahead; Joshua looked towards the long paved driveway; Anne's on her way ...she'll be here in about an hour. She's coming - oh, how I wish we could turn back the clock so that she was coming back to me....***back to us.*** What lies ahead for us..he wondered. Closing his eyes and offering up his obedience to follow His Lord...' Whatever **Your** Will is Lord, I will abide.' Pointing his finger upward and looking up at the sky, he had to chuckle... ' ..Let me re-phrase that Lord...what ever <u>**Your**</u> Will is, I will abide by it... ***Big Brother Will*** -- stay out of it...'

# Chapter Sixty

Driving down the country lane to the farm, Anne was struck by the beauty all around her...this was horse country ...and, it was breathtaking. She almost couldn't take her eyes off of the beautiful horses she saw grazing on each side of the road. Board fences, bright green pasture...Norman Rockwell should have seen this, she thought...no, Thomas Kincaid would do it justice. Seeing the crossroads up ahead, she bared off to the right, like Joshua told her...yes, there it is ... the sign announcing Butler Plantation, Est. 1800. Turning into the driveway... she made a quick prayer request.. ' Lord, Precious Lord, please see me through this with grace and dignity..Amen' She called home to let Reed know she had arrived. The answering machine...oh well, I'll try later. And with that, she pulled her car up to the front entrance to see Joshua and Grace standing on the Portico waiting to greet her.

Joshua walked down the steps and opening the car door for her, greeted her with a reserved smile. ' I'm so glad you're here..did you have any trouble with the directions..you made really good time...I'm ...glad you are finally here...please, come say hello to Grace...' Laughing softly...' I'm glad I'm here, too, Joshua...' And with that, they walked up the brick pave way to the Portico. Grace is so pretty... the years have been very kind to her, thought Anne. As she took the older woman's offered hand, then hug. ' We're so pleased to have you come to the farm...please come in...we'll go to the front parlor and have some tea and cakes.. I'll have your bags put in the front guest room - and, your car in the garage.' Then, the three of them, entered the beautiful foyer on their way to the parlor. In the parlor a delicate tea service and freshly baked scones awaited their arrival..as did two of Grace's Bichons snuggled in on the chenille sofas - One Ivory in color, the other a more of an Amber shade..' Grace, meet Chablis and Whiskey' said Joshua. Odd names, Anne thought .. and, it must have been the puzzled look on her face that brought Grace's laughter and a further explanation – ' They were named after our favorite libations..try as I did, I could never get Will to like wine, as he favored his liquor to be hard. So, it was a joke between us that wine and whiskey would one day meet head to head - as Chablis is the bitch and Whiskey is, well in Southern terms, let's say her "lover"...and yes, they did. Somewhere within these walls, there is a mottled, but lovable mutt running around.'. And , as if on cue, the tiny little bundle of soft fur appeared at the door, to which Grace said...'Anne, meet Jack Daniels, aka Jack...' Laughing hysterically, Anne fell to the floor to be lavished with loads of puppy love. Regaining her composure, Anne stood up, straightened her sweater, and joined Joshua on one of the comfy sofas by the fireplace. And so, there for nearly an hour, they chatted, laughed, and prepared themselves for all that was yet to come. With the announcement of Reverend Fields arrival, they all knew it was time to fulfill Will's last wishes and see him home.

Climbing the stairs to her bedroom, Anne was truly touched by Grace's dignity and grace under pressure. She is everything she remembered about her; and yet, after seeing this Grace, the Lady of the Manor, she couldn't imagine her out in the paddocks, or in the hayfields. Yet, Joshua assured her that was Grace, too. She is amazing to be able to do all of this. Noticing the wheelchair ramp at the end of the hall leading to the Master Suite. Yeah, she is truly amazing.

When they all convened again it was to take the walk to the Chapel. Most of the invited guests had already been seated, so the three of them entered the side room quietly and waited for Reverend Fields to come get them. And when he did, it was Grace that took Anne's hand and, looking into her eyes...' Please ..stay

with me...I have no one else...' to which Anne, squeezed her hand, and nodded.

Reverend Fields and Joshua entered, followed closely by Grace and Anne. The congregation stood in respect as Grace and Anne took their seats; and then Reverend Fields took the pulpit. 'Ashes to ashes...dust to dust...' and with that, Will's service began. Reverend Fields spoke of the generosity of both Will and Grace with regards to their community. How they both had been involved in Special Olympics. How their farm was always available for the summer and the Open Air Program to see inner city kids have a chance to learn by being on a working farm. He ended with Will's last comment to him. And, he laughed as he said Will had asked him to ' Put in a good word for me, Rev...Oh, and ask them to make sure I have a ramp to roll through the Pearly Gates..' to which the assembled guests, laughed. And then, it was Joshua's turn. Anne squeezed Grace's hand. Let him get through this...Anne prayed. And, he did.. He was strong, he was truly a Minister, thought Anne; and then, Joshua became a brother . He told of some of their exploits as kids...of how Will sometimes thought of him more as a son, than as a brother after their father had passed...how they had bonded over alcoholic parents..and how, in later life, they both came to be saved...And serve the Lord. It was poignant ..it was funny...watching intently, Anne noticed the sudden influx of tears in his eyes, but holding it together, Joshua's final words were simple...' Will was my hero...my brother and I loved him...now, he is with God...he can walk again, he can talk without pain...he is **Home**.' And with that, the congregation whispered '***Amen***' and, sent William Carson Breckenridge to his final reward.

# Chapter Sixty One

The reception was held in the front rooms, and with the huge French doors open to the patio and grounds, there was room for all. Grace moved easily between guests, thanking each one personally for their kind words and their presence. Will would have loved all of the commotion – not in his honor – but, just to have so many of their friends, business associates and community there, thought Anne. Joshua, equally at ease, drifted among the crowd, laughing and reminiscing over the old times. The sun was dipping behind the mountains as they saw the last guest pull out of the driveway. Grace literally fell on one of the sofas in the parlor, kicking off her shoes and sighing deeply. Joshua was not far behind...and Chablis and Whiskey, being released from their afternoon exile, joined in. Anne stepped to the door, and looking at the two exhausted bodies, she wondered if she should leave them to their thoughts; starting to turn to go upstairs, Grace saw her and beckoned her to join them. With her heels in her hand, Anne padded across the soft carpet to an ottoman by the fireplace. ' This day was good.. Will would have been proud...' said Grace, pleased with both the turnout, but also the honesty with which people had responded to her loss. For the next few minutes, they all sat quietly reflecting on the day... knowing that tomorrow, they would add Will's urn to those of three generations of Butler family members. But that was tomorrow. They had made it through today; and for the moment, that was enough.

# Chapter Sixty Two

Rising slowly, Grace excused herself – ' I'll have Mrs. C fix a light supper for us – maybe in the sunroom...' and, with that, she and her entourage of fur left for the peace and quiet of upstairs. Joshua was leaned back into the softness of the sofa, and, had his eyes closed... maybe he's asleep, he so needs it, Anne thought. Quietly standing up, she nearly got past the sofa, before Joshua's head popped up...' Don't go..please...not yet..come sit for a few minutes more...' With that Anne went over and gently sat down, taking his head in her lap as she eased down to the sofa. They didn't talk ...they just quietly sat there together ...until Mrs. C came in ...' Miss Grace, shes not be comin' back down fer dinner, but shes wants yualls ta no ... I's laid outs a lite suppa in de sunroom...' The elderly lady quickly left the room, leaving Joshua and Anne alone once more. Finally moving, they meandered to the sunroom; sitting down at the wrought iron table, they looked at the caesar salad, the fresh bread, the thinly sliced meats, the vegetables...and almost simultaneously laughed out loud...' My word....they call this a 'light' meal...you could feed an army on this!' Joshua exclaimed. And then the both of them laughed, really laughed. And it felt good. Anne and Joshua picked at their plates, more interested in remembering the day...the people...it was, as Grace had said...**good**. Finally giving up on eating anything, they picked up their glasses of iced tea and wandered out on to the patio. A soft wind was blowing from the South. ' No stars yet.'... Joshua was saying to Anne..' the moon is in what, the last quarter? ' Taking in the softness of the remnants of the daylight, the ringing of Joshua's cell phone brought them back to reality. Looking at the caller ID, Joshua glanced over at Anne and mouthed... ' It's Petra...' That was Anne's cue to say good-night.

Anne quietly climbed the central stairs, entered the her room, and closing the door, backed to it, thinking ...of course, Petra needs to know everything that happened here today. I do hope she is alright...that her family is okay. Undressing, she pulled on her robe. A hot shower will wash away a lot of today, she thought; but, at that particular moment, all she could think about was Joshua talking to Petra. Joshua talking to **his** wife. She jerked when her cell phone rang...'.Hello, Reed...Yes, dear...the service was very nice...reception tiring.. you know how they can be.. I just want to take a hot shower and veg for the rest of the night...everything alright there? Grace asked that I stay for a few days..if that is okay...Will probably be home Sunday afternoon...talk tomorrow?... love you, too...bye." It was good to hear Reed's voice..**my** Reed, she thought. Now for that shower..

And the shower did feel so good...she let the water wash over her tired body...been a long day, Lord. Turning the water off, she reached for a towel. Padding out of the bathroom into her room, she finally took in the true beauty of the room. The canopied four poster bed, antique for sure....the chintz covered chairs...the delicate dressing table ... my word, the wallpaper alone probably has a history dating back to the days of mint juleps and hooped skirts...the white fireplace with its porcelain tiles...this was something out of ' Traditional Southern Homes ' - wonder what stories this room could tell if it could talk, she mused. And a visual of Mammy and Scarlett O'Hara came to mind...'*Gone With The Wind*' ..that's what this room reminds me of.....the scene where Mammy is lacing Miss Scarlett up in that gown and fussing at her for not eating. The thought was a pleasant one. After all, truth be known, this Plantation probably was doing the same kind of things in **real**, not *reel* time, way back then. Wrapping the towel around her, she walked over to the tall lace- covered window; in the dimness of early evening, she could still make out a little of the side yard leading down to the Paddocks; and there is the Carriage

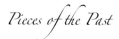

House, she thought. I can see the Carriage House from here.. the lights are on. I hope, I so hope, Joshua can rest tonight, she thought. Looking through the glass, she could just make out the slight form of someone sitting on the front porch of the Carriage House. Joshua, she thought to herself...Rest.

But at the Carriage House, Joshua was not 'resting. He had talked with Petra and all was well there..at least for the moment, he thought. Looking out on the neatly manicured grounds in front of him, he paused to thank the Lord for seeing him through today... it was important ...and, I made it through with Your help and guidance. Looking over to the main house, his eyes locked on what he knew was Anne's room...only to see Anne looking back at him.

# Chapter Sixty Three

Neither Anne nor Joshua found sleep easy that night. Joshua re-ran everything about the day in his head...the service, the reception, the time in the parlor with Anne and Grace. The quiet time with just the two of them. Anne was worried about how Grace didn't come down for dinner with them. How Petra was...and Joshua...how was he doing. And, it wasn't until the first glimmer of daylight appeared that either found any rest.

At breakfast the next morning, Grace sent her regrets, but, she had a headache and if better, she would see them for lunch. That freed up Joshua to be with Anne for the day...wonder if Grace planned that, he thought. So, when Anne came down for breakfast, it was just the two of them. They planned their day. Anne wanted to see the horses...the sheep...the farm. Maybe they could go for a ride, later. Since Joshua was not the biggest fan of horseback riding, he convinced her that a picnic down by one of the lakes would be something they **both** would enjoy. So, when leaving the breakfast room, Joshua stuck his nose into the kitchen to ask Mrs. C if she would fix them a picnic basket only to find the elderly woman way ahead of him..' .I's .heard yews and Missy Anne talkin' bouts a picnic - it's be readee when yews are..and, I's already done lets Taylor nos yew's be comin' down so as he cans have one of dem motor thingys all readee fer yews.'..not wanting to laugh at Mrs. C - he wondered to himself.. what is 'one of dem motor thingys..?

The 4 wheel Mule, aka Mrs. C's 'motor thingys', was out of the storage shed, and with their provisions of a blanket, picnic basket, a cooler and instructions from Taylor, the farm manager, they headed off to take a tour of the farm. It was huge...what 200 plus acres...most of it in pasture. Their driving through the fields didn't seem to even draw notice from the grazing stock; the sheep looked up only momentarily to observe their movement across their dinner table...then went back to their meal. The horses were in separated fields, but when they saw the vehicle, they ran down to the fences to run along side at least until they tired of the game and went back to grazing lazily on another area of their pasture. They stopped by the Mausoleum - with Grace's headache taking center stage at the moment, they would put off the internment of Will's ashes for later - maybe tomorrow. The granite building was immense. It held so much history, the reverence of the memorial striking respect in both Anne and Joshua. Looking inside the last section, they saw the latest additions, being Grace's parents and a baby that had died at birth before Grace. Then, they both caught their breath, as they read the inscription on the open drawer...

**William Carson Breckenridge**
**Born September 3, 1942 -**
**To Eternal Rest on April 29, 2012.**
**Joining his family on this the 19th day of May, 2012**

Joshua reached out and gently rubbed his fingers across the etching on the brass plate of the drawer, as if touching his brother... just ... one more time. Anne, standing behind Joshua, watched as his shoulders bent - putting her arms around his waist, she held his trembling body. No words, no tears. After a few minutes, Joshua spoke out loud...' I see death nearly everyday; I preach of God's House welcoming all that believe home; I believe, I truly believe all of His Word...I am a messenger for God's Word. And yet, here I am, wanting to undo His Will...to have my Will back...' 'Grieve, Joshua, just grieve...God understands your frustration and the depth of your loss ...He knows you are His speaker...this is for the best...Will is home...' Anne softly spoke to his back.

Getting back into the mule, Joshua looked at Anne .. 'I'm sorry for that meltdown back there...' Anne didn't say anything, just touched his sleeve in understanding. They drove on in silence until cresting the hill in front of them, they came upon the smallest of the Farm's lakes. They paused at the top of the hill, taking in the view. Joshua's mind quickly reverted to the last hill he paused at – the Mississippi River Junction. That was certainly a turning point in my life for me; looking over at Anne, he paused thinking, wonder if this is a turning point for **US**.

On the other side of the mule, Anne was taking in all of the beauty, the tranquility of this magical place she had been invited to share. What was it about being with Joshua, she wondered. He is like an extension of me. We complete one another..we always have. I do not understand, my Lord, why You have brought us back together. Why You have brought us to this crossroads at this late junction in our lives. I know You know there is so much still between us; and I know, You know that there are just too many roadblocks between us and the hope of ever being together. I know You have a plan..I know You always do. But, begging Your pardon, dear Lord... could You just **once in my life**, just **once**...let me in on the game plan? Crossing herself, she could only hope God was listening...and had a sense of humor.

# Chapter Sixty Four

Joshua pulled the mule up under a tree and turned off the ignition. Sitting there in the peace and tranquility of the farm, he and Anne were equally amazed at what beauty there was before them. The gently rolling hillside gave way to a lake in the fork of the two hills; by itself, the lake would have been beautiful, but framed by the low pastures, the rolling countryside mirrored on its surface...well, it was simply breathtaking. It was like that wonderful old movie...***Brigadoon***..about a magical village that comes to life every 100 years. Except, there was no village to gaze upon; just this pristine lake that seemed to have appeared out of nowhere. The sun glinting on its surface made the small ripples created by the wind appear like diamonds. They flashed their prism colors with each movement of the water. Lost in the moment, they both stood there, unable to move; it wasn't until they heard the far off nickle of one of the Arabians in the lower pasture that they were able to break the spell and come back in the moment. They quickly unloaded their supplies from the cargo hold of the mule, then finding a flat spot right above the lake's edge, stretched out the big blanket, setting the food off to one side. Anne sat down and pulled her knees up under her chin, still mesmerized by the beauty in front of her. Her mind wandered back to a day, much like today...years ago...a picnic at the State Park. They had spent the whole day, talking, enjoying being with one another; munching on cheese and crackers, drinking wine coolers. Peeking over at Joshua, Anne wondered if he would remember that. Joshua stretched his long frame out, almost over the edges of the blanket, with his arms behind his head. Looking up at the clear blue sky, he turned to Anne, leaning up on his elbow...' hey... do you remember that time we went to the State Park...and...' to which Anne collapsed in giggles, yes giggles. ' I was just thinking the same thing...' she laughed. That's how the rest of the day went...remembering...laughing... enjoying each other's company. When hunger finally took center stage to their conversations, they were eager to see what goodies Mrs. C. had packed them. Peeking inside only brought more laughs as they saw the cheese, crackers - even wine coolers, this time non-alcoholic ones ; how could she have possibly known? Their lunch spilled over to afternoon; the sun was so warm. Stretched out on the soft wool blanket, they nestled into each other's bodies.. shared a soft kiss...not daring to let it be more than just that. Lying there in the warmth of the afternoon sun - it was so comfortable - so natural . Before either of them knew it, they drifted off, Joshua's arm giving her head a soft place to land. Their bodies were close enough to feel each other's rhythmic breathing, yet, not too close.

Joshua awoke first. Getting his bearings, he lay there just savoring the time frozen moments still left to them. Afraid to move as he would wake her, he felt her breathing, soft and even. I don't want this day to end...just let us stay here forever, he thought. It was the sound of a wayward crow that woke her. He gingerly moved his numb arm, as she raised up on her elbows to see Joshua there - still close beside her. Raising up a bit more, Anne suddenly found herself in Joshua's arms. For a moment, only a fleeting moment, let this be, she begged her head. It was her heart that was listening... as Joshua's head tilted down and found her looking back at him. It began with a slight buss of a kiss, but this time, they both let go. All of the held back emotions let themselves come front and center. Both of their minds were racing, when finally, finally they both let go. Joshua, refusing to let her go, whispered in her ear..' Anne..it has been *so* long. I want to hold you forever..to love you forever. I need you to be with you...to make love to you. I don't ever...ever want to let you go.' Anne felt herself melt further into his arms... please don't let this moment end, she silently prayed. Anne's heart was racing and from the way Joshua was holding her, she knew he was fighting an inner battle, too. ' ***This Can Not Be*** ' ..screamed the voice in her head..while her heart was screaming equally as loud telling her head to: '**Take A Hike**'. And then, somewhere, in a voice, even she didn't recognize, someone was talking...' It's getting late; I suppose we should be going back, Joshua...' And, just where ***did that come from***? -- her heart screamed loudly. Her heart was fighting a bitter war with her head; and it looked as if, once again, rationale would win out. I am such a ***fool***; this can not be..but how do I let him go, yet again?? Remember ... ***Think back...remember***, she told herself... what Daddy told me years ago when I was a little girl: ' ***It is not the holding on that makes us strong, Anne. It is the letting go.***' Anne pulled back, trying to get her breathing back to normal..and looked up at Joshua. Their eyes met and they both knew..it was time to go. Slowly rising to his feet, Joshua extended his hand to help her up; as she came back into his arms, he took a deep breath. Big mistake - she is entirely too close. Then following his heart, and not his head, Joshua leaned down to Anne...a sweet tender kiss. Shaking his head, Joshua looked at Anne. Anne caught his look, dead on..' Me, *too, Joshua*...me, **too**.' So, without another word, they packed up and pointed the mule back to the farm, holding hands the entire way.

They arrived back at the main house just as Taylor and a couple of the grooms were bringing in the mares and new foals to the Paddock area. Anne saw Grace overseeing the migration, and could hardly wait for Joshua to stop the mule before she was running over to see if there was any chance of getting to actually pet one of the new foals. Looking at the two of them laughing and playing with the horses like teenagers, Joshua, thought.....they both appear so happy. Catching Grace's eye, Joshua yelled over and told her he was headed to the Carriage House to make some calls; he would meet them for dinner later. As Joshua was leaving, Anne was down on her hands and knees Oohing and Gooing over the tiny little foal who was nuzzling her hair under the watchful eye of his mother. With the protection of the gate between her and Joshua, Anne looked up at Grace. Grace nodded an understood unasked question ....Yes, he is gone. Anne took a deep breath; closing her eyes, she mouthed .. 'Thank you, Lord '. The little foul re-gained her attention to which Anne announced out loud... ' Now *this* has to be heaven '. And, from the look on Grace's proud face, it was obvious, she agreed.

Putting the mule away in the barn, Joshua walked the short distance to the Carriage House...make some calls, check on things at home. Then, yes, a hot, no make that a 'cold', shower to take the images of today - the taste of her lips, the fragrance of her. If his mind and memory served him right, that fragrance, it was something like lily or wildflower. It was summer, rain, morning dew, a hillside full of flowers..it was, simply put... Anne. He had never smelled that wonderful concoction since she was out of his life..and now, he was fighting to get her out of my mind. Taking off his shirt, he held it close to his face, I can still smell her.. he thought. It was like we were teenagers again...life was much simpler then, he thought. We were 'in like' he used to say; to which Anne would smile and remind him that there was a very fine line between ' like and love.' Grabbing his cell phone off of the kitchen table, he proceeded to return a couple of business calls, then called home only to get a message telling him Petra had gone to her parent's home that morning. He called the Nemonoweski residence. His mother-in-law, Anya answered the phone, in her heavy Czechoslovakian accent...'Tak...(Hello) Oh, Josuawa, isz gud so to here yer voice... hasz ben much long..'; they chatted on for a few minutes - she extended her family's condolences for the loss of his brother. ' Isz much bad to lose brudda, Nil (No)? ...zee Lord, God, our Protector..He haz yer Will in heeze house.. Nil?.' He was touched by her concern; he could almost visualize the deeply devout Anya standing there in the hallway of the big farmhouse, fingering her ever present rosary as they talked. He asked how Stavros and Roman were, finding out everyone was fine. He then asked to speak with Petra and was told she had left to go to the store; although he didn't get to talk with Petra, her mother assured Joshua that she, everyone, Petra included, was, indeed, fine...' We be fine, Josuawa...ya want Minsca (her pet name for Petra) to ring ya ?..' ' No, no..that won't be necessary. I was just checking in... tell her I called and I'll talk with her later. Hope you all have a good day and May God Bless you All.. Take care, Anya...' and, with that Joshua disconnected the call. Tucking his head, Joshua thanked the Lord for allowing Petra and her family to all be together during this final chapter, yet unwritten.

Satisfied that Petra was home with her family for the day, he smiled. Thinking out loud....' If I know Anya, there is a heavy duty Czech feast awaiting everyone, once Petra gets back from the store..dumplings, roast pork..yeah, she'll do it up right and everyone will be completely sated and happy...' Smiling broadly and content that everything at home was alright, he quickly shut off his phone, again. I really don't want to be accessible for a while...at least, until a shower and dinner is over. Shirt balled up in his hands, off he went to shower, then dress for dinner. Toweling off after his shower and then, slipping into khakis and a light shirt, his thoughts went to tomorrow. We're going back to the Mausoleum; I've been there...and I broke down; **tomorrow, I will be ok.** With that determined thought in his head, he let the screen door slam behind him and headed to the main house. Next stop...Dinner.

Going in through the kitchen door, Joshua could smell the wonderful aromas of the night's menu...whatever it is, it smells divine...and, I am starving. Walking through the pantry, he saw Grace standing in the main hallway talking on the phone. He quietly tiptoed around her and headed to the front parlor where Anne was sitting on the floor playing with Jack. ' What is it with you...did you miss your calling as a Vet ?' he teased. Looking up with bright eyes, Anne responded...' You know, back home, they don't call me Snow White, for no reason .' To which he smiled and gave her a thumbs-up sign. Grace came in just behind him, with Chablis and Whiskey mirroring her every step; and, Jack sliding in behind them, unceremoniously landing upside down at Anne's feet. They all laughed hysterically at the antics of this little ball of fur who quickly re-cooped his faux pas and was eying Chablis for his dinner. Grace asked how their day had gone and apologized for not being available earlier; but, now tomorrow didn't look too good either. No, she wasn't sick ; that had been the Estate attorney on the phone, and, it seems before she and Joshua could go any further with the Estate, she would have to go to his office and sign all of the papers to establish her as Will's Executrix, then back to the County Court House to qualify. Since the whole process would take several hours and, the attorney's office was nearly 50 miles away, she would plan to leave early in the morning, spend the night with some friends, and return Sunday sometime around lunch . ' I'm so sorry, Anne...to leave so unexpectedly, especially after asking you to stay a few extra days and, then, being unavailable today; but, I'll be back before you leave on Sunday...for sure.' Grace said with a slight smile; with that, they all walked to the dining room, with little Jack, Chablis and Whiskey leading the way.

And yet, again, sleep would allude both Anne and Joshua. Upon returning to her room, she glanced at the bedside clock. It was only nine-thirty; not to late to call Reed. Dialing his number..she waited for him to answer. It was good to hear his strong voice. Catching up on what had happened in just two days, they chatted until she could hear their canine alarm system, Mags, going off in the background. Best let Reed go as it would be useless in trying to carry on a conversation with Maggie going wild in the background. Reed said that Maggie had been barking at 'everything' since she had been gone. It's like she nervous or something...barking at every sound. It was probably nothing, he said. However, Anne begged off saying it was late and she was tired . ' Talk tomorrow ? Ok..till then... ' Reed paused...' You okay, honey? You really do sound tired..'. Anne cleared her throat.' Of course; I'm just tired from all the activity..we'll talk tomorrow... love you. Give Mags a pat on the head. Night.' Hanging up the phone, she changed her clothes, slipping into her silk nightshirt. She tried to read...No. Hit the tv on button...flipping through the channels, she finally gave up and turned off the lights; she lay there in the quiet, allowing her eyes to adjust to the darkness. The moon's rays were slowly becoming her night light, etching the pattern of the old lace curtains on the pale Aubusson rug. Rising and looking out the window, she gently pushed it open to inhale the sweetness of the night air. She didn't see any lights at the Carriage House, so assuming Joshua had already turned in, she knelt by the bed and said a quick prayer for him. 'Heavenly Father - Holy Mother...Help him through tomorrow...give him strength...let sleep be there for him to renew his soul .Your guidance will be his gift. In the name of the Holy Mother and our Savior...I say **Amen**' Crossing herself, she rose. Looking back out the window with the moonlight in her face, she suddenly recalled what she used to always tell Joshua whenever he was leaving.. going home...saying goodbye on the phone...' To the Moon and Back, My Love, I shall Always and Forever, love you...' So sleep, my sweet Joshua...sleep for the both of us, tonight. Thinking to herself...maybe *someone* will sleep tonight. I don't think it will be me.

As it was, Joshua had stayed a little longer in the main house. After Grace and Anne had said **'Good night'** and gone off to their respective rooms, he found himself sitting in the kitchen feeding dinner scraps to chubby old Henry, the kitchen cat. When Joshua asked Mrs. C. how Henry came to be the only cat allowed in the house, she just shook her head and laughed heartily as she told Joshua...' Its weren't up ta us-ems... Henree jest wanders in de bac door one days many yeers go, snoops rounds a bit, den he sits down o'er yonder ats de firplace and gits ta washin' his self – its as he news rights den, dis iz home, wheres hes waz goin's ta be and, ain't nobodys - nobodys goin's ta be mess'n wis ole Henree.. dem lil fur ball rats of Miss Grace's -- Shablee and Wiskee-- day's tryes times and times over ta gits him out... Henree, he ain't gonna have nothin' ta do wit dat; nots ta be done in. Why even wee lil Jackee gits ole Henree ups 'gainst de wall somstimes. Even dat pup gots a reel healthee respect fer ole Henree ... Henree gots him a bad rep for ' fightin and takin ' no prisoners'..now's dat's bein' bac yonders in hiz tom-cattin' days. Ones of de new grooms, he names him, Henree..he says itz jests fits him 'cause he acts likes dat King overs yonder in Inglend who done had all dem wives...' Its fits and stuck - Henree was a reel lover, bac yonda ... dats waz 'til Misser Will he sazs dat ten cats gonna bes enoug fer dis here farm, and gifts ole Henree a trip down yonda tos the vet..and ole Henree, he gits bac here a 'it' nots a 'he' no more.' Mrs. C shoulders, and in fact, her whole body, shook with laugher at relating the story. And, Joshua, thinking about Henry's all expenses paid trip to the Vet, gave Henry a very sympatric look... that old Henry totally ignored. Joshua didn't particularly like cats, but old Henry was different. Henry had a rough around the edges dignity about him that Joshua respected; he had seen him hunker down almost flat when one of the dogs came through, getting in his **"Don't Tread On Me"** stance; and, they didn't. A glance at the bristled old cat looking at the frisky dogs was enough to make anyone laugh. Henry was simply indifferent to all the comings and goings of the busy kitchen and, to anyone, well nearly everybody. However, if you offered him food, especially left overs , he was your best buddy in the whole world. Since everybody knew this was his weakness, Henry graced the scales at a healthy twenty-five pounds. So, there Joshua sat in the kitchen with an aging feline Romeo and the cheerful Mrs. C. for company. Better than being alone, he thought. Besides, Joshua was in no hurry to return to the Carriage House and the big empty bed. Mrs. C. was busy cleaning up the dishes from dinner...pausing and looking over at Joshua...she couldn't help herself. ' Misser Joshua...its bee none of me bees-wax...buts...I's sees it...I' s overhears Misser Will and Miss Grace...talkin' bout yer 'sit-u-a-shon' ... I's...' ; unable to finish her sentence, Joshua looked at the caring elderly woman, he had known for most of his adult life, and nodded his head. ' I know... Mrs. C... I know ' and his voice simply trailed off. Standing up, he slid the counter stool back under the counter, scratched old Henry's head, thanked Mrs. C. for a wonderful dinner, and bade

them both a good night. Wiping her hands on her ever present apron, Mrs. C shook her head...'I's worry 'bout dat boy...him's gots his self some bigg troubles, Henree.. .bigg troubles.'

Joshua walked the short distance to the Carriage House; but before going in, he turned and looked up at Anne's window. It was dark. Sleep well, my love, sleep well, he mouthed. Moving onto the porch, he opened the screen door, followed by the oak door, then gently closed both so as not to wake anyone who might have found the blessings of sleep. He didn't turn on the lights; entering the main room, he collapsed on the sofa. No point in going to the bedroom, he thought...not going to sleep anyway. Might as well just stay here. So with the light of the moon streaming through the window, he passed much of the night...alone with his thoughts.

# Chapter Sixty Five

They all ate breakfast the next morning in the sunroom; it was agreed -- Grace, Joshua and Anne would go to the Mausoleum around nine to inter Will's ashes; she would leave shortly after that, hopefully returning in time Sunday to bid Anne farewell. Grace excused herself after only coffee, then returned moments later dressed in her riding habit to tell Anne and Joshua she would meet them at the Mausoleum. Thinking it a bit odd, they both nodded and went off to change. Meeting back in the foyer just minutes later, they walked to the paddock area, where Taylor had the mule ready for their journey to the Mausoleum. Arriving minutes later at the revered spot, Grace was no where to be seen. They waited outside for a few more minutes soaking up the warm morning sunshine; then hearing a rush of birds in the distance, turned to see Grace trotting up on Will's favorite Arabian, Caesar, with Will's urn in her hands. She dismounted with ease, dropping the reins to the ground; released from his reins, the majestic Caesar calmly walked over to an interesting spot of clover and, began eating the newly sprouted grass. Grace quickly took off her riding cap, dropping it down on the saddle horn, and strode purposely toward Anne and Joshua. Her face was flushed from the ride, and then, with a ever- so- slight smile on her face, Grace said.. ' I promised Caesar I would show him where Will was...is ...**now**...' her voice cracked , overcome at that moment. Joshua reached out his hand to Grace; Anne looped her arm through hers, and, without another word, the three of them entered the cool dark confines of the Mausoleum. William Carson Breckenridge, aka Will, was finally laid to rest.

Grace left shortly after one, promising, yet again, to be back in time to see Anne before she left. Before she left, however, Joshua noticed when Grace and Anne were saying their good byes, she had leaned over and whispered something in Anne's ear, pulled back from her, then giving her a big hug and smile, walked down the steps to her waiting car. Anne and Joshua watched her car until it was out of sight, before re-entering the house. Going to the den, they found the room had already been invaded by the three dogs . Whiskey, who was snoring loudly half on/half off the ottoman by the fireplace, and Jack, enjoying an early lunch thanks to Chablis. Laughing at the sight of the perfect little family and, at a momentary loss as to what to do next, their dilemma was solved when Joshua's cell phone rang . He mouthed to Anne, that he needed to take this; so Anne was left to her own devices. Explore, she thought. Think I'll go down to the Paddocks and see if any of the foals are in residence. Or, maybe check out the lower stalls to see if any of the ewes had birthed any lambs this morning. Good plan, she thought. And, with that much of the afternoon was taken up - apart - but equally happy in what they were doing. At least for a few hours, time was a friend.

Mrs. C. caught Joshua just as he closed off his cell phone. What would he like for dinner...where would he and Miss Anne like to eat. After telling her not to go to any trouble, that he and Anne could eat cold cuts...she walked off, apparently in a huff, muttering under her breath to herself ...'...Cold cuts - I'z be ashames ta fixs dat ..we'z ain't eat'n likes por folk... nots in *MY* house ...' leaving Joshua to laugh at himself because he apparently had insulted her; and all he was trying to do was to give her the evening off. Wonder where Anne took off to; not finding her in the house, he assumed she had either gone upstairs for a late afternoon nap – not likely...or ...of course, she is down at the Paddocks. Taking a short cut through the kitchen to the Paddocks, he couldn't help but smile when he saw Mrs. C. working her magic on dinner. Bet those 'cold cuts' are going to be really good, he laughed to himself as the screen door slammed behind him..

Taking the back steps from the kitchen two at a time, he crossed the side lawn, entered the darkened breeze way of the main barn. I love the coolness of the barn; the mustiness invades your senses, he thought. Walking on through the breeze way, he noticed several mares in residence and, was greeted by an occasional head poked over the gates. Laughing to himself, as he knew how terribly spoiled each and every one of Grace's horses were; he spoke out loud to the beautiful animals...' No luck, today girls...haven't got a single carrot on me..maybe next time..'

Looking around the interior of the Paddock area, Anne didn't seem to be anywhere around. Seeing one of the grooms at the end of the breeze way, he asked if he knew where Anne might have gone. The groom smiled broadly and nodded his head to a nearby stall. Hearing someone humming in one of the stalls, he nearly laughed out loud - he had found her - with dirty hands, muddy Wellies, straw in her hair; she was mucking out one of the stalls. She looks so happy doing this. Stepping up on the bottom rail of the stall, he stuck a piece of straw in his mouth, and doing his absolute best ' Junior Samples ' imitation...he grinned at Anne and, asked ...' Ben doin' dis long, Lil' Lady ? If ya finds ya needs some help, jist call me at BR-549...' to which, he had to duck the handful of straw aimed precisely at his head.

Laughing nearly to the point of crying, they walked back arm-in-arm to the main house. Anne washed off her boots at the outside spigot, while Joshua tried, in vain, to get all of the precisely aimed straw off his clothes. Agreeing to meet for dinner in an hour, they went their separate ways...totally unaware of Mrs. C. smiling from the kitchen window. Shaking her head at the aging cat sitting beside her on the counter...' ..Dems, chillen'...dem's gots its bad... oh, Lordy, Henree ..what's dems gonna do...' to which Henree gave his opinion when he nuzzled up against the elderly woman's bosom looking for a head rub... ' Yous stil a lover, ain't ya ole boy? ' to which Mrs. C laughed as she shooed Henry off the counter.

A little while later, Joshua found Anne in the front parlor with a glass of Chablis in her hand. She quickly sat it down, apologizing to Joshua. 'No need to apologize, he said. I made my peace with that demon years ago...but you enjoy...if I remember correctly, you said you always liked a glass of wine before dinner. And, by the way, you look really nice, Anne...I like that deep green color on you...it brings out your eyes...' Anne felt her face flush a bit, not sure if it was the wine or the compliment. She looked up to see Mrs. C. coming through the door to announce dinner, and, she silently said 'thank you' to whatever Guardian Angel was currently looking over her. Entering the dining room, they sat down to a wonderful dinner of roast pork with apricot glaze, fried green tomatoes, rosemary potatoes, fresh bread. Joshua whispered in Anne's ear while holding the chair for her...'I told Mrs. C. not to go to any trouble tonight..that we could have cold cuts for dinner; I'm so glad she listened to me..!' to which Anne burst out laughing.

They talked all the way through dinner..about everything and about nothing. Joshua couldn't help but wonder if this is the way his life – **their lives** --could have been spent. This is us forty years down the path; this could be us...the kids..the grand kids... this could have been **us**. Anne looked across the table at Joshua, thinking how glorious these last few days had been. Thursday had been a tough one, but Friday...today...they were like something out of a novel. We could have had all of this, and more, she thought.. **if only**. They talked on a bit more, moving the after- dinner conversation to the patio. No stars out yet; the moon was just beginning to crest the lower fields. ' Going to be a full moon tonight...should really be pretty ..and, feels warm, too.' Joshua heard himself; and yet, it didn't sound like himself, he thought. I sound like some tv weather person giving the evening forecast. Why is it she unnerves me so much...her being this close to me... I can smell her perfume.. that faint, yet mesmerizing scent. I only have to reach out to touch her. And, Anne, equally frustrated; too close, Joshua, entirely too close, she thought. Trying desperately to appear nonchalant, Anne casually ventured over to one of the patio planters filled with some sweet smelling vine, she plucked a bloom, lifting it to her nose, took in its toxic sweet smell. Must get Joshua's scent out of my head...must get that raw musky scent... gone...or else. Sensing her retreat, Joshua leaned up against the railing. Gathering every bit of nerve he could muster, he looked across the patio to where Anne was. Taking in the sweet smell of the evening, he began speaking softly...'Anne...I don't know how else to say this...**I need you with me**, **in my life**, **in my world**. I truly don't have any answers as to how this is going to work out. I don't want anyone to be hurt ...anyone; you and me included. There is Petra. There is Reed. And yet, there is us. We belong together..we have been denied so much over the years. Being with you these last few days has made me even more aware of what we lost. ..we need that chance to make things right. I need to know you feel the same way, say it..please just say it..tell me that what I am saying is what you are feeling, too. I...' he paused just as Anne raised her head, she walked into his arms, stood on tip-toe to meet his gaze, and simply said ... ' I know, Joshua.. I know..' With that, she stepped back from him and walked through the open patio doors, leaving him there...**alone**.

Joshua was crushed. How could she *just* walk away from me... did I say something wrong...does she not know how much I love her. She has to know...I mean I have told her...even though it's wrong. God, please forgive me, I love her. She is everything I want - everything I need - everything. Anne is so good at just walking away. Why is it she is always leaving me, he asked himself . No.. I know no force on earth could have made me walk away from her, *not again*. Joshua felt as if a knife had been driven far..far down into his heart..his soul. Standing there for a few more minutes, he inhaled deeply of the night air; finally with an even deeper sigh, he stepped off the side patio steps and headed back to the Carriage House...to lick his wounds.

# Chapter Sixty Six

Walking up the stairs to her room, Anne was nearly in tears. This is killing me..this is like the roller coaster ride from Hell. I can not, nor will I even begin to entertain the thought of leaving Reed. And yet, I love Joshua with every fiber of my being and have, since I don't remember when. I have walked away from Joshua, yet again...left him standing there on the patio. I should have stayed, maybe, we could have made some sense of all of this. No, I couldn't stay...I... He was standing much too close. My heart was taking over, because my head had taken loss of its senses. He loves Petra, and she is going to need him so much ...it would be unthinkable for me to take his loyalty away from her ...not now. She thought about the whispered words Grace had spoken to her - what only this morning. Heavens it seemed like a life time ago. Entering her room, she didn't turn on the light, just walked over to the window, raising it to allow the sweet warm night air in. Clear my head, she thought. The late spring full moon was rising slowly.. a 'Lover's Moon'.. she thought. No lights necessary tonight; she plopped down in the softness of the chintz covered chair by the window. Picking up her rosary from the bedside table, she fingered its familiar beads, smoothed by years of believing. Doesn't matter how many prayers I offer up...I am the one who has to make the decisions ...decisions that my head refuses to agree to with my heart. She sat there in the moonlight for what seemed an eternity. Then, rising, padded across the room, opened her door, quietly closing it behind her and, slipped softly down the back staircase. Quickly exiting the Pantry, then entering the kitchen, she quietly opened, then closed the door behind and, across the side lawn she walked - with a purpose - ***do not turn back***, she willed herself. She stepped up on the front porch of the Carriage House...pausing only to catch her breath before knocking on his door. She found herself trembling. Momentarily thinking of where she was, she unthinkingly crossed herself – ' Help Me ...Lord..' Then just as she reached out for the heavy brass door knocker, she heard his voice from the dark end of the porch. 'Anne...What ?.....' quarried Joshua. Joshua was rising from his chair, not sure whether to stay or what. With a deep breath for courage, Anne calmly walked over to where he stood. Taking his hand, she raised it to her lips, gently kissing the palm ..sending a message loud and clear that she was here - at least for tonight. Anne stood on tiptoe and whispered in his ear, ' Grace told me to go to you tonight, and not think about it until tomorrow. And, I have learned to always listen to my elders...' With that, he took her hands in his; walked over to the big oak door, opened it...and, ushering her in, gently, ever so gently, closed the doors behind them. Knowing full well this might be all they would ever have, Joshua told himself... Reality can wait until tomorrow.

In her hurry to go to the Carriage House and Joshua, Anne had failed to even notice Mrs. C. filling the dishwasher with the dinner dishes. Mrs. C. raised up just as the back door was closing. Walking over to the open window, through the moonlight, she could see Anne walk up the steps of the Carriage House. Wiping her hands on her apron and smiling broadly...' I's told ya, Henree...dems n love..Lord bless dems chillen..' to which she turned around to see Henry sitting on the counter beside her looking out the window. She would have sworn she saw the ole boy smile, too.

# Chapter Sixty Seven

Anne awoke just moments after the dawn had broken. Thinking back to last night, she wondered how she ever found the courage to go to Joshua. In so many ways, last night should have never happened. And, in so many ways, last night **had** to happen. And it was wonderful ... so wonderful. Being in each others arms... again...loving one another...again. It was just so right...and then, quickly chastising herself ... so wrong. I absolutely refuse to think that my kind and loving God... my forgiving God...could not see it for what it was. Redemption. Redemption for all the time lost ... for what could have been. Feeling the first warm rays of sunshine on her face, she stretched, gingerly moving the covers only to be re-pinned completely by an enormous arm thrown over her entire body...' And, just where do you think you are going, my love?' a sleepy Joshua asked. 'Back to the main house before the entire house wakes up, and figures out I'm not there, if you must know...' she laughed in his ear. ' I don't really care *who* knows ...' he growled at her. Moving slightly, he easily pulled her on top of him, and, raising up a bit, kissed her good morning. ' And, now that you have totally messed up my plan to stay in bed all day, I intend to keep you here as my prisoner for as long as I possibly can..' whispered Joshua. To which Anne laughingly asked him...' And what, do tell, crime is it that I have committed to make me your prisoner, kind Sir?' Without hesitation, Joshua replied... ' You stole my heart...'

An hour later, Anne, once again, made the attempt to leave the Carriage House, this time being a bit more successful. Straightening up on her elbows, she looked at the sleep-eyed love of her life and murmured in his ear...'Joshua ...I **need** to go...what if Mrs. C. sees me sneak in...you may not care, but I do; see you at breakfast, and, Joshua.... act... **'normal'..'** and eased out from under his arm. Reaching out for her, he nearly fell out of the bed, to which Anne almost collapsed in laughter. She fled the bedroom laughing hysterically at Joshua trying to disentangle himself from the sheets; then carefully retracing their steps from the night before, retrieved her clothes as she went.

When Joshua walked into the breakfast room, there sat Anne reading the Sunday paper on the divan surrounded by all of the dogs. There was no place for him, he thought jealously. Picking up a piece of bacon from the breakfast table, he was able to at least bribe Whiskey to leave his spot, but Chablis and Jack held firm ignoring his offered bribes. Anne laughed at his obvious attempt to get the dogs off the divan, teasing Joshua in the process by standing up and kissing him soundly on the lips. They ate breakfast...sneaking treats to the dogs...reading and discussing the paper ... a normal Sunday morning before Church. Anne knew Joshua missed his church; they had agreed, at some point, last night to attend church this morning . Today ... today, he could just listen and be a parishioner. Besides in only a few weeks, he would be returning to that world. His world of the ministry, of Petra, her parents, everything that he had become and was now. There would be no room in it for her, and she understood. She was not angry ... she was not regretful of one moment they had spent together, nor, was she remorseful. We may have sinned in Your eyes, God, but it was not intended to hurt anyone; Petra will never know; Reed will never know. It is only **Joshua** and **I** and *You*; we will know that we...*No* ... I refuse to think we sinned because loving someone is **not** a sin. Before the tears could well up in her eyes, she quickly stood up and kissing Joshua on the top of his perfect bald head, said she was off to take a hot shower and, dress for Church. She would meet him back downstairs in an hour. Joshua raised his head, from his newspaper, caught her hand, and smiling broadly, asked as he winked at her...' Want

some company?' ' Joshua !' exclaimed Anne and off she went laughing and shaking her head..

When they agreed to attend Church services, it was decided that it would neither be Catholic for her or Episcopalian for him. They would go to the Church that Will and Grace had attended. Their destination would be the Church of the Holy Resurrection. Pulling into the parking lot, they both took in the beauty of the centuries old church. From the grey limestone cut rock block walls, the exquisite stained glass windows latticed with wrought iron work, it was Old World in every sense of the word. Upon entering the huge front doors, they were greeted by many of the same people they had met at Will's service. They entered the sanctuary, accepted their programs from the ushers and quietly took their seats. It is such a beautiful old church, Anne thought..reminds me of that Greek Orthodox Church she and Reed had visited in Washington several years ago. It just oozes reverence. The service began with the Assistant Minister's welcome to all this morning, and, looking over at Anne and Joshua, expressed his, as well as the congregation's sympathy at Will's death, but also their extreme joy at seeing them here today to worship with Will and Grace's family. After a Bible reading and the morning hymn, Reverend Fields stepped to the Pulpit to begin his service. However, the first part of it was momentarily lost to Anne...as Joshua reached over and gently pulled her hand to his lap...nonchalantly as if it was the most normal thing in the world for him to do so. But, for Anne she had to figure how and why the entire University of Alabama Drum Corps was playing loudly in her head.

With the final hymn and prayer of invitation, the congregation began to file out. Nearly everyone who had not already spoken to them, made a point to express their sympathy for Joshua's loss, and to extend their assistance ...if they could help in any way. This was the South, Anne thought. We truly care about each other. Reverend Fields caught Joshua's eye as they were leaving, so Joshua halted to talk a minute more with him. Anne stepped into the Vestibule, thankful to feel the cool rush of the a/c in her face. Looking back to see if Joshua was coming, she felt someone gently touch her sleeve. Standing in front of her was a tall attractive woman of about 70, graying hair and impeccably dressed. Reaching out to take Anne's hand in hers, she started to speak... ' Hello - it's Anne, right... I don't know if you remember me, I'm Susanna Langston. Pierpoint.. Grace and I were Sorority Sisters at Southern Seminary - in Virginia. My heavens that was so long ago...anyway, I was at the reception yesterday. I just wanted to tell you how sorry we all are for you and your husband's loss... Will is... was a very special person to all of us here..please tell Grace, again, that should she need anything, just let us, my husband Ross and I, know. Again, it was so nice to meet you -- and, see Joshua again. Heavens, I haven't seen him since he was knee high to a grasshopper. The two of you make such a lovely couple, dear.. you both look so happy, and, so much in love ...just like Will and Grace were for so many years.. Please come back and see all of us real soon...ya here? '

Momentarily stunned by what had just happened, Anne quickly gathered her composure and thanked Mrs. Pierpoint graciously. Then turning, she caught a glimpse of Joshua entering the Vestibule still talking with Reverend Fields. She watched as Mrs. Pierpoint stopped to greet Joshua; and, leaning up to catch his ear, whispered something to him. Responding to whatever she had said, Joshua bussed her cheek, and walked away with a huge smile on his face. 'Okay, I give up'... Joshua whispered to Anne as they headed back to their car. ' Just what were you and Susie chatting on about...' When Anne didn't answer, he said with a smile... ' Okay, I'll tell you what she said to me... she said for me to hold on real tight to you - **real tight** - 'cause you were a ' **keeper..**'

On the drive back to the farm, Joshua noticed Anne had been quiet for most of the trip. Thinking she was thinking about the return trip home she would later make, he asked if she had packed yet. ' No, not yet,' she answered vaguely. Pulling in the driveway to the farm, Joshua stopped halfway; exiting the car, he walked over to Anne's side and opened the door. Helping her out of the car, he put his arm around her waist and together they walked over to the board fence. Several of the horses were down here in the lower pasture, apparently all Sunday gussied up as they had their colorful moisture blankets on, and being nosy, they trotted over. Always looking for that **one** person who just might have a spare carrot in their pocket, two of them reached their beautiful heads over the top rail. Anne caught the bridle of one of the mares, Athena, a real beauty, and began softly speaking with the gentle animal, rubbing her muzzle and whispering; she appears to have entered another dimension, thought Joshua . He leaned across the fence to pick a single wild daisy. **'*She loves me, She loves me not..*'** Joshua recited the age old poem, hoping to, at least, coax a smile from Anne. When he offered the half de-petaled daisy to her, she looked at him up at him, her eyes beginning to tear... 'Joshua...that lady, Mrs. Pierpoint...she thought...we were husband and wife..' Anne told him. ' Ah... so that explains her '**keeper**' comment,' Joshua said. Taking her into his arms, he kissed the top of her head... ' I'm so sorry, Anne...' They held on to each other; neither one wanting to let go. Their hand was forced, however, when Athena reached across the top of the fence and very impolitely stole the half plucked daisy out of Anne's hand and proceeded to enjoy her snack. It broke the moment; with a final rub to the nose of the thief, and Anne still laughing at the daggered look Joshua shot the mare, they were back in the car and, were, once more, headed for the main house.

Walking up to the front steps, Anne turned back to look at Joshua, still seated in the front seat of the car, talking on his cell phone. To who..he didn't say..it was probably Petra, she thought...his **"real"** wife. She walked up the staircase, into her room, and began packing her things in her suitcase; sitting down on the bed, she went over and over in her mind the events of the past three days and nights. We have to talk...before...she heard her cell phone ring, and answering it she heard Reed's strong voice on the other end... '...Yes...I'll be leaving in a few hours..am packing as we speak...should see you before dinner...oh yes, let's cook out on the grill.. love you too...see you in a few hours... she waited to close off the call when she heard Reed clear his throat... ' Anne...I'm glad you're coming home.. Back to me...to all of us.. ' Me, too'...she said; with that, Reed hung up the phone. Finishing her packing, she turned the hot water on...' Shower ' she said out loud.... ' Wash away my sins.'

Coming down the backstairs from her second floor bedroom, Anne was hoping to catch Mrs. C. in the kitchen. She wanted to thank her personally for her hospitality and to say good -bye. Walking into the sun filled room, she noticed Henry curled up in a ball in his favorite rocker. Leaning down to rub the old cat's head, she raised her head to see Mrs. C. coming in from the side porch with a jar of pickles. Smiling and walking over, Anne took the work worn hand in hers and said.. 'Mrs. C...I just wanted to thank you for all of your kindness these last few days... your cooking has spoiled me so much that I wish you could come home with me...' Anne laughed lightly. Mrs. C's broad smile indicated that she truly did appreciate Anne taking the time to thank her. 'Yews be levin, Missus Anne?...I's sure has njoy havin' yer smilin' face 'round heres ...ycws puts lots of smiles on faces 'round her.. I's hopes yer be bac... soes wes ain't go'n say no good byes... Misser Joshua, hes gones ta mis yer fer sure..and sos wilt I.. ' the elderly woman paused. Then patting Anne's hand gently... ' Missus Anne...I's gonna prays fer yer and Misser Joshua...ya nos, de Lord, He works n mysterious ways...He's gonna makes its all works out..somehow.. He wills, I's jist nos Hes will... yer takes care yerself, yer here..and yer comes back her reel soon...we's all be waitin'...' and, with that the elderly woman enfolded Anne into her big loving arms; Anne held on dearly ... while old Henry took it all in from his throne by the fireplace. As Anne let go of the comfort of Mrs. C's loving arms, she headed to the Library and Joshua. **Remember**, she told herself ... **what Daddy said. Remember**.

Downstairs, Joshua was in the library...pacing back and forth. Good thing he had called Petra, before they left for Church. He didn't think he could have talked with her at that moment; but, they had talked earlier – about his weekend, about her health, how she was feeling, the dogs...' ... the Estate work will hopefully be done in a few weeks; I'll be back..maybe even before that. Grace sends her love..take care of yourself....bye.. love you' Thinking back to the call in the car, he wondered why Anne had looked so distressed when he said he had to take it as they were just pulling up to the front steps. His phone had rung, he answered it; realizing it was Grace telling him she was on her way back home, he was just about to tell Anne when , he looked up to see Anne hurriedly exiting the car and heading up the front steps. And, now she was standing in the doorway. He felt his heart plummet to the wood floor beneath his now unsteady feet. Anne began to speak....' Joshua , we need to talk..' And so it was...he heard all the words coming out of Anne's mouth; witness to the pained look on her face. She continued... 'This - **we** - cannot be and you and I both know it. This is going to be hard. ..so hard to walk away, yet again.' And then, there they were; the words he never wanted to hear again. ' We must leave here as just friends, for both of our sakes. You have to ..you **must** .. go back to Petra with a clear conscience. And I, to Reed. I will always and forever love you.. **Please, please... Never forget that**. *And, Never Question It.* And maybe, just maybe... someday, someway, Fate will smile on us again. Then, maybe it will finally... *finally* be 'OUR' time. At least, we had this weekend to let us know what might have been. In dying, Will gave us one last chance to see what we would have had...could have had...*if only*... I love you so much, Joshua...this is killing me..my heart is breaking all over again..' with her voice faltering. Anne felt the sting of the tears she had been trying so hard to keep from falling, break free. Joshua stood there trying to digest everything she had said. All he wanted to do was to reach out, take her in his arms, hold her... love her like he had done last night...*forever*. His heart disagreed with everything she was saying, but his head knew she was right... yet again. He was willing his mouth to open - say something; do something. Anything that would ease this moment..but not a word would come out. How could he let her go, yet again? He finally found his feet, and crossing the room in huge strides, pulled her trembling body into his arms, kissing the top of her head. He felt his heart break yet again...for everything that they had shared this weekend; and, for everything they would lose when she left today. I now know what Will had meant. I can't go through this again, he thought. The pain is too great...too deep. They stood there simply holding on to one another until the dogs started to bark announcing Grace's return. They hesitantly let go. There were no words left to speak now...looking at one another, they both knew this might be the last time they would ever be together. Anne thought, through the pain..so this is **Karma**. This sucks.

The Lady of the Manor was home and, they must greet her. Grace entered the front door; bending down to accept the lavish welcome homes from her babies. She watched with amusement as satisfied with the attention they had just received, Whiskey and Chablis trotted off. Where was Jack, she wondered. Grace saw Joshua and Anne coming out of the library, looking at their faces, she knew what had happened. But even worse than that, she *knew* what was going to happen. Anne's bags were in the foyer; her car parked at the front entrance. From the tears in Anne's eyes, she knew full well, her heart was breaking; and, Joshua, he looked like he had just been sucker punched in the stomach. Grace hugged them both; make this easy for them, she thought. Don't let on you see what is going one. Regaining her composure, she saw out of the corner of her eye, the fluffy ball of fur that was Jack, headed straight for Anne. He tried to stop, but on the slick slate floor, his efforts were for nothing. The happy little pup plowed head on into Anne. They all broke out laughing at his antics. At least, it broke the tension in here, thought Grace. Bending over to gather up the little scamp in her arms, she heard herself telling Anne she was glad to have gotten to know her and, there was an open invitation to come back to the farm - anytime. Hugging her and kissing her cheek, she stepped aside to let Joshua walk her to her car. Putting her bags in the trunk, Joshua walked over to where

Anne stood. Opening the car door for her, he folded her into his arms, then bent down to kiss the top of her head. They reached out to one another with one last kiss. Grace felt her heart go to the bottom of the floor. How can I watch this, she asked herself. But she found herself glued to the scene before her; I **have** to be here... **for Joshua**. Will told me to. Anne stood up on tiptoes and whispered something in Joshua's ear. Grace watched as Joshua held on for another minute before letting his hold loosen. Anne climbed into her car; he closed the door. He reached out his hand to touch her sleeve - just once more. She started the engine, and eased the car out of the driveway, slowly making it down the long driveway to the main road. Joshua never moved until he could no longer see her car. Then he slowly turned around, head tucked and walked back up the pave way to the Portico where Grace stood waiting for him. They had said good - bye, yet again, he thought to himself; but this time – **this time**, it had been for all the **right** reasons. Grace reached out her hand to him, hugging him to her; she wrapped her arm around his waist, and gently asked him what Anne had whispered in his ear. Joshua momentarily let go and, turned away from her; looking back at the driveway, he lowered his head... she said...

**'... Let Go, Joshua...Let Go.....'**

# *Epilogue*

Joshua went back to Louisiana...to his ministry..to Petra. His world began to crumble as first Petra's mother, Anya passed suddenly. Then only a few months later, her father, Stavros. Joshua preached their final services ... his final gift to them. Roman, Petra's brother, sold the farm and moved to town to be closer to Petra. Petra seemed to be taking it all in stride, until she was caught in a sudden rain storm and took a cold; try as she did, she could not shake it. She continued her down hill slide, until finally nearly a year to the day of Will's death, Petra *'Minsca'* Nemonoweski Cantor Breckenridge slipped her earthly bonds with her Joshua and Roman by her side...and, Lady, Tramp and Mischa on her bed. She was 57.

Anne returned to her life...Reed, Emerson, Wright, and the twins, Brennan and little Emma. Back to her canine babies, Mags and Vanna. She kept in touch with Grace. Slowly her world had drifted back to normalcy. This was the way it was supposed to be. And, then, out of the blue, Grace called to let her know Petra - was gone.

And, now the story continues with .... ***Pieces of the Heart.***

# Pieces of the Heart

## By Bree Matthews

# Prologue

'What do you mean this is for nothing...it can not be... we have endured too much..and, suffered through too much. I refuse to believe that there is nothing else that can be done...' Anne asked incredulously, her eyes filling with tears as she spoke. 'There is always **"something"** else that can be done...' her voice trembling.

# Chapter One

A nd the congregation said...'**Amen**'.

Rising slowly, friends, co-workers, neighbors all begin to exit the tiny church in Debrussiae Parish, LA., having just attended the Memorial Service for Petra Nemonoskoweski Cantor Breckenridge, Pastor, and beloved wife of Pastor in Residence, Joshua Crayford Breckenridge, on this the 25th day of April, 2013.

The Memorial Service had been poignant...heartfelt...and, joyful; Petra had gone home to our Heavenly Father's House. And yet, the gathering was tinged with sadness for a faithful servant and true believer gone too soon. Joshua had preached many a final service, but this one he just couldn't handle. His assistant Pastor and the Pastor from their sister Church in Montpeiler would do the honors. His sister-in-law, Grace-Katherine Butler Breckenridge had come to Debrussiae Parish to be with Joshua...to try and repay the kindess and understanding he had given her almost a year ago when her beloved Will, his brother had passed. Grace thought back to that time, remembering how Will had fought a brave fight with MS; and now, Petra was gone too. She had courageously fought the devastating illness that one by one had also taken her parents in the last year. Grace knew full well the pain of losing someone you loved...and, she could see the reserved sadness in every line of Joshua's face. He had beena a pillar of strength, reassuring everyone that he was, indeed, coping. But, he had not yet, at least not in Grace's presence, given in to the deep grief she knew he was dealing with inwardly. He had helped her with the arrangements, selecting the cremation urn, the marker, a few of Petra's favorite hymns and Bible readings. While being efficient and dignified in every decision, she had seen he was on Auto-Pilot. He was physically with her, but not mentally. And all the while, she kept hoping that he would let her in to help him cope. The only crack in his steeled armor was when he was selecting the verses for the memory card. He went back to one that he, as well as Petra, had always favored:

God saw you were getting tired; your body failing but your spirit strong. He reached out his loving arms and bade you...
**'Come Home to Me'.** You left us behind to enter The Gates of Forever. Your work is now done; through the tears, we bid you Farewell.
**'SleepWell, Sweet Angel...Sleep Well.'**

Yes, Joshua had been the poster child of reserved dignity; he had handled grief many times over since becoming a Man of the Cloth. In the past year, he had seen Will, Petra's parents, Anya and Stavros Nemonoskoweski and now, Petra to their final rewards. And, grieved in private...asking only for strength from his Lord to fulfill His designated plan. But Grace knew Joshua...and she knew that it was time for him to take off the Mantel of the Robe, and be just a man. He needed someone to lean on, someone he trusted and loved with all of his heart. She knew that the only person he would be able to turn to...and, yet couldn't turn to was...Anne. And since he would not allow his grief to become hers, he did not ask it of her. But, Grace could...and did.

Sitting in the front pew, alongside Grace, Joshua was immersed in his thoughts...beautiful service, must thank John...and Peter for speaking so eloquently...And, the choir...beautiful music...Petra loved music almost as much as she loved her faith...in death, they allowed her to be called 'Pastor'...but not in life...Flowers....so many flowers. Petra loved flowers...thought Joshua. And so many people.. so many people loved her...her gentle ways...he laughed inwardly to himself, her warped sense of humor, oh, and the language transfer...

did that ever cause many a gasp, laugh or puzzled look from people. Good memories of the past twenty years. Now, standing in the vestibule beside Grace, they graciously thanked each and every one for coming and extended an invitation to attend the afternoon brunch to be held in the Church Activities Center.

As the last of the mourners filed out the font doors to walk down the pathway to the Activities Center, Joshua reached over and took Grace's hand in his... 'Thank you so much for coming. I do not think I would have been able to do this without you; this must be so hard on you, with Will gone less than a year...' his voice trailed off. Grace smiled at him, knowing that he was truly hurting. Petra had passed so quickly, that there was little time to take it all in... much less prepare for this outcome. After all, it was 'just' a cold... 'just a cold'... but her weakened system just could not counter. So, within a few weeks, she was gone. Tucking her head so as not to let Joshua see the emotion on her face, her eye caught a movement from inside the Chapel. Catching her breath, she smiled, then nodded her head in acknowledgement of the person she saw walking down the aisle from the back section of the Balcony. And then, came the voice**...'Joshua...turn around..'** echoing slightly in the emptiness of the Chapel. Joshua turned slightly around from Grace, who still had his hand in hers...which was a good thing, because Joshua nearly collapsed at the sight of Anne standing there close enough to touch. 'She is here ...finally she is here. Thank you, Lord for sending her to me -- someone for me to lean on...I truly needed her and You knew it..' he said to himself. Momentarily looking at Grace, he knew that it was she who had made the call...told Anne to come...for Anne would not have come if it were not asked of her. She would never intrude; at the farm she said she would be there if I asked...but, I didn't think it would be fair to impose my pain on her...and yet, here she is. Looking back at Grace, he mouthed silently...'Thank you..' to which Grace patted his hand, and quickly slipped out of the vestibule. This moment belonged to Anne and Joshua.

The journey continues... **Pieces of the Heart** is forthcoming.

# About the Author

## Bree Matthews

Having been born, bred and raised near the beautiful Blue Ridge Mountains of Virginia, Bree Matthews has spent her entire life as a country girl. She and her husband are both now retired and are enjoying immensely the freedom to truly savor life. Having been an English Major, one of her life long desires - her 'Bucket List,' if you will, was to author a novel and have it published. Writing has always been a passion for Bree and one of her main hobbies. Her objective with **'Pieces of the Past'** was to tell the story of first love, the heartache and the joy, as well as the many twists and turns it can take.

The sequel to ' **Pieces of the Past'** - ' **Pieces of the Heart'** is forthcoming.

CPSIA information can be obtained at www.ICGtesting.com
Printed in the USA
LVOW10s1007241215

467722LV00001B/82/P